MURDER IN THE OLD VILLAGE

James London has had a home on the Island for over twenty years, having been a regular visitor since the 1980s. He loves its quiet pace, its history, and the gems of English life that unexpectedly reveal themselves there.

The Island is a microcosm of the world, capable of revealing good and evil that is everywhere, which he shows through the activities of Detective Inspector Bruno Peach – The Island's Murder Squad detective, with a sharp eye for a clue.

By the same author:
The Folks That Live On The Hill
The Island Murders
One-Way Ticket to Ryde

MURDER
IN THE
OLD VILLAGE

James London

Discript

First published in the United Kingdom by
Discript Limited
67 Fishbourne Road West
Chichester
PO19 3JJ

www.discript.com

A catalogue record for this book is available from the British Library.

Murder in the Old Village is a work of fiction. All incidents and
dialogue, and all characters, are products of the author's imagination
and are not to be construed as real. Any resemblance to actual persons,
living or dead, events, or locales is entirely coincidental.

ISBN 978-1-9163613-7-9

Designed and typeset in Minion Pro
Printed in Scotland by Bell & Bain Ltd

For Winifred,

because she is always interested.

CHAPTER 1

IT STARTED as a pretty much routine Monday morning for Detective Inspector Bruno Peach. Nothing had come in over the weekend demanding his attention after a busy summer so far. In late July he was looking forward to fine weather in August when he and Janet could slope off to the mainland for a couple of weeks, stay in a five-star hotel, relax and release the pressure that their individual professions continually put them under.

Schools had broken up the previous Friday and after Janet had completed the outstanding end of term paperwork, she was free until the end of August, when she had to plan for the new school year, and receive two classes of four- to five-year-olds to begin their school life.

Bruno knew he would be lucky to get away in August. The holiday season always saw an increased workload for the Murder Division, which was perpetually understaffed. There weren't many murders on the Island but a second often followed a first, then there would be a gap.

Secretly Bruno didn't mind giving up his summer holiday to hunt for a murderer, whose breed were invariably evil bastards without compassion or respect for human life. In twelve months from now Bruno would reach retirement age, after thirty-seven years as a policeman, a job he loved.

Until now, with the grace of Chief Superintendent Barlow, he'd continued for an extra year and he'd been assured, during his recent annual review, that he'd let him stay for a further year. This made him very happy, in fact the happiest he'd ever been because with Janet his partner of four years, he had become a better policeman and a better person. She had given him a purpose, unlike all of his years as a bachelor, when flings and unstable relationships had just kept him on the right side of normal.

While she shared in his police work with a helpful opinion now and then, he enthusiastically helped in renovating their Grade II listed home on the edge of Newport. He had finally completed the rebuilding of the drystone wall that ran along the eastern edge of their cottage.

For many policemen the inflation-protected pension after twenty years' service was their holy grail. Not Bruno: for him policing was a vocation and when justice was not done, or even seen to be done, it depressed him. But he'd always managed to move on with a new challenge seeking the often-unattainable goal of justice for everyone.

Janet had broadened his approach to life and this was reflected in his every action and thought. His one regret was that he'd not met her years before.

Before an hour had passed Bruno and his sidekick, Detective Sergeant Andy Bowen, were summoned to Chief Superintendent Barlow's office. Andy Bowen had worked alongside Bruno for nearly a year since transferring from the Hampshire constabulary in Southampton. His wife had accepted a nursing appointment at St Mary's hospital in Newport, and as simultaneously he had been promoted to Detective Sergeant, he'd applied for the vacancy as Bruno's number two in the Island's murder investigation team. He liked Bruno and knew that in the couple of years that remained of Bruno's police service, he'd learn a huge amount from the Island's most experienced murder detective.

With the Chief Superintendent they never knew what was coming: sometimes an inconvenient, unsolvable crime, involving late night inclement weather observation.

Bruno got on well with Barlow, as they shared a mutual respect for each other's skills. He was as usual pleasant and polite, and began by introducing Detective Glenn Pimley from the London Metropolitan Police force, an expert in vehicle crash analysis.

He started by recalling a vehicle crash in Shanklin High

Street that had occurred two weeks previously and had wrecked the annual Shanklin Carnival. The crash was comprehensively covered in the local press and, because of the casualties, had been the main Island topic of discussion ever since.

It happened on a Tuesday evening, 12 July, just after 7 p.m. at the start of the annual procession which celebrated the crowning of the Shanklin Carnival Queen. Every Island resort town celebrated the crowning of its Carnival Queen on different evenings throughout the summer. They attracted large crowds of locals and holiday visitors and raised large sums of cash for Island charities.

Shanklin Carnival was the major event in the town's summer festivities. There was great excitement throughout the town, centred on the High Street, where the spectators and street vendors gathered, creating the Carnival atmosphere. The procession proceeded at walking pace through the town. A Carnival committee was responsible for getting local companies and organisations to sponsor the vehicles, and for recruiting the volunteers who collected the contributions to charity in white plastic buckets during the procession.

To become the Carnival Queen, you had to be a resident of Shanklin. The displays were mounted on low-loaders and open backed commercial lorries loaned by local businesses. The leading vehicle carried the Queen of the Carnival. Routinely they assembled in the early morning on the edge of town in Popham Road, a quiet traffic-free back street. It took several hours to adorn the floats. Then at 7 p.m., to the sound of many local brass bands marching between the vehicles, the procession led by the beautiful young Carnival Queen and her attendants, two Carnival Princesses and two Maids of Honour started their journey through the town. Usually they moved at an ordinary walking pace for the entire journey, but on this occasion the leading vehicle carrying the Carnival Queen moved out of Popham Road, slowly gathering pace down the gentle slope of Church Road, until travelling fast through the S bend at the bottom of the hill, the driver did not, or couldn't, apply the brakes. Out of control, it crashed into the ancient stone wall of the picturesque Crab Inn, causing the ten-foot-high wall to collapse, bringing down the heavy cast-iron post carrying the pub sign onto the driver and the Carnival Queen, whose steel canopy, in which her throne was fixed, was crushed by collapsed concrete and stone. The Maids of Honour and the Carnival Princess were thrown or jumped from the vehicle as it crashed, escaping with minor injuries, scratches and bruises. Fortunately, there were no customers sitting in the Crab patio as the vehicle turned on its head.

Instantly pandemonium broke out, as no rescue of the driver or the Carnival Queen could be attempted by the public. The road through the Old Village was blocked by the highest part of the wall that fell across the road without damage to any member of the public. In fifteen minutes, an ambulance, police and the fire service arrived to search and retrieve the bodies of the casualties, the driver and the Carnival Queen, all buried in the wrecked vehicle, covered with rocks and rubble from the collapsed wall. The Carnival was disbanded and the spectators lining the route through the town drifted away, aware of the disaster that had befallen the main spectacle.

In fatal crashes the police appoint a specialist vehicle crash analyst, whose task is to determine the cause of the accident. Detective Glenn Pimley was from the London Metropolitan Police vehicle crash division. After a lengthy two-day examination of the vehicle, he reported unusual defects in the brakes, and the steel structure erected on the open loader to support the Carnival Queen's throne. His report concluded that the vehicle had been deliberately made unsafe in a manner that would result in a serious accident and possibly the death of the driver.

He illustrated with a diagram the low-loader's hydraulic braking system where the brake cables had been cut, rendering the moving vehicle unstoppable using the brakes and loss of control, even when descending gentle slopes.

He demonstrated with an engineering drawing the brake pedal attached to the Master hydraulic cylinder by a connecting rod. Technically the force of the driver's foot on the brake pedal when applied is converted to hydraulic pressure, forcing the liquid through the brake lines to the drum brakes. The hydraulic liquid is drawn back to the master cylinder when the brake pedal is released.

The second defect lay with the steel lintel supporting the metal roof under which was secured the Carnival Queen's throne. The cast iron lintel should have been fixed with eight steel bolts. Pimley produced a diagram showing that only two bolts were in place at one end of the lintel, and none could be found in the wreckage.

The weight of the lintel fixed by two bolts rendered it unstable. It would collapse if subjected to any serious jolt or crash, collapsing the supporting roof on to the head of the Carnival Queen perched on her throne.

"Access to the braking system would have required motor engineering knowledge, and both defects required tools. Almost certainly these had been done by the same person," concluded Detective Pimley. "This crash has been clearly planned to appear like an accident by a person whose motive was not personal gain. Perhaps a form of revenge?" Pimley theorised.

"So, gentlemen, this crash is now a murder enquiry, for motives that are as yet unknown, which you have to discover," said Barlow

Bruno, seeing his planned holiday disappear up the spout, waited for the anticipated response from Chief Superintendent Barlow.

"Here is a copy of Pimley's report gentlemen, Glenn will

remain with us through tomorrow, please avail yourselves of any questions while he is with us, and can I ask you to take on the assignment of finding the murderer of this young lady and the vehicle driver."

"Thank you, sir," said Bruno, in a manner of someone receiving an unwanted gift.

Barlow knew he was scuppering any holiday plans these two detectives might have, and he appreciated that Bruno would never complain. He'd always cut him some slack when appropriate.

"Can we ask Detective Pimley to accompany us to the wrecked low-loader and show us his findings hands on?" requested Bruno.

"That can be arranged," said Barlow. "Good luck, keep me posted," he said with a smile.

"Thank you for your assistance, Glenn. We'll let you know how we get on," he said.

CHAPTER 2

Pimley had arrived with a manual of the vehicle's make and its year of manufacture with tools and instruments to conduct his diligent examination. Whilst showing them the sabotage of the braking system he provided Bruno with a vital clue that he'd not mentioned earlier.

"The angle of the cut cable was done by a left-handed person. This angle is very difficult for a right-handed person, and unnatural." He demonstrated the actions.

As a right-handed person Bruno experienced the same difficulty as Pimley accessing the brake cable. The lintel was of cast iron set in a skull-crushing roof support structure. Pimley explained that the steels on the base had been properly fixed with the correct complement of bolts, firmly tightened, but the 150-pound lintel bridging the top of the cage was missing three quarters of its securing bolts. He had collected hand and fingerprints from the structure and the lintel which might prove a match with a suspect, but they were not clear and most likely those of the rescue workers. He had filed these with the records office in case they were needed in future.

Pimley presented Andy Bowen with the vehicle's service manual that contained illustrated diagrams of the braking systems on the front and rear wheels, and Pimley's drawing identified the damage. He had also green taped the severed rod which was easily visible to them on examination of the wreckage.

The steel structure lay beside the vehicle in a mangled state. The supporting lintel weighed 150 pounds, but could be lifted by a youthful labourer. The weight of the canopy had easily severed the two bolts on impact. The structure supporting the throne had been assembled by a local blacksmith named Barney Puff, who lived in the Newport Road three miles from Shanklin.

After Pimley's departure, Bruno and Andy remained in the Newport Police vehicle compound with the collapsed steel structure that housed the wooden throne. Beside the vehicle in which two innocent people had been murdered by a cold-blooded killer they experienced a sombre moment.

They discovered that the driver, Mick McClusky, was a well-known pillar of the local community who helped run the Shanklin Scouts; and the pretty seventeen-year-old, Gillian Napier, who'd been selected as the Shanklin Carnival Queen, was an A level student at a Shanklin Comprehensive School.

Barlow was confident that Bruno Peach and Andy Bowen would catch the killer and had guaranteed that the case would be conducted in complete secrecy throughout their investigation with no press coverage.

The funerals of the deceased had not yet taken place and would be further delayed because of the need to perform a post-mortem to confirm the health of the driver, who could have suffered a heart attack or have been under the influence of drugs or alcohol. This delay could be useful: attendance at the funerals of murdered victims sometimes helped the police determine a motive for the crime or identify a suspect, especially as in this case where there seemed to be no tangible gain by the killer.

The crash was the place to begin. While Andy picked through the wreckage of the low-loader, Bruno studied the accident report completed by the police officers, who were the first to arrive at the site of the accident. As the vehicle entered the Old Village, out of control, it was just seconds before it crashed in the Crab Inn wall. The only witnesses to the crash were three thirteen-year-old boys from Purley in Surrey, on holiday, who were interviewed by PC Peter Tinkler from Sandown Police Station.

A team of police officers had arrived in the Shanklin Old Village within twenty minutes of the crash whilst the majority of the spectators who had witnessed the accident with young children had left the vicinity. Others who had tried to assist in the rescue had pulled debris from the vehicle, but were held back because of the risk of further collapse of the damaged high wall and potential fire to await the imminent arrival of the ambulance and fire engine rescue team.

Most of the public had returned to their drinks at the bars in Holliers Hotel and the Village Inn, except for three thirteen-year-old schoolboys, who sat together on the bench outside of the front of the Village Inn drinking Cokes. They were mesmerised by the crash, hoping an ambulance would arrive quickly to rescue the driver.

The crowd that gathered around the Crab Inn forecourt were helpless to approach the upturned vehicle, covered in the disintegrated stone wall weighing many tonnes, in which the driver and possibly the Shanklin Carnival Queen lay buried.

The arrival of the police saw them seal the Crab Inn with blue tape. After clearing everybody from the scene a police constable approached the Village Inn and spoke to the boys.

"Did you see what happened young men?"

"Yes sir, we did, we saw everything."

"Can I take your names as witnesses to this accident and would you like to tell me what you saw?"

"Yes sir, my name is Ernest Wright and these are my friends Zach Bush and Tom Coombs."

"Where are you from?"

"We are all from Surrey sir, Purley to be exact."

"Sir," said Ernest. "Do you mind if I get my dad before we carry on?"

"Of course," said the policeman.

At which point, Ernest disappeared into the Village Inn, only to reappear after less than a minute with his father, with three more Cokes.

"Yes, Officer, I believe you want the boys to tell you what they saw?"

"It would be helpful to have an eyewitness to the crash. Here is my card, sir," on which was written: POLICE CONSTABLE PETER TINKLER.

"Okay, Officer, ask the boys anything you wish about the crash, but just two things I'd like to say. First, they are young boys, so I do not want what they say to be used as evidence in any court hearing that I imagine the crash will be heard in; and second, they are not to be regarded as giving witness statements that could be used as evidence."

"I understand that sir."

"Will you note my comments in your little black book?"

"Of course, sir, fully understood."

"That's fine then, I'll let you carry on. Tell the officer exactly what you saw boys, don't make anything up or elaborate."

The boys nodded at the instruction.

"Where would you like to start boys?"

"I'll start sir," said Ernest. "We were sat here waiting for the procession to appear we thought it would be at walking speed. Then this low-loader careered round the corner at breakneck speed and headed straight towards us. It was terrifying."

Zach continued: "I saw the whites of the driver's eyes, sir. They were frightening, open wide, staring at us while trying to wrench the steering wheel."

"We jumped up together," said Tom. "Just as the driver had wrenched the vehicle around the chicane through the village. By then he was totally out of control as it headed into the ancient Crab Inn brick wall, decapitating the old Crab sign, which fell down onto the wreckage."

"We were lucky sir, the driver saved us, he might have crashed through us into this place. To us he is a hero, he pulled it round, missing everyone," said Zach.

"So, a lucky escape boys."

"Yes sir, and we are still here drinking Cokes. We are worried about the driver and the Queen. She couldn't get out. As the lorry turned away from us the four girls on the back of the lorry were thrown off into the road, along with the furniture. I don't know if any were hurt, but they were picked up by adults and taken into Holliers Hotel. I think they were hurt," said Tom.

"Sir, I know my father said we are not to be used as witnesses, but we'd be happy to show up in court if you need us. We saw it all," said Ernest.

"We'll swear an oath sir," said Tom, holding up his right hand and offering the palm of his left as if he were holding a bible.

"Thank you, boys, but I think your father will have the last word on that," he said, looking at Ernest.

"Dad is a very busy man – and very important I may add – so we'd prefer you not trouble him. We catch trains by ourselves all the time, we'd just take a day off and be there," said Ernest.

"You mean play truant?"

"No sir, we'd clear it with the Head."

"Okay boys, we'll bear that in mind," said PC Tinkler. "I hope you enjoy the rest of your Coke and your holiday."

"You'll need us in court sir, we saw it all," said Zach, as Tinkler departed with a generous smile.

Both casualties had died instantly at the scene at the moment of impact. The high stone wall that had stood for a hundred years surrounding the Crab Inn, had been struck with great force by the front of the vehicle, bringing down the ancient stone wall, crushing the driver's cab and the steel cage housing the Carnival Queen's throne, which had been buried in rubble from the collapsed wall. This tangled wreckage lay in a corner of the police compound and could offer no further insight into the murder.

Bruno decided to start with a visit to the owners of the low-loader transporter, a building materials company located at Ryde St John's, a semi-industrial area one mile from

Ryde. It was a medium sized company called Westlake's Builders Merchants, owned by Malcolm Westlake who had started the business in his twenties, thirty years previously, now employing sixty-five people.

Malcolm Westlake ran an efficient business. As an employer he was liked and respected by his employees and all his customers who knew him.

His low-loader was a write-off and the subject of an insurance claim which the insurers would pay out in full. The damage to the building and the claims by the two accident victims' relatives might cause problems, if the accident was proven to be the result of sabotage.

Bruno had to divulge the result of Pimley's report to Westlake in order to get his views on the cause of the accident. His pleasant manner explained why he enjoyed the respect he did from everyone he came into contact with.

"I knew Mick McClusky very well," he said. "He'd worked for me twenty years ago, until he found another job which suited him better in a different field. It was not just as the driver of my low-loader that we knew each other. Mick ran the Shanklin Scout group, which I also support by supplying some of their equipment, tents, portable stoves and waterproof clothing. He was on the Shanklin Carnival charity organisation and for the past seven years I was pleased to release one of our vehicles into his care for a couple of days. He was a good driver with an HGV licence. He is a great loss to us all. It was a tragic accident, and I am completely mystified why anyone should want to injure Mick. He was a genuine person who gave to the community."

"Did you have anything to do with the servicing of the vehicle?" said Bruno.

"No, our vehicles are held on three-year leases, during which time they get one hell of a bashing, then we upgrade to new vehicles. Mick's vehicle was in its third year and was regularly serviced on time or mileage and I ensure that the low-loader I lend to Mick is in tip-top condition. Leasing contracts include a schedule guaranteeing regular servicing, which maintains the vehicle's resale value. Our vehicles are maintained by Kennedys in Shanklin."

"Could we have sight of the maintenance record of the vehicle?"

"Of course, I will get my office assistant to bring it up."

While they waited for his lady to appear with the maintenance record, Westlake expressed his sadness at the death of Gillian Napier, the Shanklin Carnival Queen.

"Such a young life, her parents will never get over it."

"They have lost the most important part of their future."

The file contained the maintenance record since the purchase of the vehicle and Malcolm Westlake provided Bruno with a photocopy to take. Several pages recorded everything that had been done on the vehicle since the date of purchase. Later scrutiny of the service history showed no defect on the braking system during the thirty months it had been leased by Westlake's.

Kennedy's log was signed at the date and time of each service by the mechanic who had carried out the routine work. Three mechanics had worked on the vehicle during its thirty-month period of lease with Westlake's. The most recent service was done on 23rd May, six weeks prior to the accident, and carried out by Robert Proctor.

"The sabotage to the braking system could only have been done immediately prior to the parade," observed Bruno, "while the vehicle was parked in Popham Road awaiting the start of the Carnival, or it could never have been driven to the start. What time did the vehicles assemble before the parade starts at 7 o'clock in the evening?"

Andy Bowen had found out from the parade organiser that the vehicles assembled early, sometime before 6 a.m. After that the vehicle decorators arrive, throughout the day, with flags and bunting to set up their displays.

"Mick's fully serviceable low-loader was in place at 6 a.m.," he said. "At the start of Popham Road, to be the leader of the procession."

After they departed Westlake's, Andy said: "Any time after 6 a.m. the saboteur could have climbed onto the vehicle and cut the brake cables and removed the bolts from the steel lintel. Anyone noticing him would have assumed he was decorating the vehicle. Whilst in Mick McClusky's care the vehicle was kept in a secure place. So let's make a visit to his home."

CHAPTER 3

THE MCCLUSKY FAMILY lived in a detached house between Lake and Sandown, with a drive that led to a rear hard standing capable of supporting a commercial vehicle and where the low-loader was parked in the build-up to Carnival Day. It had been parked behind his house to await decorating by a group of like-minded men and women known to McClusky who, on Carnival Day, would walk alongside of the vehicle with collection buckets in aid of the Carnival nominated charity. They were community volunteers and friends who had known each other for half their lives and who loved Mick deeply and his death had stunned the local people.

Bruno believed that when it became common knowledge that McClusky had been murdered someone might come forward with information that would help the detectives find his killer, but for now it was the long slog, starting with a visit to Robert Proctor at Kennedy's workshop and then to Barney Puff, the blacksmith responsible for fixing the canopy. Their visit to McClusky's home confirmed that the saboteur would not have inflicted the damage on the vehicle there.

Bob Proctor, aged about forty, was an experienced mechanic who had worked for Pat Kennedy for twenty years. They serviced and maintained all types of commercial vehicles and operated a body shop for crash repairs. Proctor worked on Westlake's vehicles, which were all of a similar type. The service record of the vehicle confirmed its 40,000 mile service had been completed in accordance with the manufacturer's instruction manual. Without divulging any details of the defective brakes to Proctor, Andy asked him to describe his examination process.

"It's a heavy vehicle which can carry up to ten tons of building materials, sand bags of cement, bricks and steels, so an examination of the brakes is always thorough, and if there is any wear the part is replaced."

"How about the linkages, hydraulic connecting rods, for example?" said Andy, demonstrating his newly acquired knowledge of commercial vehicles.

"Everything is done according to the manual and all defective parts are repaired or replaced. It's straightforward," he said. It was an informative answer from a professional who confirmed the recent state of the vehicle.

Proctor knew Mick McClusky and believed the police's health and safety interest in the vehicle. In his opinion it was not a problem with the brakes that caused the crash. However, Bruno did ask him to examine the vehicle post the crash, which might reveal something to his experienced eye. He considered taking him into his confidence, for his knowledge might point a finger, but he left that to another time.

"I think he must have passed out at the wheel. It was a shame it was on a downhill section of the parade or he'd have just stopped, and those two people may still be alive," he said.

"Did you have anything to do with the Carnival?"

"Nothing at all, but Malcolm always called me over to make sure the vehicle was fully serviceable and ready for the parade before Mick came to collect it from him."

"Thank you, we may come back for more details about the vehicle, if we discover anything amiss," said Bruno.

Their next visit was to Barney Puff, or "Puff the blacksmith", as he was known, who did the welding and built the canopy to house the Carnival Queen's throne.

He was at work in the barn that housed his forge behind his bungalow when they arrived. Set on a three-acre smallholding on the Newport Road, three miles outside of Sandown, his wife successfully grew root crops for sale to the public from a roadside shed.

Barney was a tall, strong man with the physique of a body-builder, genial and happy to speak about his work on the Carnival float, which he had undertaken in previous years.

"I built the frame that supported the canopy a few years ago. I took it down at the end of the season and stored it out the back," he said, pointing to a covered area behind him.

"Mick drove over a couple of days before the crash with the truck and we bolted it onto the floor. It took us a couple of hours to secure. We checked it and he took it away, same as previous years."

"Did you know Mick well?"

"Quite well, he was an estate agent. I met him when I bought this place," he said referring to his present home. This place has got everything we need and it works for us, I think Mick did us a favour."

"Tell me about the canopy?" said Andy.

"It was an aluminium frame and it could never have been blown off if the weather was bad and windy. It was secured to a steel lintel with eight bolts, four each end."

"How easy was it to fix?"

"The lintel stabilised the aluminium canopy by its weight. The structure was supported by galvanised scaffold poles secured to the base of the truck. The throne sat inside it. It was solid and could not move."

"The bolts that secured the lintel, were they tight?"

"They were, eight metal bolts, which held the frame together, four at each end of the steel."

"Could they have been taken out by anybody?"

"They could have been taken out by anyone with the right tool, you'd need an adjustable spanner."

"Why would anyone do that?" said Puff.

"We are not saying that anyone would, but six of the securing bolts could not be found amongst the wreckage?"

"I can assure you all eight were tight in place when I set it up and a crash would not have loosened them. It must have been one hell of a crash to sheer those fixings!"

Bruno thanked Puff for his help and they drove back to Newport.

"Is he a suspect?" said Andy in the car.

"Not the type," said Bruno. "Murder would never enter his head. He is a person of interest only because he built the canopy, but as far as we know he would have no reason to murder someone. If we showed him the lintel, as it is now, he might have something to say."

"We'll come back again in a few days when he's had time to think about it," said Bruno.

It was clear that the people with a professional interest in the vehicle could not help in identifying the murderer, so Bruno's investigation had to begin with two victims who came from different backgrounds. So, who would want to kill one of these two people?

The delicate task of meeting the relatives of the victims lay ahead for them.

Over a relaxing supper with Janet, Bruno broke the news to her about the police discoveries regarding the wrecked vehicle and Barlow's decision to give him the case. The thought of a vanishing summer holiday did not perturb her. She understood police work and the thought of helping her partner solve a difficult problem would interest her.

She was aware of the accident and had joined in school prayers for Gillian and her family on the day after the accident.

CHAPTER 4

THE DETECTIVES AGREED that this murder was not intended to kill the Carnival Queen, which meant that the target was McClusky, so it was with the persons connected with him that Bruno's investigation started.

Andy Bowen believed they should not ignore the parents whose daughters had not been selected as the Carnival Queen. Bruno disagreed: he thought that too extreme, but his suggestion was not so fanciful as to be discarded immediately.

"Let's build up a picture of McClusky, his family and business associates first," said Bruno.

The vehicle was in his possession for two days from the time it was released by Malcolm Westlake until the evening of the accident. Throughout this time, it had remained parked at the rear of McClusky's garden, out of sight of the road and his house, except during a visit to the blacksmith to assemble and fit the throne housing. Anybody could have had access to the vehicle whilst it was parked in Popham Road awaiting decoration on the day of the Carnival and its early evening start, suggesting the murderer was familiar with the pre-Carnival activities.

Mick and his wife, Eileen, had two children, a son and a daughter in their early twenties. His son, David, was in the Royal Navy and lived in Portsmouth, and his daughter, Melanie, was a trainee solicitor, commuting to Portsmouth on the hovercraft daily from Ryde. Eileen worked in an NHS Clinic in Shanklin as a receptionist. They were a contented married couple who attended St Augustine's parish church in Shanklin, where they had been married twenty-four years ago. The Vicar, the Reverend Peter Singh, knew the family well.

Mick was a Chartered Surveyor and from their estate office in Newport worked for a Southampton headquartered company called Middleton's Land Agents, who sold property, woodland and farms on the Island. Mick had become well-known on the Island and turned in handsome profits for his employer every year.

Although grieving the loss of her beloved husband, Eileen was fully co-operative when asked by Bruno if she would talk about Mick and his life and work. The public still believed the crash was a tragic accident, with no indication of foul play. However, Bruno informed her that during a police experts' examination of the vehicle they had discovered problems with the periodic service schedule and their investigation was continuing into certain clerical errors. He was careful not to reveal their belief that her husband's death was part of a murder plot.

Because it was their opinion that Gillian was collateral damage, they did not intend to jump to conclusions about any person connected with her.

Eileen revealed that Mick had planned with Eileen to set up his own business. He could rely on the loyalty of Island people, many of whom were his personal friends.

"After twenty years with Middleton's, Mick was the cornerstone of their business and he was confident that he could start his own business, and that it would succeed," she said.

Every significant land transaction, buying, selling, renting went through Middleton's Newport office. He had developed the Newport branch so that it was the most profitable estate agency business on the Island. It was a gold mine, but Tom Middleton, the owner, couldn't acknowledge that without Mick running it, it would not be the business it was.

Mick had asked Tom to be made a partner a couple of years ago, but he ignored him and he was frugal with his remuneration package. Staff came and went with Middleton's, but Mick held it all together establishing and maintaining a proper professional image.

"When Mick said to me that he was leaving Middleton's

and setting up on his own in Ryde, he wanted me to run the office for him. I was thrilled that we could work together and build a family business. A medical receptionist in today's Covid world is a crap job. No one has a pleasant word to say to you," Eileen explained.

"After we decided we could do it, Mick, out of courtesy, told Middleton what he was planning to do. He went crazy. He accused Mick, who had built the business up from nothing, of disloyalty and theft, and threatened to sue him for everything you could think of. He couldn't accept that nobody has a divine right to a customer in any business. Mick had nothing to fear but there is no doubt that Tom frightened him. It was not the kind farewell with good luck wishes he deserved. He suffered anxiety for weeks about leaving, but I kept him resolved to set up his new business. I gave in my notice straight away and as soon as he decided, we found our premises in Ryde, with the help of a solicitor friend of his. We had savings to cover the lease and set up, but more important than that was once the Island farmers got whiff of what Mick was doing, they promised to hold back instructions until we'd opened up, which was to be four weeks from now."

Eileen shed a few tears at this disclosure and whispered to herself, "Poor Mick, who did this to him?" revealing to Bruno that she felt that perhaps this was not an accident.

She was a woman whose life had been ruined, but with family wasn't ready to be beaten by her husband's death. She continued to tell Bruno about his plans, which she was determined to implement, and Andy within earshot, did his duty and made tea.

"He'd been a modestly rewarded employee for twenty years, and the denial of Middleton's blessing could have affected his concentration that night," she said. "His threat to sue him had worried him for weeks."

"I don't know what caused the accident but Mick was an

excellent HGV driver. There must have been defects with the vehicle, so someone must be to blame," observed Bruno.

"Well, the threat to Middleton's is not going away," she said. "I have signed a ten-year lease for the office and written to all Mick's contacts thanking them for their loyal support over many years, and saying that David our son was starting the family business using his name David McClusky.

"David and Mick were very close. David used to work with him during school holidays. After work in the summer, they'd go sailing, they had a great bond between them and David learned the business from Mick. He joined the Royal Navy at eighteen and went to officer training in Dartmouth and excelled as a cadet. He passed out as a Midshipman and after one year was promoted to acting Sub-Lieutenant and now, he is a full Lieutenant, but he has developed bad eyesight which limits his scope for any sea jobs, and your success in the Royal Navy is related to your sea time in command of a ship, like in the Royal Air Force, where you must have wings and have flown an aircraft as a pilot to achieve the highest rank.

"When David learned of Mick's death, he offered to resign his commission and take over Mick's role. He said he knew many of dad's clients from his school holiday jobs at Middleton's, and he'd build from there. It's the silver lining I never dreamed would happen."

Eileen's face lighting up, briefly dispelling the gloom of grief.

"Now it's like I have got Mick back, and I intend to put Middleton's out of business on the Island. Do you know, he has never contacted me since Mick's accident? After twenty years' service from Mick, you would think he would speak to his widow?"

It was an astonishing omission, thought Bruno, who felt relieved at Eileen's story. For her it was hope for the future and a kind of happy ending, and she had given them their first suspect, Tom Middleton. Two weeks after the crash, if he was in anyway involved, he may be thinking he'd got away with it.

CHAPTER 5

WHEN THEY CALLED to speak to Gillian Napier's parents they were as accommodating as Eileen McClusky. Frances and Bob Napier were in their early forties, and their grief was all embracing. Gillian had been their only child and her death had left a gaping hole in their lives.

Frances, an attractive woman, thirty years before had also been elected as the Shanklin Carnival Queen, and for some years had become determined that Gillian would follow in her footsteps. Because of the family connection with the church she had got herself elected to the Shanklin Parochial Church Council who were responsible for choosing the Carnival Queen for the year. There were seven members of the council and she openly tried to ensure that the others pledged their support for her daughter. However, securing the role for Gillian was not straightforward.

Bob Napier was upset about the Carnival Queen selection process. Everyone knew how the voting had gone at the selection meeting, and if Frances had not been so persuasive, somebody else may have been chosen. Nevertheless, Bob had suppressed any feelings of blame that he might have harboured and accepted all the blame himself as her father.

Frances was just about coping with the emotional distress of losing her daughter in pursuit of her desires, and sat quietly as Bruno explained their reason for visiting: "We bring condolences from the police and feel that with such an accident we should offer you the chance to talk about anything concerning the accident."

Frances Napier's demeanour indicated that she believed it had been her fault and she should not have been so obsessive about wanting her daughter to be the Carnival Queen.

Bruno responded by saying what she needed to hear. "You

must not blame yourself Mrs Napier, you were doing your best for your daughter."

"But I got her chosen," she said.

"Did she ever say she didn't want to be the Shanklin Carnival Queen?"

"No, but I know she was doing it for me."

"I am sure she was," said Bruno. "She was a pretty young lady that you have a right to be proud of."

She lowered her eyes and shed a tear and took hold of her husband's hand.

"Mr Napier, is there anything you would like to say about the accident?"

Bob Napier asked about the reliability of the vehicle.

Bruno ensured him that all of Malcolm Westlake's vehicles are maintained regularly to high standards. He said that they had visited the vehicle owners and inspected the service record of the vehicle and nothing in their mechanic's report after each service suggested there was any potential problem. Being less than three years old it had not required an MOT. Nevertheless, the police had asked a specialist in vehicle crashes to look at the wreckage and report anything suspicious, and they would pass on their findings to the Napiers if there was anything unusual in their report.

"I am surprised the vehicle went straight down the hill into the Crab Inn wall," he said. "Have you checked the steering?"

"We've checked everything," said Andy.

"We believe the driver was trying to avoid the crowds lining the pavements, so he kept to the road as much as he could," said Andy. "The medical report on the driver did not find any evidence of a heart attack, as has been suggested by some.

"We saw her set off from Popham Road and were following the procession on foot, so we didn't witness the accident, but we've been back to the site of the crash since."

"We understand there were several candidates for the role of Carnival Queen. Can you tell us about those girls?"

"They were all given roles as princesses or attendants, except Elizabeth, the Martin's daughter. When Gillian was chosen, she withdrew. She was younger than our daughter and the Martins said she'd try again next year. I think Jane Martin was pleased."

"What about the other mothers of girls who applied to be Carnival Queen?"

"They were all lucky to have escaped the crash. Sadly, Gillian was trapped inside the steel canopy."

Bruno had learned as much as he could from the Napiers, so it was time to let them grieve privately and figure out how they could rebuild their lives which seemed an impossible task without the light of their lives.

"Mr and Mrs Napier, thank you for seeing us, and please contact either of us if you want to talk about anything that happened around the time of the accident or since," said Bruno.

"Do you think that there's something suspicious about the accident?" said Bob Napier.

"Yes, we do," said Bruno. "But we have not discovered the cause of the accident yet, which we must do before we finalise our conclusions," said Bruno. "There could be health and safety issues that could affect all these annual Island Carnivals. Until we are satisfied this is an accident, we shall continue our investigation. Please don't read anything into routine police activity. A number of civilians could have been injured or killed but for the bravery of the driver, who in that awful moment when he realised he had lost control, did everything he could to avoid the crowds which might have cost him his life. It was his tough call. These Carnivals are annual events on the Island, and are run by volunteers who spend most of the year fundraising. The Town Council is responsible for the routes they take, so every aspect of this event must be looked at in depth in the interests of public safety," said Bruno. "If we discover a cause of the accident, of course we'll let you know."

"Thank you for explaining that," said Bob Napier. "I agree public safety is paramount."

◈

"Let's talk to the other members of the Shanklin Parish Council and get their take on the election of the Carnival Queen," was Bruno's next suggestion to Andy, once they had left the Napiers.

"They meet the first Monday of each month at 6 p.m. in the bar of the Shanklin Theatre, so let's wait until next week and tell the Chair we'd like a chat at 5.30, before their meeting.

"For now, let's focus on McClusky's business activities and visit Middleton's head office in Southampton and his office in Newport and speak to his colleagues. Twenty years is a long time to work in one location and we need to get an in-depth knowledge of his business activities. He was a pillar of the community but not without enemies, his wife pointed out, namely with Tom Middleton. Why has he not visited her? That's a question we should put to him."

"She certainly didn't like him."

◈

Middleton's Land and Estate agents occupied the former Westminster Bank building on the southern corner of St John's Square in Newport. Terry Matchett had run the office for years, and was responsible for the admin, accounts and seeing the staff gave a high level of service to their clients. It was a thriving business, due to the dedicated efficiency of Matchett and the sales skills and Island-wide contacts of McClusky.

Matchett responded eagerly to Bruno's invitation to visit the Police Station, an option he chose in preference to Bruno visiting their offices.

"Everybody knows the police, especially the locals, so I'll

come to you," he said.

At the appointed time after lunch, Terry Matchett showed up at the station and sat with Bruno and Andy in Bruno's office. They weren't questioning a suspect, so one of their basic interview rooms with a clock and a camera and see-through glass was inappropriate.

"How have the office staff taken the death of Mick McClusky?"

"Badly," he said. "He was the longest serving member of staff and well-liked by clients."

"He recruited every person who works in the office."

"Everybody liked Mick," said Matchett.

"How is everything going without him? I believe Mick was the chief salesman?"

"And brilliant he was too."

"So far, we are maintaining our level of instructions, and I have no doubt we shall achieve the asking prices. But it's early days," he added cautiously.

Matchett was small, one might have said petite, at a guess five feet five inches, wearing a suit, a tie, polished black shoes with leather soles and a decent watch. In all he seemed a pleasant, serious man. By Bruno's estimation he was an excellent number two, who would not be averse to plotting against number one, if it could be of benefit to him.

"What is the secret of success in your business?" said Andy.

"Obtaining instructions. Without instructions we have nothing to sell."

"Most things don't sell themselves," said Matchett. "It's our job to create a desire. Everything has its price, and every buyer has a limit. Our job is to match them."

"And Mick made all the sales at Middleton's?" said Bruno.

"He did the face-to-face stuff. I did the marketing and advertising, which is indirect selling. Selina took the photographs, measured the property and produced the sales literature. Harry drew the site plan on the computer and I did the advertising schedule for the County Press property page. Sometimes Middleton's take two pages. Then there are the auctions. There's a lot of legal packs to assemble when we decide to auction farms and small holdings. Mick did none of that."

"So, in spite of losing your chief salesman, whose valuable connections brought in the instructions, everything will go on as normal?"

"Probably," said Matchett. "We might even do better, which will please Tom Middleton."

"Did Mick and Tom get on?"

"They appeared to. Tom thought the business should do more. But in truth we were as profitable as we could be, and working flat out, and Mick was happy being the big fish in a small pond. We could have opened an office in Cowes or Ryde, but Mick didn't think he was paid enough for what he did do, certainly not for what he'd have to do with a second office to run."

"Did you know that he was planning to leave Middleton's and set up his own business in Ryde?" said Bruno.

"Yes, but I didn't think it would happen. When he talked to Tom he threatened to sue him if he took any business from us. So, I expected Mick to back off and drop the idea. You see, if he'd taken our business, we'd all be out of a job."

"Wouldn't he have taken some of the staff with him?"

"He might," said Matchett. "But all the while we were doing the business and 90 per cent of us live in Newport. Tom Middleton lives in Hampshire. He doesn't know any of the Island farmers."

"So, although Mick was the key man, you did all the work in the office?"

"Mick was not the whole show. Now he's gone it's up to me to retain the existing business and build."

"Can you do that?"

"I think I can."

"Do you know of anyone who had a grudge against Mick who might want to harm him?"

"I'd be surprised if no one bore a grudge given some of the deals he pulled off over the years."

"Can you give an example?"

"I won't go that far, Inspector, but sometimes when a buyer wants a property that's under offer, he will offer sweeteners and Mick would pick those up for himself. That's the business."

"Have you got any proof of that?"

"He'd come in with chocolates for all of us."

"That's not proof," said Bruno. "That's something for us to think about. If you can put a name to any of those deals we'd appreciate it."

Matchett looked Bruno in the eye unsure whether to disclose details, but decided not to, or couldn't.

"Who are the majority property players that you've dealt with on the Island?"

"There are developers, those who buy dilaps to improve and sell on. They are pretty sharp operators and all seem to make a fortune, but are always moaning about someone. Now if that's it, Inspector, I'll take my leave and go home to see my lady for tea?"

Matchett had demonstrated that he was a good office manager, but Bruno doubted he could hold it together without Mick as the frontman who brought in the instructions and completed the sales. With Mick in place, he had a job, with him as a competitor running his own business, Middleton's might disappear and Matchett with it.

"He would not have murdered Mick to put himself on the line for a job he didn't think he could do, would he?" said Andy.

"He is a person of interest. We need to know more about

him."

"We've spoken to Puff and Matchett. Who's next?" said Andy. "Do you think either of them would know anything about the vehicle's hydraulic system?"

"You can find out anything on the internet. Key in the type of vehicle and you can see the detail in drawings, just like Pimley's report," said Bruno.

CHAPTER 6

WHEN THEY COMPARED NOTES of the conversations with Terry Matchett and Barney Puff the blacksmith, Matchett was smooth and overconfident and might have had something to conceal. Barney Puff had played his role and nothing more.

Matchett portrayed McClusky as out for himself, a wheeler-dealer, without producing any evidence. His comments said more about him than McClusky, with the implication that McClusky's demise was more about Middleton's property business than it seemed by the nature of the accident.

Bruno suggested they see Middleton on Monday after he'd dealt with his visit to see Matchett, who'd said he'd planned to visit Newport that day.

"You would think he would be all over the business without McClusky running it," observed Andy.

"Perhaps he is, but it seems that his principal interest is himself."

"If Middleton doesn't come to the Newport office on Monday, we'll go to Southampton to see him and find out more about McClusky. After twenty years he should be able to tell us what his relationship with McClusky was. His side of the story about McClusky's threat to set up his own business might give us a lead."

"I'll call him," said Andy. "And make an appointment, then he can't block us and we shall know if he is coming."

"If he does try to duck and dive, tell him we will see him at our convenience on Saturday morning in Southampton," said Bruno.

When he called the Southampton number that Matchett had given him a lady put him through to a pleasant sounding man who agreed to meet on Monday at the Newport Police Station at 2 p.m. Bruno would have preferred to visit

Middleton on his home patch, but his friendly willingness to visit the Newport Police Station was a start.

✦

Over supper with Janet at their Friday evening gourmet meal, which she prepared with great enthusiasm, they discussed the McClusky case. She believed that there was something fishy about the Middleton business, as it appeared to be at the centre of everything.

"Tom Middleton runs it as if it were in another country, not ten miles away or a short ferry ride from where he lived," said Bruno. "He could have commuted to Newport from Southampton daily rather than show up monthly to collect the takings. He's lucky the staff haven't stolen the business years ago."

"Did McClusky ever visit the office in Southampton?"

"We don't know, we will find out from Tom Middleton and then we'll visit his Southampton office."

"Don't give him any notice," she said. "What does Andy think?"

"He doesn't eliminate suspects easily."

"There's a good balance between you then," she said as she placed lobster thermidor on the table.

"McClusky and Matchett don't sound like small-time dummies to me and Middleton definitely sounds a mysterious character," she said.

✦

Janet's observation was confirmed when Middleton appeared at his office at 2 p.m. on Monday afternoon for a friendly chat with Bruno and Andy following his lunchtime meeting with Matchett.

He was younger than Bruno had expected, early forties, at least ten years younger than Bruno and fifteen years older than Andy.

"Thanks for dropping in," said Bruno. "Whenever someone dies in mysterious circumstances it's the job of the police to interview the nearest and dearest and as his employer you fall into the first category. What can you tell us about Mick McClusky?"

"What were the mysterious circumstances?" asked Middleton.

"The driver lost control of the Carnival float," said Andy.

"Did he suffer a heart attack?"

"The post-mortem did not reveal anything abnormal. He was fit and healthy."

"Regarding Mick, he was a first-class manager of our Island business."

"Tell us about the rest of your business on the mainland."

"Middleton's land agency business was started by my great-grandfather in 1892 and occupied offices in the business district of Southampton," he began. "It grew rapidly to become the largest land agency in Dorset, Hampshire and Sussex. I was educated at Winchester and attended Cirencester Agricultural College, joining the family business after five years of working for Strattons, a London property business where I qualified as a Chartered Surveyor."

His condensed history revealed nothing about him or his present role in the company or what the company now did.

To Bruno's question, "How is business on the mainland?", he replied, "Buoyant, very buoyant."

He was a different person to the one Bruno had envisaged from Terry Matchett's description.

But then Matchett, who'd spent his entire life living and working on the Island, had only dealt with Middleton through McClusky.

Middleton explained that the office staff in Newport were happy and loyal, contrary to Eileen McClusky's opinion and added that they were all paid well with excellent working conditions and a generous annual bonus linked to performance. "We wouldn't have kept the same staff year after year if they had not been perfectly happy."

Although he spoke well of McClusky there were one or two aspects of his recent activities relating to specific clients that were not in line with the company's professional standards.

"Give me an example?" Bruno said.

"Recently we valued two farms west of Cowes with adjoining sea frontage. Both were sold quickly to a single London buyer at the value determined by Mick. In spite of our good connection with both vendors, we were not officially instructed to sell either property. These two farms were sold through a firm of solicitors in Ryde called Jarreds. They handle Island property deals, and specialise in farms, woodland and sea frontages and in select residential districts such as Seaview, Bembridge, and Cowes. Lawyers are not normally the first to know if a landowner wishes to sell, so they develop good connections with the land agents which, on the Island, was with Mick at our Newport office."

"Any others?" said Andy.

"None that I am aware of," said Middleton.

"Are you certain that the request for the valuations came from the vendors and not from Jarreds? It would seem strange that both vendors came to Mick for valuations of their farms at the same time, and then both subsequently did not instruct you? Unless Jarreds were acting as sales agents."

"Matchett believes there was something irregular about the transaction, and in the normal course of business Mick, on receiving a request for a valuation from the vendors, would have been given the heads up to sell them."

"Did Mick, in his professional capacity, ever do valuations when you were not instructed to sell?"

"There were occasions," said Middleton.

"So, what did Matchett think was irregular on this occasion?"

"Before we could agree a sales contract, we were contacted by Jarreds in Ryde who informed us that both farms had been bought by an individual in London. We had no knowledge of the identity of the purchaser or the name of the individual. Mick claimed he knew of Jarreds, but not the purchasers."

"So, you lost the sale?"

"The two vendors say they were contacted by Jarreds and were made offers which exceeded their asking price, so they accepted these offers."

"Terry Matchett says that only Mick knew these properties were coming to the market. That was obviously not the situation," said Bruno.

"What about your office?"

"Inspector Peach I am not speculating on what might have happened in these sales, but Matchett believes Mick did some deal with Jarreds that financed the offices he was setting up in Ryde."

"Really?" said Bruno. "And do you believe that?"

"It's a possibility," said Middleton.

"Does that mean you do believe Matchett?"

"It's possible Inspector," he repeated.

"So, Mick knew Jarreds well?"

"I don't know if well is correct, but Middleton's have contacts with most Island solicitors."

"Are you suggesting that he took a commission on the sale for himself?"

"I don't know," said Tom Middleton. "It's probably more a case of, I'll scratch your back, if you scratch mine."

"When did you become aware of this?"

"Recently from Matchett."

"Why would he tell you that story after McClusky had died? Surely with a big deal at stake it was a discussion that should have taken place at the time."

"What does it suggest to you?" Middleton did not answer Bruno's question.

"Can you tell us anything that might help us in our investigation?" said Bruno.

"I think the sale of these two farms might have had something to do with the crash in which McClusky died, but I don't know what. The death-in-service claim that we shall submit to Zurich which covers the death of a key staff member will be high."

"How high?"

"High six figures."

"Who are the beneficiaries?"

"The company, because of its loss of the key man, and Mick's family. It's always a fight with a big claim," he said.

"Can we see the death-in-service insurance policy?" said Andy.

"Is it relevant to your case?"

"We don't know, but it is a box we'd like to tick."

"I am sure that can be arranged."

Middleton departed in a friendly manner, promising to keep in touch, without the slightest intention of letting the police see McClusky's death-in-service insurance policy.

Nevertheless, Bruno had enough to get back to him with as his investigation developed.

"We need to speak to Matchett again, so he can explain to us his suspicions and the basis for them," said Andy. "And then there is Jarreds. Let's visit them. We should get truthful answers from lawyers."

"Don't kid yourself," said Bruno. "The sale of these farms was a big money deal and the vendors probably had no intention of selling their business until the person whose idea it was, who is not from the Island, made offers that couldn't be refused. These vendors wanted professional valuations, hence McClusky was hired to provide them, but not to sell the properties. Farmers are financially very smart they wouldn't have sold their farms without negotiating the best possible value. The fees for Mick's valuations went through Middleton's business, so all was above board."

"Probably," said Bruno.

CHAPTER 7

MICHAEL JARRED agreed to see the detectives that after-noon at 5.30 after his office in Ryde closed. There were still people working when they arrived, and a smartly dressed lady showed them to the meeting room where Michael Jarred was waiting. Coffee was offered by the lady before she departed and the three men introduced themselves and the detectives exchanged business cards. Jarred was in his thirties, smartly dressed and as friendly as he had sounded earlier on the telephone.

"Gentlemen, you are investigating the cause of that terrible accident. How can I help?"

"Yes Mr Jarred, we are investigating suspicious circumstances surrounding the death of Mick McClusky in a motor accident in Shanklin three weeks ago. In discussions with his employer, Tom Middleton, and his office manager, we understand that he was involved in the sale of two adjoining farms in the north-west of the Island, and that Jarreds were doing the legal work?"

"Let me first express my sadness that Mick should have died in such a way, and that the young lady should have also died in the crash. I have known Mick for several years. He was honest, professional and always a pleasure to do business with. I am pleased that the police are investigating this accident, because it doesn't seem possible after safety standards imposed at all public functions that this could have happened. Something must have been wrong with the lorry."

"We have had an expert from the Met in London looking at the vehicle," said Andy. "And we should have his report next week."

"Regarding the negotiations for the sale of Westhill and West Ridge farms, the situation was not as you might understand it. Jarreds have been buying farmland on the Island on behalf of mainland clients for fifteen years. I have permanent instructions that if this or that becomes available to inform my clients immediately.

"I know Mick very well, I've worked with him on many deals. He was a brilliant negotiator and easy to deal with – unlike Matchett in his office. Have you met him?"

"We have, and we probably agree with you," said Bruno.

"I also know the owners of every big farm on the Island, not just the big farms, the strategically situated. When my client expressed an interest in buying any farm of 1,000-plus acres in the west if the Island, only a handful qualified. I know all of the farmers with this size of farm, so I spoke to them all. I asked them, are you looking to sell? And if so, when and how much? Two of the owners who were getting on expressed an interest and asked me to obtain an offer. I advised, for correctness, that they obtain a valuation. And I asked Mick.

"I already had from my London clients their proposal and offers but the vendors wanted an independent valuation. Mick did the job, they agreed to sell, and they accepted my clients' offers, which were higher than Mick's valuations. He didn't undervalue, they paid a premium to stop an auction, and as both farms were for sale at the same time there was a premium for them.

"Detective, I am not a land agent or a broker. I wanted an independent valuation from a man who knew Island land values. So I asked Mick, who I admit was surprised they had not instructed him. When he assumed I would invite Middleton's to sell them I told him our position and he was happy to have helped me. He gave me his valuation documents properly stamped which I presented to my purchaser and they bought from the vendors direct. There was no need for them to incur agents' fees. How Mick's involvement was viewed by his company, I don't know.

"Mick was a professionally qualified valuer and surveyor, and we paid a Middleton's invoice for the work he did."

"What would the commission be for the agent if he'd sold the two farms?"

"One per cent of the selling price or a negotiated fee based on the sale price achieved. So, if the sale for each of those two farms reached £5 million, 1 per cent would be £50,000 times two, might be £100,000. Not many of those around," said Jarred.

"Would Tom Middleton know about these two farms?" said Bruno.

"Definitely," said Jarred. "And he would be kicking butts in their Newport office for not getting the instructions to sell them. Mick said to me recently that he was planning to set up on his own, so I did the legals on a lease in the right part of Ryde for him. As we had a good connection, I imagined that we would continue to do business together. Now I understand that his son is going to set up the business in Ryde."

"Will you help him get it off the ground?" said Bruno.

"Certainly I will."

◆

It was late when they left Jarreds, so they went to Yates Hotel opposite his office for a beer to recap on their day.

"Nothing untoward with him," said Bruno.

"No, Mick was a victim of circumstances. He'd expected to be instructed, but Jarreds' client was there first, and no agency fees, but they earned professional valuation fees," said Andy.

"Considering the size of his business on the mainland, Tom Middleton's reaction at not getting the instructions was a bit over the top," said Bruno. "Matchett has led him to believe that Mick was involved with the sale of these two farms, because he was leaving to go it alone. Mick wouldn't have done anything that would have laid him open to the wrath of Tom Middleton. He did the valuation under the Middleton umbrella, so everything was open and above board. We have to check with Matchett on that. We'll ask him to show us the fee note for the valuations."

◆

"Tell me about Middleton?" asked Janet at supper that evening.

"A tricky businessman from the mainland, a deal-doing estate agent type. Needed McClusky to front his Island office. He inherited the business from his father, which operates from Southampton. We saw Jarred this afternoon, a professional lawyer with excellent city connections making a fortune down here on the Island."

"Could the missing bolts have been an accident?" suggested Janet. "Could the person building the throne have forgotten to finish it?"

"No," said Bruno. "It would have been a very careless omission and Barney Puff is not that person."

"Perhaps it was an evil act of jealousy by someone connected to the Carnival," she said.

Bruno acknowledged that jealousy could have been a motive for this crime. "But so far neither the Napiers, nor anyone else, had given any indication that Gillian was a target and for us to pursue that would be a waste of time."

"If Gillian was not the target, Mr and Mrs Napier might have been for reasons you need to find out. You'll get a better idea when you speak to the PCC," she said.

Halfway through a bottle of red wine it was the time for Bruno to switch off from his detective work and relax watching *Line of Duty* about bent coppers, and enjoy Janet's supper.

CHAPTER 8

MATCHETT AGREED to a second interview on Thursday afternoon, and in view of his aversion to police turning up at Middleton's office, Bruno suggested they meet informally at his home, to which he reluctantly agreed as well as bringing the valuation fee note for the two farms.

He lived a fifteen-minute walk from St Thomas's Square in Newport, in a three bedroomed bungalow, opposite Newport Town football clubs run-down stadium. When Bruno and Andy arrived Debra, his girlfriend, was in the house and primed for their visit. Matchett was not the lonely bachelor he might have seemed.

He lived alone, but Debra was an almost permanent fixture in his home. She cooked and cleaned for him and often stayed over, when she could escape from her widowed seventy-seven-year-old mother's grip, for whom she behaved in the same slave-like manner that she did for Terry Matchett.

She had no official job. She was an unpaid carer for her mother in receipt of Carers Allowance. She was an ordinary lady, probably in her mid-thirties, unmarried, a caring woman with few personal needs, secure in the knowledge that when her mother died, she would inherit the family home, and maybe live permanently with Terry Matchett. That was her sincere hope.

To Debra, Terry Matchett was god-like and his delusions of grandeur might have been the result of the admiration she showed him, almost as an acolyte. He was undoubtedly kind to her, in return for which she did all she could for him. Bruno was pleased for Matchett: it showed his positive human response, and answered some of Bruno's questions about his personality and his capacity for an evil response to McClusky. He came to the conclusion that his attitude towards Mick rested on the threat he posed to the business and what his departure might mean to him and the staff at Middleton's with potential job losses.

The highlight of Debra's life with Matchett was their annual two-week holiday together on a Fred Olsen cruise ship, departing and returning to Southampton, usually in September, which gave substance to their claim to have travelled the world together. Without Matchett she would never have been taken to Egypt to ride a camel, or to see the midnight sun in Norway, or to watch the dancing girls at the on-board evening extravaganza after shaking hands with the ship's Captain at the gala Champagne reception.

On a cruise they enjoyed the company of other passengers at their level, and the comfort of a superior cabin with a balcony. They kept contact details of new friends, married couples who lived mostly in the North of England to whom they sent Christmas cards. The local Newport travel agency always ensured they had the best on offer from the shipping company, and the reward points earned guaranteed their return cruise.

Matchett kept up with local events through his office contacts but was not an overly social person. They frequently went to the cinema and afterwards dined in Chinese or Indian restaurants. Matchett's dress and manner indicated him to be a bit of a ladies' man.

Bruno was finding it difficult to detect a trait in Matchett that would lead him to commit a crime of this complexity or a motive for him. He did not display any pleasure at the demise of McClusky, as someone about to inherit his position might show in the subtlest of ways.

"Who will replace McClusky at Middleton's?" he asked him. "Could you do his job?"

"Of course, but I would change the way the business is run. Promote a young negotiator, let him do the spade work. I think I could expand the business considerably."

"Middleton will have other options?"

"Maybe, but if he has, he hasn't mentioned them to me yet. I shall wait until the dust settles. If he doesn't appoint me to run the business, I shall tackle him," he said. "The staff need to know who is in charge. Even if he wants to appoint someone else, he's got to give me a chance first."

"Has he?" said Andy.

"If he doesn't, I will probably leave. I own my own house, no mortgage, and I still have my parents' nest egg which I could use to do what Mick was planning. If get a chance and I find I can do it under Middleton, why couldn't I do it on my own?"

From where Andy sat, facing the rear garden, at a distance of 30 to 40 metres, he spotted what he made out as an old green vintage single decker bus. It was an unusual piece of garden furniture.

During a lull in Bruno's questioning he asked Matchett, "Do you use that old bus as a garden shed?"

"Definitely not," he replied. "It's a 1932 Vectis AEC Regal single decker, the only one on the Island. It is in pristine condition, you can't see it properly from here. It's here because we are showing it at the annual Chale show in a couple of weeks. I drive and Deb is the ticket collector. We wear authentic Vectis uniforms of the period. We also go to other shows on the Island during the summer, then store it in the museum in Ryde during winter where I'll give the old bus its annual MOT, grease the suspension and clean the plugs."

His enthusiasm for the old bus and his capability to keep it serviceable, shone another light on his personality. It also opened the detective's eyes to the possibility that with his mechanic's knowledge he could have been responsible for sabotaging the Carnival float.

Bruno's summary of their visit to Matchett was positive. He'd opened up as a fairly normal person, unlike the cautious office clerk he'd at first seemed. Andy's view was that he was their first suspect who had the skill to sabotage the

Carnival float, and with Andy's keen nose, Bruno could not eliminate him as a suspect.

Matchett and Tom Middleton believed Mick was to blame for the loss of the instructions to sell the two farms, although the evidence from Jarred proved otherwise. Matchett confirmed by bringing and showing the police the fee note that the valuations undertaken by Mick were paid to Middleton's. Matchett was not afraid that he would lose his job, because if Middleton was the shrewd businessman he portrayed himself to be, he would be aware of Matchett's contribution and plan to keep him, understanding what a threat he could be as a competitor.

McClusky had planned to leave imminently and set up in competition. Now the McClusky family was going to run the new business targeting Middleton's clients, so he had to maintain continuity by appointing Matchett with a salary and bonus to match.

"There is something I don't get about Tom Middleton, and that is that he seems totally trusting in his employees running his business for him, and at the same time he doesn't seem to trust them as individuals."

Bruno doubted a happy ending for Middleton. However, with what they knew about both men, it still did not put them in the suspects category, so, persons of interest they remained. It was time to look at the participants in the Carnival Queen selection process.

Gillian Napier's parents were devastated at their daughter's death and Frances Napier's influence in choosing Gillian for the role of Carnival Queen was a disastrous, self-inflicted wound, which would not heal.

The Shanklin Parochial Church Council chose the Carnival Queen from applications by young girls who live in the Parish. It was usually straightforward with an outstanding candidate, but this year there were several contenders, two of whom were daughters of council members. The Reverend

Peter Singh who chaired the seven member PCC on Monday evenings invited the police to attend and speak to the group the following Monday at 5.30 p.m. in the bar of the Shanklin Theatre.

◈

At home in their delightful part-renovated period house in Newport, Bruno fed Janet an up-to-date résumé of where he had got to. The one person he believed to be innocent of any involvement was the blacksmith.

Barney Puff, who had fixed the canopy on the rear of the truck insisted that eight bolts were needed to keep it rigid. Detective Inspector Pimley, the vehicle expert from the Met, found six missing, and agreed that eight bolts were necessary, which suggested the Carnival Queen was a target but so far nothing else suggested that.

CHAPTER 9

THE MEMBERS of the PCC attended their first meeting after the accident in the bar of Shanklin Theatre where they expressed their sorrow to Frances Napier, who suffered the loss of her daughter Gillian, known to every member of the PCC. Father Peter said prayers for the family and spoke beautifully about her.

The theatre was closed on Mondays, so the meeting remained uninterrupted and enabled each member to show their love and understanding towards Frances during a time of bereavement and despair in which it is impossible to come to terms with what had the potential to wreck the lives of Frances and Bob Napier. That she attended the meeting was a sign that she was trying hard to come to terms with the tragedy and accept the situation in which she found herself.

Father Peter began by introducing Bruno and Andy from the Island police to the six members of the PCC by name.

Mrs Linda Peploe, in her early sixties, was the senior member of the PCC, being its longest serving member, and as a magistrate a member of the Newport Magistrates' Court.

Frances Napier represented the parish wives' group. George Martin, a surveyor and insurance assessor, aged forty-eight, provided professional knowledge to guarantee the church was properly insured and ensured that it conducted its business in accordance with legal health and safety laws and were never exposed to claims for negligence. Sally Bots, aged seventy, the widow of a once prominent Island medical consultant, who too had been a churchwarden. Harold Belson, aged sixty-five, a retired solicitor and Eddie Jackson, aged sixty, a churchwarden and chairman of the Shanklin Conservative Club, provided a living connection with the town community and members of other church denominations. They were as a group generous, kind, helpful, understanding, and knowledgeable of the problems of some of the inhabitants of Shanklin.

Bruno respectful, calm, and friendly, explained why they were attending.

"Before we can accept the crash of the Carnival float as an accident, the police have to be certain there was no foul play, and to date we have not been able to establish that fact with certainty. So we are asking everyone with a connection to the Carnival and the victims to tell us about any unusual circumstances they may have noticed, on the day of the accident and in the days leading up to the day of the Carnival, and what they might have learned from other people about this disaster. Gossip sometimes brings forth surprisingly observant comments. The prime interest of the police is the health and safety of all the participants and members of the public who lined the streets as spectators.

"We are convinced that it was the bravery of Mick McClusky that prevented the vehicle from swerving into the path of the many pedestrians lining the route. So we must honour his bravery and ensure that if the crash was caused through negligence, it does not happen again."

Father Singh, an Anglo/Indian, had entered the Church of England after taking a degree in Theology at the University in York. After ordination he had served as a curate, assistant to the Bishop of Portsmouth and after two further church appointments in rural Hampshire was appointed the Vicar of Shanklin and Sandown. He was well liked, efficient, had excellent connections in the diocese, and likely to be promoted in the near future. His wife was enthusiastic and hard working in the church, promoting the wives' group, the guides and scouts. They had two boys, aged twelve and fourteen, who attended Ryde Grammar School, on full fee scholarships.

Father Singh began by explaining to the detectives the PCC's role in the Carnival.

"Inspector, Shanklin Carnival day is a very busy day for me because there are several floats and organisations and charities with which my wife and I have a personal connection, which I physically visit and to which I give my blessing. The vehicles start to arrive very early and park in Popham Road in accordance with their allocated starting position. I speak to as many participants as I can, wish them luck and say a prayer. It takes me all day and evening. It is always a happy occasion because of the young people involved with their parents, whose job is to see that everyone is fed and watered with sandwiches and tea and coffee before we start at around 7 p.m."

"Father, you say the vehicles assemble from early morning?" said Andy.

"Yes, during the day various supporters arrive to decorate and arrange the displays."

"So, all day the vehicles stand unattended in Popham Road?" said Andy.

"Supporters come and undertake a variety of tasks on the vehicles, which might include mechanics fixing things, carpenters, even painters, anyone with a special skill will turn up do their job and leave. Would you include strangers?" said Singh.

"The vehicles are accessible throughout the day anybody can climb aboard to do a job. But they would be known to someone?" said Andy.

"Not necessarily," said Singh. "They came from all over the Island."

What that meant to the detectives was that the saboteur, a stranger, could have arrived, unnoticed, cut the brake cable and extracted the securing bolts in a few minutes and left without anyone seeing them arrive and depart. It was the obvious time to do the damage before the procession began, while the vehicle was parked. But the saboteurs would have had to have been familiar with all the aspects of the Carnival.

"We said prayers before the procession started and as Gillian was the Carnival Queen this year, I went to her float and spoke to her. She was very happy and I thought she did credit to the PCC's choice of girl. I noticed nothing untoward during my visit to that float."

"Father, can you remember whether, once the lead vehicle starts the procession, it has to slow or brake at all before it reaches the top of the hill?"

He thought carefully before answering Bruno's questions.

"I would say neither. It is a gentle downward slope along Church Road, but by the time you reach Holliers Hotel it gets steeper. On the left you would need to brake before the steep slope into the Old Village, otherwise you might lose control through the chicane, which is what happened, so the vehicle went straight into the stone wall in front of the Crab Inn."

"Detective Peach, my name is Linda Peploe and I am a magistrate on the Newport bench."

Bruno had heard her name mentioned in the station, both favourably and unfavourably, for years but he seldom visited the magistrates' court. She was a well-preserved sixty-year-old lady who liked to be noticed.

"I am presuming that you are investigating this accident because you suspect that a crime has been committed?"

Bruno thought to himself, "If it has you will soon know about it."

"Thank you for your question, ma'am. Yes, the police are investigating a serious accident that cost two lives and threatened members of the public, not necessarily a crime at this stage. Rather, we are interested in the health and safety aspects," said Bruno.

"What have you discovered so far, Inspector?"

"Very little," said Bruno. "However, as your legal experience would appreciate, we are not in a position to divulge any details of our investigation."

"Was the vehicle unsound?" she continued regardless, which was just as well and might have prevented him giving a nosey magistrate a rude answer.

"We are working on every possibility Mrs Peploe."

Having demonstrated her magistrate's competence she smiled and shut up, in order to think of an awkward question to put to Bruno and his colleague, as magistrates were trained to do. They believed it was their duty to be on the side of the defendants in unfamiliar surroundings.

"All the members of this PCC have some involvement in the Carnival," continued Father Peter, "which raises considerable sums for the Island charities. Has anyone anything to say about this year's build up?" he asked the meeting. "Was there any competition about which charities you should support?"

As the PCC treasurer, George Martin explained how the collection was conducted on the night and the donations were made.

"Our major donation this year was to be to the Mountbatten Hospice in Newport. Two other major donations were promised to the Shanklin Manor Care Home, and to the St Mary's Hospital Covid support fund. The other Carnivals in Sandown and Ventnor have promised to help us if we cannot rely on our more generous supporters to donate a little more."

"Is choosing the Carnival Queen straightforward?" said Andy Bowen.

"It usually is," said Father Singh. "But this year we had two candidates: the daughters of two of the members of this committee. It was very unusual and both girls had outstanding merits. As chairman I exercise the casting vote in the event of a tie, and for the first time voting was three votes for each candidate, so I had to vote and chose Gillian, ahead of George's daughter, Elizabeth, for the reason that Gillian was by several months the eldest, and George's daughter could try again next year."

"Was that difficult for you?" asked Bruno.

"I understand George's wife, Jane, was not too pleased with me. However, I have since learned that Jane preferred to see her daughter have a clear run next year."

Then Frances Napier spoke.

"Ladies and Gentlemen, and Detective Peach, I hope you will forgive me but I would like to go home. I can't bear to travel over the accident any more. I have your number, Detective, and I will call you if I have anything to contribute."

"Mrs Napier, thank you for coming this evening and convey our sincere best wishes to your husband," said Bruno.

At Mrs Napier's decision to leave, George Martin also gave his apologies and they left together.

"I think she was very brave to show up," said Sally Bots. "I didn't go the Carnival this year. Too old. But I know that years ago there was always hot competition among the young girls of the parish to be the Carnival Queen. Nowadays they don't seem interested. You have to attend the charity functions throughout the year with people like me, so I can't wonder at it."

"How do you decide on who should be this year's Carnival Queen?" asked Andy.

"Easy. We all have one vote," said Sally Bots. "I voted for Elizabeth, I don't mind telling you it was equal three for each girl, and Peter had a casting vote."

Sensing there was something more revealing to come from Sally Bots, Andy asked, in an innocent manner, "Who else voted for Gillian apart from her mother and the Reverend?"

"I almost abstained," said Harold Bilson, "because I thought neither of these girls should be chosen as they were children of members of the PCC and with the high level of local interest a different girl would have been more representative. It looked too much like favouritism to me. In the end I was persuaded to vote for George's daughter, by Eddie. Isn't that so Eddie?" he said referring to Eddie Jackson, the senior churchwarden at St Augustine's.

"That's true," said Eddie. "But it's no satisfaction that she didn't win."

"If you three voted for the other girl and Father Peter used his casting vote to decide and voted for Gillian Napier, then Mrs Peploe, Frances Napier and George Martin voted for Gillian?" said Andy.

"Exactly right," said Sally Bots.

"Has George ever mentioned why he didn't vote for his own daughter?"

"Yes, he has," said Father Singh. "Jane said she'd prefer her to do it next year."

"But we all really know why," said Sally Bots.

"We don't all know why Sally, and perhaps you should keep your fictitious theories to yourself?" said Linda Peploe, sensing that Sally Bots was about to say something controversial. "You shouldn't be introducing gossip into this meeting, or you'll give the detectives a false impression."

"False impression of what?" said Sally Bots. "Linda, you're the biggest gossip I know! There isn't much we don't know about your fellow magistrates and the criminals who you gleefully send down."

Linda Peploe never got anywhere when taking on Sally Bots, so she shut up.

"Jolly lucky that she did," said Harold Bilson in a matter-of-fact way.

"Now you know that George Martin voted for Fran's daughter and not his own daughter, you've got something to work on, Inspector," said Linda Peploe.

"Have I?" said Bruno. "Can you explain?"

"We are only trying to be helpful," said Sally Bots, as if to rescue Linda Peploe from the need the explain something she couldn't.

Changing the subject, Bruno said, "Did anyone witness the accident?"

"I was in the Village Inn restaurant opposite the Crab,"

said Harold Belson. "The noise of the crash was earth shat-
tering. Emptied the lounge bar. Lucky it didn't catch fire or
it would have burnt the Crab down, and it could have gone
directly into the lounge bar of the Village Inn. That would
have killed a lot of people! But all they saw was the collapsed
wall. The vehicle was buried in rubble. It was impossible to
see the cab of the Carnival Queen's cage, which had collapsed. The Carnival procession was halted, although police
and ambulances took an age to arrive."

"The members of the PCC have no hands-on involvement
with the Carnival, we just administer the Carnival charity
collections and see that whoever the committee decides to
give a donation to is done properly and quickly. There are
receipts issued and signatures for every bucket transfer of
money," said Father Peter.

Before thanks to the members of the PCC for attending,
and leaving the meeting, Bruno asked that they think about
the build-up to Carnival Day and if any unusual incident
came to mind to call him or Andy. They gave business cards
to them all and left promptly after about an hour. Apart
from the Father Peter, who said prayers, none of them were
involved with the Carnival.

"It's not in their remit," said Bruno. "They are there to see
the church is run properly."

◆

The following morning, as Bruno expected, he received a
phone call from one of the members of the PCC. He knew it
would be someone who was not prepared to broadcast their
opinions to everyone at the meeting and if he'd been asked
to bet on who was calling, he would have won.

It was Sally Bots. "Inspector, it was nice of you to come and
see us yesterday evening. As those who chose the Carnival
Queen, we feel guilty in some way for her death. In truth, we
all feel we should resign from the PCC."

"Surely that wouldn't be necessary?" said Bruno.

"Inspector, there is one thing I thought I must tell you privately, and that is the reason for my call. It concerns Frances Napier and George Martin."

"Carry on," said Bruno.

"You witnessed their departure together from the meeting yesterday?"

"We did," said Bruno. "And I can understand that Mrs Napier could be very upset discussing her daughter's death in the manner in which we were."

"Detective, what I felt you should know is that Mrs Napier and Mr Martin are having an affair."

"That is none of your business," said Bruno. "How is that connected to our accident investigation Mrs Bots?"

"There is something, Detective. I am not sure what, but it doesn't add up?"

Mrs Bots suffered from that old lady syndrome, of wanting to be the centre of attention by inventing or sensationalising everyday occurrences.

"Mrs Bots, there is something I forgot to ask the meeting yesterday. When did you vote and choose this year's Carnival Queen?"

"It was a couple of weeks before the Carnival as I remember," she said.

"Anything else Mrs Bots?"

"There is something but I am not ready with it yet."

"Don't leave it too long. Thank you for calling Mrs Bots. Every bit of information or gossip could be helpful. We policemen must be careful that when we add two and two together, we don't make five. If you think of anything else, please call me straight away. Goodbye Mrs Bots," he said, while his mind returned to a key piece of information he'd learned at the PCC meeting, which he put to Andy for comment.

"Father Peter said that the floats had remained parked in Popham Road throughout the day of the Carnival, from

6 o'clock in the morning while men and women came and went, decorating and fixing displays. That provided the opportunity for any person to climb onto the vehicle, and in the cold light of day. Using the right spanner, as Barney Puff said, you could extract the retaining bolts that secured the lintel to the Carnival Queen's frame. With another tool you could cut the brake fluid connector, and quietly fade away. We have a list of the participants, so let's ask them if they noticed anyone working on McClusky's float at any time during the day."

"The Carnival committee will have details. I will get onto it straight away, sir," said Andy.

Sid Owen, the committee chairman was able to provide Andy with a complete list of each participant and, on listening to the police need for information, agreed to email them all with a general enquiry. "Did anyone see work being done on the Carnival Queen's float driven by Mick McClusky on the day of the Carnival?" was a simple question.

"I will call if I get any replies," he said. "They are all pretty security-conscious, so if anyone has seen anything they will tell me."

It was not quite a shot in the dark, but a long shot, they agreed.

When Bruno relayed his conversation with Sally Bots to Andy, he thought the call was well-intended, without malice, and something to be thought about.

As Napier and Martin did not stay until the end of the meeting it presented them with an opportunity to see them a second time individually.

The key piece of information gained from Mrs Bots' call related to when that decision was made on who the Carnival Queen should be. It gave the murderer time to plan and render the vehicle in the state that caused the crash.

What was she referring to when she said something did not add up?

She didn't enlarge on her point, but she will. She has become our Miss Marple.

"Marple usually solves the crimes," said Andy.

"I don't care who solves this murder, as long as it's us," said Bruno. "We will leave Napier and Martin for a few days then talk to them separately. Meanwhile let's visit Tom Middleton in Southampton, where we'll get a true picture of him. We will show up at his home first and then the Middleton business offices."

CHAPTER 10

Tom middleton lived in a suburb of Southampton off the Shirley Road, in a house he had inherited, where well-off professionals lived whose wives drove 4×4 cars to transport children to fee-paying schools, and while cleaners and gardeners tended to the household chores, they lunched together or played tennis, went running or went to yoga classes.

It was an elegant Victorian house, set in a garden with a wooded area on one side, and on the other side a hard surface tennis court. The house did not have a swimming pool, considered a liability by most owners of large houses. Inside it was full of possessions, oil paintings, handmade furniture, a library full of dusty old covers and a full-size snooker table and brass ornaments, all of which must have been there when Middleton inherited the place. The kitchen had been extended to accommodate modern living, leading to a comfortable lounge with huge television. It was an old-fashioned house, needing daily help to keep it clean and in tip-top condition.

Middleton, at Bruno's request, had agreed to meet early Monday morning at his home. In Bruno's experience some men were always willing to meet in their homes, so they could show the less affluent the trappings of their wealth. However, these men were usually less successful than their appearance.

First Tom Middleton introduced Bruno and Andy to Sonia, his wife, who was anxiously preparing to go out. She was an attractive lady in her early forties, who Tom claimed worked as the regional director of the National Trust in South Hampshire. She was friendly and after comments on the beautiful sunny morning weather, made and served coffee to the three men in their family lounge. She said goodbye to the two detectives and left the house with Tom, who saw her to her car.

On his return, they began their discussion, led by Bruno. "We are trying to build a picture of Mick McClusky's activities. As his long-term employer you might help us by clarifying your relationship with him, and open a window or two into his personality that would help us in our investigation."

"Your investigation Inspector?"

"Yes, the vehicle crash was not an accident," said Bruno.

"Do you have proof of that?"

"We have evidence that the vehicle was tampered with before it set off leading the Carnival procession which caused it to crash. So, we need to build a picture of the man, his friends and after-work activities."

"Did you know Mick well?"

"Quite well, not personally. I did meet his wife, Eileen, a couple of times, but that was all. I did not go to his home."

"He worked for you for such a long time. It would be unusual not to have enjoyed some social contact from time to time?"

"I used to go to the Newport office for a staff Christmas lunch every year, a couple of times Sonia came along and I lunched with Mick every month, when he presented the branch figures and we discussed potential business."

"He was obviously good at his job, but were you happy to let him go when he threatened to leave and set up on his own?"

"I wasn't happy to let him leave. In fact I would say the opposite. Mick had been threatening to leave for years. He had an inflated opinion of himself and believed he was solely responsible for the success of the Newport business. He thought he was worth more money and was reluctant to acknowledge the contribution of Terry Matchett and his backup team, and the professional way they ran the office which contributed to its success for which he liked to take all the credit. Without them and my support, he'd never have made it on his own."

"So, you had nothing to worry about if he'd left and tried it? But you threatened to sue him if he took any business from you."

"I would have protected the Middleton name on the Island and the goodwill, Inspector. I have long thought that Matchett could run the business without Mick, so now I may give him a chance," he added.

"Does he know that?"

"I'm still thinking about it. I am uncertain about his sales skills. I am going to Newport on Friday morning to discuss the business, and possibly offer him the job."

"I don't think he will be surprised," said Bruno.

"He deserves the chance," said Middleton.

"If you doubt his sales abilities, isn't that too big a risk to take?"

"I will be more hands-on myself for a while. I think it will work."

"You could take over from Mick yourself, living as near to the Island as you do?"

"I am not an estate agent, Inspector. Working in a office day in, day out, is not what I do. I am an entrepreneur."

"Can you tell us about the relationship between Mick and Matchett?"

"They were a team. No complaints from me," said Middleton. "I didn't involve myself with office politics. Mick encouraged the staff to speak to clients because he believed that was the way to network, build up relationships that won you new instructions, and he was right. By showing the clients a family side of the business as well as the professional, they trusted him."

"Trust is what you need in the property business. Matchett will do things differently, and hopefully be just as successful?"

"He could be more successful!"

"Isn't it a risk to try Matchett if he can't sell?"

"We shall see," he added with a confident smile.

"If we said to you that the vehicle, modified to transport the Carnival Queen, had been sabotaged; the brakes had been disconnected so that the driver had no way of stopping the vehicle downhill, which made the crash inevitable and resulted in the death of the driver and the Carnival Queen; what would you say to that?"

"Are you saying that Mick and the young lady were murdered?" said Tom.

"Correct," said Bruno. "As the driver was your employee, we think you might be able to help us find the killer. His death could be connected to Mick's business activities, your business activities if you like."

"Really?" Middleton looked puzzled and serious. "In what way?" he said, as if offended by the inference.

"Putting it bluntly, Mr Middleton, this so-called accident was the murder of your key man in Newport. A person you have worked with for twenty years, and know well. Is there nothing you can tell us about him, apart from your belief he might steal your business? Anything that might give us a clue as to who might have killed him?"

Middleton looked puzzled and said nothing.

Bruno elaborated: "With your in-depth knowledge of what went on in Newport, what can you tell us that will help us to find Mick's murderer? When you visited the Island what did you talk about? Surely not everything would have been plain sailing all the time?"

"You don't think that I killed Mick, do you, Inspector?"

"Don't put words into my mouth Mr Middleton. But I would be interested to know why you have not visited Mick's wife and family. Isn't that somewhat remiss of you, when he worked for you so long?"

"I suppose it is, Inspector, but since I learned of his accident, I have been very busy."

"Doing what?" said Bruno.

"Besides the Newport office business, I have been concerned with many other property deals."

"Mr Middleton, you had a motive. Mick was planning to leave and start his own business and take your clients away. So far you are the closest thing we have to a suspect."

"I still believe it was an accident, Inspector."

"I have just explained that McClusky was murdered, we have evidence to that effect, now we are looking for his killer, and you are our number-one suspect."

"This is a frightening revelation. Why would I murder Mick? He always achieved what was asked of him by myself and by the clients. I never heard a bad word against him. We had few differences from time to time. Don't be so sure we would lose any business to him, if he set up on his own."

"Apart from his business plan, was Mick working on something he did not tell you about?"

"It's possible Inspector, but I trusted Mick."

"Totally?" said Andy.

"Over twenty years nothing ever happened that caused me to distrust him. If somebody wanted to kill Mick, it wouldn't have been connected with our business," he said.

"With your knowledge of your business, please would you take a look at his recent activities, contacts and appointments when you visit Newport on Friday and tell us of anything unusual that has happened recently? He or one of your office staff must have been responsible for his diary and that might reveal something to tell us."

"I will do that, Inspector," he said.

"And finally," said Bruno. "You promised we could have sight of Mick's death-in-service insurance policy."

"Sonia has all of that documentation so I'll ask her about it."

"Ask her to forward a copy to me," said Bruno.

"Yes, Inspector."

"We must ask you to keep our visit confidential. It is not

released police information that McClusky was murdered. We want to retain an element of surprise as long as possible, and not alert whoever tampered with the vehicle. One last question: did you know that Matchett was a vintage bus enthusiast?"

"Yes, it is his hobby. He owns a 1932 Vectis single-decker, which he takes to summer fairs and vehicle shows. In the winter he stores the bus in Ryde Bus Museum, where he works on it."

"He would be an experienced mechanic to do that, wouldn't he?" said Bruno.

"I believe so," said Middleton. "Is he one of your suspects, Inspector?"

"At the present time we do not have a list of suspects. As a connected person naturally he is of interest."

"Like me, I suppose?" said Middleton.

"Yes," said Bruno. Sensing Middleton's unease at Bruno's nonchalant response, he added: "We cast our nets wide at the start of every investigation where the killer is not known."

"If I can find out anything from Matchett when I meet him on Friday that I think can help you, I will call you."

"If you would do that without disclosing our interest, we would be grateful," said Bruno. "Anything that might help us find the killer. McClusky's diary might be helpful."

◆

"Did we worry him?" said Andy to Bruno on their way back to central Southampton.

"Yes, if this murder has anything to do with Mick's job at Middleton's, he might turn it up. He has questions to answer."

Bruno felt they had learned something of use from their meeting with him.

"He was evasive," said Bruno, "as if something has been going on. Before we return to the Island let's take a look at the Middleton office here in Southampton," said Bruno.

"I am interested in what he does when he's not visiting the office in Newport, the size of his business in Southampton. How do we find out where his business is?"

"An estate agent should know where to find Middleton's," said Bruno.

They had driven to Southampton via the Lymington car ferry, so they were not stuck in one place and reliant on the local police for transport.

Several estate agents had never heard of Middleton's and the city list of estate agents and property companies did not have any by that name. It was the desk officer at Southampton Chamber of Commerce who provided answers.

Fred Winter, a late middle-aged gentleman, had known of the company many years before when it was run by Jack Middleton. "It went broke as the result of dodgy land deals down in the docks," he said. "For probably fifty years it had been a well-established successful business. When it folded it had massive debts, but it was a limited company so the directors escaped unscathed except for their reputations. If it had been a partnership, which those businesses usually are, they'd have all sunk together. It was the banks that caught a serious cold for millions. Now there is no Middleton's in Southampton, but it does still trade in other parts of Hampshire because it was bought from the official receiver by one of those big London firms, but no one in the family is involved."

"How long ago was that?" said Bruno.

"Ten years, maybe longer," said Winter.

"What about his son, Tom Middleton?"

"He worked for his father and must have been part of the debacle, but fortunately for him he was not a signatory on anything, so he too avoided bankruptcy. When the dust settled, he set up on his own as a land agent but no one around here would touch him, so he lasted a few months and packed it in."

Bruno was not surprised by Fred Winter's story.

"I was suspicious of how easily he agreed to meet us at his home," said Andy. "A successful businessman would have wanted to show us a thriving business."

"If there was one," said Bruno.

"Jack Middleton must have left his children a few quid?" said Andy.

"As part of a multi-branch operation, the Isle of Wight would represent a minor part of the Middleton empire, important as a branch, and as long as it made money, the larger business would accept it. It was obviously established as a separate company, or it would also have been acquired with the rest of the business. Now it looks as if it might be the entire business, which puts the departure of McClusky and his threat to set up on his own in a different light. I'd be surprised if Tom Middleton is officially the owner of the Isle of Wight business. Perhaps it is in his wife's name?"

"Who told us that Middleton's were the leading land agents in the South of England?" said Andy.

"They might still be, but nothing to do with Tom Middleton," said Bruno.

"Would the staff in Newport know that?"

"I would say not," said Bruno. "He obviously trades off it, though."

"How does that change things?"

"It suggests that McClusky was more of a threat to Middleton personally than we had thought, and if Matchett fails the business will fold, and Middleton will lose his livelihood."

"We know very little about Middleton and his wife," observed Andy. "Do they have children? What does he do when he's not counting the profits from the Island office?"

"Check on the National Trust and see if Mrs Middleton is what he said she is," Bruno requested.

"He said she was the regional director for South Hampshire."

"Maybe she is, but let's make sure that's not bullshit."

"I'll do that, sir," said Andy.

"Let's go and talk to Matchett and find out what he really knows about his employer."

CHAPTER 11

WHEN BRUNO CALLED MATCHETT, he was still sensitive about detectives calling into the Middleton office and agreed to come into the Newport station when the office closed at 5.30 p.m. That was okay by Bruno because it offered him the opportunity to be more direct, and an interview on police ground always brought more out of the interviewee. Matchett arrived promptly and behaved as if they were old friends, obviously after a good day at the office.

"Mr Matchett we asked you to come in to discuss a few things. How well do you know Tom Middleton?" enquired Bruno.

"Not very well. Whenever he came over, he saw Mick. He said hello to all the staff, but they always went out for coffee or lunch, to which I was never invited, and after lunch Mr Middleton wouldn't return to the office. I used to prepare monthly accounts for Mick who'd provide Tom with a copy. Mick was not a bank signatory. Office expenses such as heat, light, water, rates and the salaries were paid from the Southampton office. Salaries were paid direct to our personal bank accounts on the last working Friday of the month. Petty cash was recharged monthly with a cash cheque from Southampton; we have a float of £100. There were never any holdups over payments to staff or to local traders. Nothing was lavish with Tom Middleton. Mick had to fight hard to get everyone a pay rise every year, which he succeeded in doing while Middleton would use every excuse to limit the amounts."

"Were the staff underpaid?"

"I wouldn't say any of us were underpaid and we all felt secure in our jobs, or at least we did when Mick was in charge. Now we are not sure. He is coming to the office on Friday, so we shall know more then."

"Will he offer Mick's job to you?"

"He might. He hasn't much option really, but I can't do Mick's job as well as my own, and who will do my job?"

"He might expect you to do both jobs?"

"Then he'll have to get someone else in, because I am flat out already. Make no mistake. Mick worked extremely hard to keep us as the number-one land agents on the Island. He put his heart and soul into it because he loved it. If Tom Middleton had offered him a partnership he'd have been honoured and satisfied, but Middleton is not that kind."

"What are you going to do if he offers you the job?" said Andy.

"I'll see what else he offers and then decide," said Matchett.

"I think you've already decided," said Bruno.

"He could send someone over from the mainland, of course," said Matchett.

"What do you know about the mainland business? Have you been there?"

"I've never been there, but Middleton's advertise in the Estates Gazette. It's the industry periodical, so it's a pretty big company."

"The Middleton's you see advertised is nothing to do with Tom Middleton," said Bruno.

"It was until a number of years ago."

"Now you are a standalone business?"

"That's not what we tell everyone," said Matchett.

"Well, those are the facts, and when you see Tom Middleton on Friday ask him."

"We've checked Middleton out," said Andy, "and he doesn't have a person he could send over from Southampton."

Matchett listened while Andy shattered his belief that he worked for a big company. If the police were right, he'd be working for a one-man band, and that might worry him.

"What else does Tom Middleton do?" asked Andy.

"He runs the mainland business in Southampton, or that's what we all thought."

Bruno now saw the need to examine Middleton's activity and movements closely. Middleton senior had controlled the business with his son as an employee until about ten years ago when, according to Fred Winter, it had collapsed. Since then, apart from a brief period, Tom Middleton had taken the profits of the Island office regularly which, if that was all he did, implied a degree of avarice and laziness. With little else to occupy him it was surprising that he didn't involve himself more in the Island business.

"How often did he visit you at the office in Newport?"

"Monthly, more in the holiday season, but as I said he only dealt with Mick and they did not discuss business in the office. It's an open plan layout which doesn't lend itself to confidential exchanges. We were always pleased to see that head office took an interest in us. It gave us comfort that we were an important part of the business and a feeling of security."

"Did he always visit as a foot passenger?" said Andy.

"Usually, but not always," said Matchett. "Occasionally he came by car and I remember once he brought his wife, who he introduced to everyone. She was the kind of lady you'd expect to be the wife of a business high-up, or that is the impression she conveyed to us."

Bruno realised that the Island employees had not been aware of the limited substance of the so-called Middleton empire. Following Middleton's visit on Friday, Bruno asked him to call in and tell them what his proposal to him was.

"I am interested in what reporting to his office in Southampton he'll ask you to undertake, and his response to your request for help with taking on McClusky's job."

"I need to employ an experienced negotiator and take on the overall responsibility. That would require no increased investment," said Matchett.

"Okay," said Bruno. "Let's meet again after your meeting on Friday."

"Why would you want to speak to me again? I told you everything I know about Mick's activities."

"You have," said Bruno. "But I want to know about Middleton's plans for the Newport office now you are soon to become an established competitor to McClusky's wife and son."

"What's that got to do with me?"

"Just say that you are still a person of interest to us, and part of our investigation. If you are going to make a success of your new appointment, Middleton's response to the McClusky's threat will involve you, so I'd like to know his plans."

Matchett nodded but did not speak because he couldn't understand why Inspector Bruno Peach should be interested in Middleton's business plan, and he left the station visibly uneasy about the police's continued interest in him.

"He should leave and offer his services to Mrs McClusky's new venture in return for a partnership," Andy Bowen suggested. Bruno was impressed by his young detective's solutions to other people's situations, which were always food for thought and revealed possible motives and avenues for investigation.

The question occupying Andy was: did Middleton's doubtful character and business behaviour make him capable of murder? He wasn't convinced. Middleton was malleable but not vindictive or stupid enough to prejudice his lifestyle by murdering his key employee.

"That's a question we might find easier to answer after Middleton's next visit," said Bruno. "Meanwhile, try to find out what he does in Southampton when he is not making his occasional visits to the Island and what he was doing from the time McClusky collected the low-loader, three days before the crash, and if he travelled to the Island by car during this period. I'm interested in any visit he may have made by car during the three-day window and if he did not visit the Newport office. Matchett will have a note of his office visits – if he did visit."

◆

Andy Bowen decided to begin his investigation into the Middleton's by checking his membership of the Royal Institute of Chartered Surveyors, of which he claimed to be a member during his visit to Newport Police Station. As a qualified surveyor after the demise of the family business he would naturally return to his professional discipline and resurrect the career that he had abandoned in order to work in the family business. When Andy accessed the computer database of qualified members, against Thomas Middleton's name it stated his practicing certificate had been withdrawn 2016.

The RICS membership office in London would not provide any information on Tom Middleton's membership activities. But they did confirm that the withdrawal of his practising certificate would stop any qualified member from working as an RICS surveyor.

To find out why they had disqualified him, Andy presented himself to the membership secretary at his office in London at 11 a.m. the following morning, a stone's throw from Waterloo railway station, with an email letter from the Hampshire Chief Constable requiring access to the information on why his practising certificate was withdrawn. He was presented with a confidentiality document for signature by Peregrine Pleever FRICS, a serious man from whom a smile would have cracked his face. In an exchange of business cards Andy read that Pleever was the manager of the Institute.

"What do you want to know about Tom Middleton?" he asked in a manner that indicated he had prepared his answers.

Andy explained that the Isle of Wight police were

investigating a motor crash in which two people died. One of the casualties was employed by Tom Middleton. The vehicle on inspection was found to have mechanical defects that could only have been engineered by a knowledgeable mechanic and everyone connected with the casualties, even loosely, were being investigated about the accident. Middleton as the employer of the vehicle's driver was a person of interest to the police as someone who might shed light on the crash.

"Middleton had his practicing licence withdrawn as a result of malpractice; he approved all the structural calculations for a building at Southampton No. 2 dock. It was called the Cartwright building, financed by the local authority and built by the Samson Construction Company, which has since been wound up," Pleever explained.

"Middleton had certified steel supports throughout the building that were unable to take the weight of the concrete laid on the floors above. The entire structure had been constructed using the cheapest materials. The size of the steel supports where wrongly specified by Middleton. By the grace of God no one was killed when the building collapsed late one night causing enormous damage to adjoining buildings. The specification of the steel structure could never have supported this completed building, Middleton had a fortunate escape, avoiding a manslaughter charge had the building been completed and occupied.

"When he was sued by Samson's he declared himself bankrupt. His house in Southampton was in his wife's name. His professional liability insurance was totally inadequate and Samson Construction folded.

"This kind of incident happens occasionally, it's professional incompetence and cost-cutting by the builder which our members should resist, and they do. The local authority lost several million pounds as a result.

"I don't know what Middleton is doing now but if he

applied to have his license reinstated, I doubt of the council of the institute would do that. It was criminal incompetence. They could not risk it. I am surprised when you say the crash victim was an employee of Middleton. I don't know the laws of bankruptcy, but as an undischarged bankrupt he'd not be permitted to employ people in a business."

Peregrine Pleever's statements were supported with a copy of the Chartered Institute's minutes, and their disciplinary report referring to the Cartwright building and the reason for withdrawing Middleton's certificate as a member of the RICS.

◈

When Andy Bowen reported his meeting with Pleever to Bruno, he said it made their dealings with Middleton easier. He was not a man of substance, and from Pleever's report an undischarged bankrupt.

"Do you think McClusky knew the score with Middleton, and would it have changed their relationship?" Andy wondered aloud. "I'd be surprised if McClusky had not found out about his background. Could he have been blackmailing him?"

"That's food for thought," said Bruno. "But McClusky was a professional surveyor himself, so no. It raises the questions that Middleton's in Newport acted as a professional surveyor in some of their work, and without Mick they would not be able to offer that professional service."

"It would make it easier for McClusky to steal the business. As an undischarged bankrupt, Tom Middleton could not claim ownership of the Island branch but he could work for his wife's business."

"I think the best he can do going forward is to visit regularly, be quiet and keep taking the money."

"Let's paint a new picture of Middleton," Bruno said to Andy when he arrived back at Newport Police Station late afternoon.

"The family business that had existed for over sixty years was destroyed by Jack Middleton's dodgy property deals along the Southampton dock area. His attempt to recover by starting a small estate agency failed because he couldn't do the work. A one-man business demands everything. Near completion of one of the signature projects, the central tower containing the lift shaft and services collapses, by the grace of God no one was killed. The building company was wound up and as a limited company none of the directors lost a penny. The banks lost the money and everyone sued Tom Middleton, whose professional indemnity insurance didn't exist, so he was struck off as a practising surveyor and made bankrupt.

"In the background the Isle of Wight's business flourishes under the new ownership of Mrs Middleton. He creams off the profits for them both. He gets away with it all until the key man, Mick McClusky, hands in his notice, who then dies unexpectedly in mysterious circumstances. This threatens any remaining source of income.

"You will find the house is in his wife's name. It always is with these professionals. They are all frightened of making the big mistake," said Bruno. "The Island business is also in her name, and she signs the cheques."

"I'll check all that," said Andy.

"As an undischarged bankrupt with a trashed reputation it will be the only money he'll get his hands on, so he is a desperate man and that makes him, at the moment, our main suspect," said Bruno.

Andy replied, "I will have the information about any journeys to the Island in the three days prior to the accident tomorrow morning and, as The National Trust county directory does not name Sonia Middleton as the regional director of Hampshire, I will go to their office in Winchester and check her out."

CHAPTER 12

THE FORENSIC EXAMINATION of the bodies of Mick McClusky and Gillian Napier revealed nothing suspicious. He was not under the influence of alcohol or drugs and physically he showed no signs of any condition that might have contributed to the accident. Gillian Napier likewise, so their bodies were released to the families for burial.

The funeral of Gillian Napier would be an emotional experience that Bruno was dreading and with Andy Bowen it would show a police presence that he would prefer to avoid. For two police officers to intrude on this personal family occasion seemed inappropriate, but there lurked in Bruno's mind a suspicion, a hunch, that he should attend. It was an opportunity to see the people close-to who were connected with the Napier family. Sensing his uneasiness, Janet offered to accompany him.

There had been no sign during their investigation that the beautiful schoolgirl had been the target for this gruesome murder, so the absence of the retaining bolts on the metal structure supporting the Carnival Queen's throne was a mystery. It could have been an oversight during the assembly that would have held except for the stress caused in an accident. A more sinister theory could be the murderer wanted the canopy to collapse over the driver's cab ensuring the certain death of the driver. For the time being they had to accept Barney Puff's assurances that all the bolts were in place when he assembled the canopy.

As the Head Teacher of an Isle of Wight Primary School, Janet had a personal interest in an Island girl dying in such a manner. The health and safety of all Island schoolchildren she considered part of her responsibility. Her presence alongside two plain-clothed police officers was acceptable and diluted their presence and quelled Bruno's anxiety.

With Janet by his side, the detectives became mourners. She represented the educational establishment, attending on behalf of all young people on the Isle of Wight who spent their time on Island Carnival activities to raise money for the many Island charities.

There were representatives from St Mary's Hospital, all seven PCC members, the St John's Ambulance, her teachers, friends from school and her relatives. There were one or two strangers and several of the parents of the girls who had been unsuccessful with their application to be the 2022 Shanklin Carnival Queen, and who were involved in the Carnival Queen's charity program.

Bob Napier had promised Andy Bowen to tell the police if any person, male or female, unknown to them came to the crematorium, and to find out who they were. The crematorium chapel was full to capacity, with representatives of the Island press attending. Everyone was invited for coffee and refreshments, arranged by the vicar's wife at St Augustine's church hall in Shanklin after the service.

Janet agreed to go and mingle with the family, enabling Bruno and Andy, having paid their police respects, the polite chance to leave. She understood what Bruno wanted to find out and her pleasant manner would likely elicit anything of value that their presence at the family coffee gathering might not.

◆

Later over an evening supper at their favourite Newport fish and chip restaurant, Janet reported on Gillian Napier's wake at St Augustine's church hall. Two strangers who did not seem connected to anyone were representatives of the Mountbatten Hospice Trust who were eternally grateful to the Island Carnival organisers for the generous Carnival charity donations.

The official groups who attended the crematorium did not go for coffee, which left about twenty family relatives and the members of the PCC. As far as Janet could tell no one from the McClusky family attended the funeral.

"The PCC attendees were as you described them," she said. "Father Singh, Linda Peploe, Sally Bots, two gentlemen, Frances Napier, and George Martin. All were of interest because it is too early to rule some of them out from being involved. Frances Napier and Jane Martin did not speak to each other, relying on the brief acknowledgement with a courteous smile and nod. Jane Martin knew Frances Napier on more than a casual acquaintance level. No tearful message of condolence, and for a woman of her age not to put an arm around Frances and engage in a quiet personal conversation demonstrated an unusual cold-heartedness between the two mothers, one having lost the most precious possession in such horrific circumstances. Her obligatory attendance was probably because George Martin was a member of the PCC. There is clearly an issue between them which should not have stopped her expressing her friendship," said Janet.

"What about Bob Napier?"

"He was a man who behaved as if he had lost his whole world, a little lost but attentive to the goings on. He will need some counselling. It was obvious their daughter meant everything to them, and if Frances is involved with George Martin, on a personal level, his marriage has an uncertain future."

"How did you find Frances Napier?" asked Bruno.

"She is grieving and guilt-ridden, because she feels solely responsible for her daughter's death, and she is also frightened that somebody has targeted her. "

"Go back to the PCC and pick up on the gossip and get them talking. What they say could lead you to someone who is responsible for the crime. A lot of harm has been done to Frances Napier and she will feel she is the target of the killer, not her daughter, and that they have unfinished business," suggested Bruno.

"But she was not the target," said Janet.

"How do we know?" he persisted.

"Not physically; psychologically she will have suffered immensely. If she was the target then the killer will have achieved their aim. We don't know what that aim was, but if this murderer has mental problems, she would be right to be afraid," Janet said.

Bruno had not considered that.

She continued, "There may have been some backbiting connected with the choosing of the Carnival Queen by some mothers of the contestants, and one of them might know something? It is not certain the killer or killers meant to murder – possibly they only intended to wreck the display and the vehicle? If so then they are living in fear of being found out for a crime they never intended. So you should not just look for a murderer. Have you spoken to any of the mothers?"

"Not yet," said Bruno.

"One of the parents could have a grievance," suggested Janet. "Find out from Father Singh how many girls entered the competition, speak to the mothers, get their take on the accident."

◆

So far Bruno had given low priority to speaking with the mothers of the other contestants for the honour of election as Carnival Queen. Taking Janet's advice, he set Andy Bowen the task of obtaining a list of applicants who'd entered the Carnival Queen contest from Father Singh. It was something they might have forgotten. Concentrating on McClusky's activities and plans had taken priority. Nevertheless, Bruno believed Gillian Napier's death unfortunate, and a case of the murderer's plan gone wrong.

"Let's not forget the missing bolts," was Andy Bowen's thoughtful response to Bruno's summary. He was inclined to look closer at Barney Puff's involvement.

"There were six missing and we should have found them if

they were in place at the time of the crash – unless the person who extracted them took them?"

◈

From Father Singh, Andy Bowen obtained a list of eleven applicants for the Shanklin Carnival Queen who were interviewed on a Saturday afternoon three weeks prior to the Carnival. All the contestants were invited to attend at the same time for tea and cakes in the church hall and each applicant was asked one question only: why do you want to be the Shanklin Carnival Queen?

Their answers were similar and wisely connected with the charity activities that the Carnival Queen was expected to participate in during the summer. All said they were determined to raise record amounts for the charities supported through the Carnival's activities.

Five girls were, in Father Singh's opinion, too young to undertake the commitment, which involved speaking to groups about the Carnival's objectives. Two of the more mature candidates stood out. Both were outstanding and capable of the obligations demanded of them: Gillian Napier and Elizabeth, Jane Martin's daughter. According to Singh the unsuccessful candidate's parents understood the Carnival Queen's obligations during the summer, and appeared to be relieved at what seemed the Vicar's fair decision, satisfying the young girl's ambitions with a promise of inclusion next year. All members of the PCC felt unhappy that the two candidates were both daughters of members of the PCC but satisfied the competition had been fair.

"I suggested they should share the honour," said Father Singh. "But no one could see how that would work, so we conducted the selection as usual, by a majority vote."

"Were you surprised by the outcome of a 3/3 split by the PCC?"

"Not at all. George Martin was under pressure from Jane to withdraw Elizabeth, so he voted for Gillian."

"Any reason for that?"

"George said Jane was too busy to give her daughter any support during the summer. As I saw it, Elizabeth would have her turn next year. This is Gillian's final year at school so she could be anywhere next year, working or at a University off the Island."

When Andy examined the list of parents, he concluded that their applications were the result of pressure from the girls, who, nevertheless, could claim some kudos from being a shortlisted name. Having happily accepted Father Singh's comments they could relax, discharged of the obligations all summer of supporting the Carnival Queen.

◆

Andy Bowen had a gossip's gift for wringing out confidential snippets of useful information in little private chats with connected parties, as he regarded the members of the PCC. And so, it proved, when he took the opportunity to speak to Sally Bots, the widow of a local surgeon and GP. Acting as her husband's secretary she had had access to the medical records of all his patients and as curiosity and nosiness was a key element in her personality, she read up on everyone, even strangers she had no connection with.

It gave her a godlike feeling of power, but she was careful not to be the source of information that could have only come from her husband's confidential patient records. It was her connection and friendship with the small Island fraternity of GPs and surgeons that provided her with the essential elements of her contribution to the gossip's agenda. As a doctor's widow, having lost touch with the Island medics and contact with her husband's patient database, she relied on old friends the Women's Institute and her husband's past associations, including Shanklin Cricket Club, of which he had been a long-time member and past President and in his young days a fine opening batsman.

On any short shopping expedition to the town, even at a

bus stop, she could meet a friend, where they would evangel-
ically update each other with events and current affairs. Her
natural inquisitiveness provided enough interesting material
to remain the town's best gossip, and she had a take on everyone. It is often said that gossips make the world go round,
which is the reason that handsome Andy Bowen called to
see her at her very pleasant house in Victoria Avenue in
Shanklin.

The fabric of the building was well maintained by local
tradesmen, and Bill her gardener of twenty years continued
the planting cycle instigated by her late husband, which kept
alive pleasant memories of their very happy lives together.

Andy knew that with a blend of respect for age and senior-
ity which she believed she was due as the widow of a well-
known former GP, he would discover more about the PCC's
decision to select Gillian Napier as the Shanklin Carnival
Queen.

"We all knew what the result of the ballot would be,"
she said. "You see, George Martin is besotted with Frances
Napier, you can tell. They arrive at our meeting together and
they leave together, and I know they invent meetings so they
can go somewhere together."

"How do you know that?" said Andy.

"I will tell you, Inspector."

"It's actually Detective Sergeant, Mrs Bots."

"I am sorry, I know it is that charming Detective Bruno
Peach who is an Inspector. When I called George to speak to
him about an insurance claim on a collapsed stone wall at St
Augustine's, June Martin told me that he was out and she'd
ask him to look at it and get him to report to the PCC at our
next meeting. I didn't mention the date to her as it was a full
two weeks until our next meeting."

Sally Bots continued: "After I had spoken to Jane at 6 p.m.
I called Frances to tell her I'd asked George to look at the
church wall. Bob said she was at a PCC meeting and George

had given her a lift. He simply confirmed what we all thought all along."

"All? Who is 'all', Mrs Bots?"

"The other members of the PCC."

"And what did all the PCC members think?"

"That they are having an affair. We think they should resign from the PCC, but it gives them an opportunity to meet, so why would they? We have our reputation to protect," she said.

"How will it damage the reputation of the PCC?"

"People talk, and they will think that's all there is to us."

"Does Father Singh know about this?"

"Of course he does. At least, we all think he does. When our meetings finish, Linda, Harold, Eddie and I stay behind and have a drink in the theatre bar. Father Singh goes home, and the love birds go off. So I know what they all think."

"What is the relevance of their relationship to this awful accident? People have these clandestine relationships all the time," said Andy.

"I know that, but they don't end up like this," she said.

"End up like what?" said Andy. "I venture to say that their relationship hasn't ended up. This is simply a catastrophic accident involving Frances' daughter."

"The connection between the couple and the accident is for you to work out, Inspector. I am not saying there is a connection. That would be awful if it was true, wouldn't it?" she said.

"Do you have any other ideas Mrs Bots?"

"None," she said, and after a pause added, ". . . at the moment. You should speak to Jane Martin. Men don't often get away with having an affair without their partner knowing about it, because a woman owns a marriage, she protects it and Jane Martin is more savvy than most I would say. You've heard the expression 'hell hath no fury like a woman scorned' Inspector?"

"I have, Mrs Bots. I take it you're referring to Jane Martin?"

She was comfortable calling him Inspector, and perhaps she didn't realise the significance. It was the first time Andy had noticed that she really was a forgetful old lady, so he let it pass.

"Mrs Bots, thank you for speaking to me. I'm sure you've opened up a new line of investigation. As you suggest I will speak to Jane Martin. You have been very, very helpful."

"It is my absolute pleasure, and Inspector, please call me Sally."

"Mrs Bots, I have to keep our relationship on a professional basis," replied Andy praying she didn't take it the wrong way.

He felt he had learned that Sally Bots was an influential voice on the PCC. He was unsure of her assertion that George Marti and Frances Napier were having an affair. More than likely they had other problems they were consoling themselves over.

And the parents of the contestants were helpful people seeking to give their little girls what they wanted – a place to shine in the sun, with nothing to hide.

Andy was able to satisfy Bruno's concerns about the parents of the other contestants and concentrate on the next task of understanding more about the Middleton's starting with a visit to the Southern offices of the National Trust in Hampshire.

CHAPTER 13

A NDY BOWEN travelled from Cowes to Southampton as a foot passenger on the Red Funnel car ferry to meet Sarah Grayson, the managing director of the company, who was reticent when he called enquiring about passenger journeys from Southampton to the Isle of Wight. However, it was a police request, so she agreed to meet him. The Red Funnel dockside terminal was the company administration, bookings and data centre for all travellers and the place to find out if Tom Middleton had made any visits to the Isle of Wight by car in the three days prior to the accident that killed McClusky and Napier.

Red Funnel is the original and first Isle of Wight ferry. It celebrated its 160-year anniversary in 2021. However, there was nothing outdated about its present-day operation.

At the request of the Southampton city police unit assisting Andy he was able to obtain a record of every vehicle to and from the Island for each departure in the three-day period leading up to the Shanklin Carnival date.

Bookings for car ferry sailings are made online, requiring the car registration, driver's name and the number of passengers. Sarah Grayson a pretty lady in her early thirties, understood everything about Red Funnel. She was naturally inquisitive, asking questions that Andy did not answer precisely. She remained with him while an office assistant in front of a computer screen checked the driver's names for the three-day period. Andy was in luck when Tom Middleton's name appeared on the passenger list twice the day before the Shanklin Carnival day, departing early morning, returning early evening on Carnival day.

This was an unexpected discovery and focused their investigation onto the dubious Tom Middleton. It was possible that this visit was business-related, but it demanded investigation, beginning with a discussion with Matchett at the Newport office, which Andy would undertake on his return that afternoon. Sarah Grayson had provided a copy of his booking with ticket details for police evidence.

Andy then took a taxi to the regional office of South Hampshire National Trust on the western shore beyond the Southampton docks. He was intent on killing two birds with one visit. The twenty-three-room former home of the brother of Lord Montague of Beaulieu was surrounded by manicured lawns and well-tended beds of summer flowers.

He hoped to meet Sonia Middleton and learn more about the Middleton business in Southampton, which did not seem to exist. He wanted her take on the accident and Mick McClusky who, according to Matchett, she had met once or twice in Newport, and her husband's reaction on learning of the accident in which his key employee had died. After all, he had not, according to Eileen McClusky, responded as a good employer would by visiting the family with his condolences and an offer of support especially financially.

At the reception desk of the South Hampshire National Trust office the response to his request to speak to Mrs Middleton was immediate. 'We have nobody of that name working here.'

Andy then asked if he could speak to the person in charge of the office.

"Our local director is Caroline Shuttleworth. Who shall I say is calling?"

"Detective Andy Bowen from the Isle of Wight Police."

She relayed the information to a voice on the telephone whose reply he heard: "I will see him in the interview room in ten minutes."

Progress, thought Andy, continuing his so far successful morning. The female voice sounded friendly and coffee came quickly followed by Caroline Shuttleworth. She was a stylishly dressed, middle-aged lady.

Andy produced his identity.

"How can I be of help, Detective Bowen?" she said reading from his business card.

Andy adopted a casual attitude to explain his calling without an appointment.

"We are investigating a vehicle accident that took place on the Isle of Wight three weeks ago, in which Mrs Middleton's husband's manager and a young lady died. As one of the casualties was employed by the Middletons, we thought Mrs Middleton might help us with our enquiries. So, we are speaking to every person who had any connection with the driver who was killed. We met her briefly last week, while interviewing her husband, but we called at an inconvenient time and did not have a chance to speak to her because she was leaving for work. Her husband was unsure of certain timings and we are sure she'd be able to clear these up. We understood from her husband that she is a director of your organisation and expected she would be here."

"Detective Bowen, Mrs Middleton is no longer working for us. She left very recently."

Her reply was not a total surprise. Once again it confirmed Bruno's hunch that her early departure from the home the previous week was to avoid being drawn into a conversation with the police.

Mindful of the complex rules contained in data protection law, he asked if she could elaborate on her departure and why she no longer worked for the Trust. He did not have to prise the reason for her departure out of Caroline Shuttleworth. She was more than willing to explain to a police officer.

"In the Trust we are continually trying to improve the methods we use to be faithful to the work we were established to do," she said. "One of these tasks is to improve the access to the properties we maintain by road widening, eliminating dangerous bends on access roads, ensuring we protect and make safe river banks, and creating car parks. Many of these improvements require the purchase of small parcels of land and, where redundant, the sale of the occasional plot of land or sheep grazing. There are many such sites on the Isle of Wight, which you may be familiar with, with spectacular views. If you 'Walk the Wight' on the annual pilgrimage, taking the coastal path, you will come across dozens of National Trust open access land. To help us we use local estate agents, surveyors and auctioneers to maintain and keep these walks safe, protecting the public from landslips and erosion."

She continued: "Mrs Middleton's job was to instruct estate and land agents to sell the parcels of land that our surveyor designated surplus to our requirements and to negotiate with local authorities the improvements we were planning, which usually require some form of official planning approval. She did the work very well. Sales were made and the size of the proceeds on sales seemed okay. We then discovered that all the major sales were made through FLA – short for 'Flanagan's Land Agents', as they styled themselves, whose sole employee was her husband Tom Middleton, who in this part of Southampton, I subsequently learned, was regarded as a businessman with a clouded reputation. Sonia Middleton never disclosed that FLA was her husband's business, and when we looked at the seventeen deals they had bought and sold on our behalf, FLA had made a tidy sum. We informed the Southampton Police but nothing illegal had taken place. FLA acting as agents were entitled to a commission, so they weren't interested in helping the trust pursue a civil action against FLA, unless we had proof that the values achieved were substantially lower than expected, which if I am honest, they were not. It was the substantial commission earned by FLA that upset us. You see, we are a charity and many of the people working for us are volunteers."

After a pause, she continued: "We eventually discovered that FLA was a business registered in the name of Sonia Middleton in Jersey in the Channel Islands, and that her husband was a salaried adviser. A low-salaried adviser she added. The argument put to us was that in any auction the parcels could have fetched less or remain unsold, whereas FLA had been 100 per cent successful."

"That's interesting," said Andy Bowen. "If you provide a list of parcels of land bought and sold by the trust, we shall look into it."

"I'd be grateful if you would," said Caroline. "We have a duty to preserve the value of the property that has been passed to us. I don't know what Mrs Middleton is doing now. What I do know is that she is a very clever lady. I will print off a list for you now. Obviously we do not have their sales and purchase records which would reveal their profit. It was certainly tens of thousands of pounds on some Isle of Wight deals," she said.

"Not all of the business was conducted on the Island. There were sites on the New Forest and at New Milton and Lymington."

Andy drank more coffee whilst she went to get the information on the deals that Sonia Middleton had placed with FLA. She returned with pages of details with maps and exact locations from which Andy could see that Sonia had set up quite a successful business for Tom Middleton to run. It did not take a genius to see that substantial money had been made by the Middletons.

Andy departed with thanks to a very pleasant, helpful lady, who had advanced their investigation considerably, and returned to Newport with a clear picture of the Middletons, and probably the reasons for Tom Middleton making several trips to the Island at unusual times, which may or may not be connected with visits to the Newport office. And visits to Newport were not their purpose, those trips may have been to buy or sell, or survey on behalf of the National Trust disposals of land and property that was surplus to requirements.

If the Southampton police had already investigated these

transactions and found nothing illegal, the Island investigators could accept that.

◆

Back at the station Andy reported the details to Bruno, who noted that his findings did not reveal a motive for Tom Middleton to murder Mick McClusky, and explained his various visits to the Island.

"We have a clearer picture of the kind of people the Middletons are, but are these two money-making crooks capable of murder? Does the Island business mean that much to them that they would murder to stop it being stolen by Mick?" queried Bruno.

He did not think so. Clearly the Trust property scam was her idea. How much did they cream off for themselves and what do they do with their money? They've no children or close family we know about, so what is their game? We need to find out his movements on his overnight visit to the Island before the day of the Carnival, if only for the record."

Caroline Shuttleworth had revealed the nature of the Middletons. Once they had more information on Tom Middleton's clandestine visit to the Island before Carnival Day, they might bring him in for questioning. The Jersey-registered company should not be hard to identify, and an audited set of their accounts should complete the police picture, and Middleton could still shed light on McClusky's contacts.

CHAPTER 14

BASED ON a prompting by Sally Bots, a visit to Jane Martin was necessary. She was remotely connected with the accident but one could not see her meddling with brake cables or taking bolts off a steel frame.

"Let's visit her for her take on the accident and find out if she believes that her husband is having an affair with Frances Napier, as other people seem to think," said Bruno.

"Well Mrs Bots knows about it, but it is just gossip from an old woman who seeks attention," said Andy.

Bruno was glad that Sally Bots was Andy's friend and not his, and he liked the manner in which Mrs Jane Martin welcomed the two detectives into her comfortable detached family home in the Fairway district of Lake, where the houses were occupied by the professional classes.

"I'll have tea ready as soon as I boil the water," she said. She was friendly and made a good first impression on them.

"Mrs Martin, there are matters related to the vehicle loaned to the Carnival organisers by Malcolm Westlake that made it unsafe to drive, and in the condition we found it, Health & Safety would not have allowed the vehicle to participate. We are asking everybody even remotely connected who might be able to help us in our investigation. As your husband participated in the selection process of the Carnival Queen, which involved your daughter Elizabeth, we felt you might have a valuable opinion about the accident."

"Inspector, Frances Napier and I attended the same primary School as children, Gatton and Lake in Shanklin, over forty years ago. She is not a friend, never has been, and I've had no personal contact with her since. I did meet Gillian once to say hello, a nice young lady. I am sorry about the accident. It was a terrible thing to happen to that family."

"By the grace of God, it wasn't your daughter?" said Bruno.

"You might say that, Inspector. I've seen where it happened. It's quite a twisty section of the road there."

"Mrs Martin, the police believe that the crash that killed Mick McClusky and Gillian was not an accident. The vehicle, a low-loader, had defects which could only have been introduced by a person with evil intent. We've no idea who that might be, yet. Is there anything you could contribute that might give a better understanding of why somebody might want to wreck this year's Carnival Queen show?"

Her facial features did not change at this question except that a thoughtful silent manner overcame her.

"There are always people who want to wreck things, Inspector, just for the sake of it. But the thought of someone committing that act is quite alien to this Island community," she said. "And the Carnival is quite a joyful occasion for the town. It was an act of which I did not think we would be capable," she said.

"Someone had a motive to wreck the Carnival, which they did, or had a score to settle with the driver," said Bruno.

"I've no idea who would do that Inspector, no idea at all."

"Have you seen Mrs Napier since the accident?"

"I felt I should," she said. "Just for few minutes, very briefly to extend the family's condolences. She was politely receptive when I visited and thanked me," she said, failing to disguise her coldness that indicated her visit had been an obligation that had probably been forced upon her by her husband.

"If we assume that Mr McClusky was a target, do you know of anything that he was involved in to cause a violent reaction such as this?"

"McClusky was well-known on the Island and almost certainly knew some dodgy people. Lots of things go on here that are cloak-and-dagger," she said.

"Any examples?" said Bruno, smiling as if she was winding him up.

"People put grand schemes together for property and land that they do not own, and they try to acquire it cheaply."

"Do you know of any of these schemes?"

"I know there is something going on in Cowes on the promenade, the section that was opened by Edward VIII, who was our King in 1936. And the Bembridge Harbour project is a grand scheme involving money from the mainland. There are others which I don't know about, Inspector. I am just a middle-aged Island housewife who works in a garage, so I don't have contact with these kind of people."

"Where do you work Mrs Martin?"

"I am the accountant-receptionist in Southbridge Motors showroom in Ryde. I've worked there for five years."

"Did you know that your husband voted for Gillian Napier in the ballot for who was to be this year's Carnival Queen?"

"I do. It was my idea, Inspector. Elizabeth is eligible next year, and this year I wanted her to concentrate on her school work. This time next year she'll have finished her exams and have time to do the fundraising for the charities."

"Did the other members of the PCC know it was your wish for your daughter to stand down?"

"I am sure George would have told them."

"That is why he voted for Gillian," said Bruno.

"I bet that old witch Sally Bots told you something else . . ."

"You know Mrs Bots?"

"Of course. Everybody knows her. She spreads lies about you," she said.

"Some people think that gossips make the world go round Mrs Martin," said Andy.

"Only in her small little world, Detective Bowen. She came into the showroom three weeks ago and sat down for a chat while she was waiting for her car. She said she was pleased

to see me, and how lucky I was that our daughter came second in the Carnival Queen vote. She expressed the feeling
of guilt felt by the members of the PCC that Frances and
George voted for Gillian. 'The Carnival Queen would have
died whoever it was, so don't feel guilty voting for Gillian,'
I told her. Mind you I don't know who she voted for, she
never said."

Bruno felt they were straying from their mission with Jane
Martin. They should be exploring her personal insecurities.
If she was aware of or believed her husband was in a relationship with Frances Napier which could only end in pain
for both families, Jane Martin was letting it happen, behaving as the innocent party which would probably see her win
possession of the marital assets in a divorce court if it came
to it. She had a plan and was happy for her husband to experience the pain. Things are never what they seem between
husbands and wives and no one except Sally Bots believed
Frances Napier and George Martin were in a relationship.

So far it did not seem that Jane Martin could reveal anything helpful towards their investigation because they could
not see any connection between her and Mick McClusky, so
they thanked her for her time and departed.

⁕

"There is more to her than that," said Bruno to Andy over a
ham and cheese sandwich at the Cliff Top café overlooking
Shanklin Sandown Bay.

"I don't believe she is the passive housewife watching
events take place that she had no interest or involvement in.
Do you know where Southbridge Motors is?" Andy replied.

"It's on the corner as you turn left to go to Fishbourne
ferry, about a mile before you descend into Ryde. It's a medi-
um-size business. I'd imagine a receptionist there would run
the office and do the accounts. Maybe she is part-time?" suggested Bruno.

"She'd certainly know a motor mechanic or two in the

workshop who could fix the brakes on the Carnival Queen low-loader," said Andy Bowen. "Food for thought, sir."

Janet's take on Jane Martin, after Bruno ran through his day's business with her over a beer in the garden on a warm sunny evening, was that she had something to hide.

"Jane Martin is on a mission. She disposed of her previous husband and left with all his money. She has a plan to dispose of George Martin and take what he has. She has a young lover, who she could never marry, but he runs the business where she works."

"What's the mission?" said Bruno.

"Jealously," said Janet. "Something she has lived with her entire life. A former school friend in a relationship with her husband should enrage her, and Janet believed she could respond in a violent manner towards Frances. Either she was happy for it to continue to justify her own plans, and seeing George Martin slide into a relationship with Frances Napier might be just her luck. She would be seen as an innocent divorcee, not a woman on the make. It is not beyond the bounds of possibility that, with her connections, she could have engineered the sabotage on Mick McClusky's low-loader with the aid of someone from the Southbridge Garage. It may not have been her intention to murder Mick McClusky or Gillian. It was just an unforeseen consequence of the accident."

Then she went on: "You haven't scratched the surface of Jane Martin. Speak to George Martin, he should confirm what kind of person she really is. A friendly chat with Sally Bots about spreading false gossip might help, if it is false gossip."

Janet had summed up his day pretty well and the idea that Southbridge Motors could play a part in the investigation had to be explored, as did the rest of Tom Middleton's Island activities.

CHAPTER 15

WHEN BRUNO CALLED MATCHETT, he was willing to share his diary in which he recorded dates and times of Middleton's visits to the Newport office. Mick's wall chart was also there to fill in any gaps. Unsurprisingly, the days Middleton had driven to the Island using Red Funnel ferries he had not visited the Newport office. Neither had the office any note that their boss was on the Island on those days.

Bruno accepted that Middleton's connection with the office would always have to be planned and notified to McClusky and Matchett in advance. There would be no reason for him to just show up, as it could unsettle junior office staff and might signal to McClusky that he didn't trust him, and they would want to know his reason for these visits.

Janet's believed the murderer may only have intended to wreck the Carnival Queen's float and may be deeply remorseful at the outcome. What had started as a vengeful act for which retribution would have been relatively minor was now a murder hunt. This may have frightened the saboteur, who may now make amateurish mistakes during an interview as a suspect.

Tom Middleton, Terry Matchett and Jane Martin all had to be regarded as persons of interest.

An examination of its ownership and accounts revealed Southbridge Motors was a profitable business that employed thirty-five people and had four directors. Alan Southbridge, aged forty-three, was managing director and owned 80 per cent of the company shares. Elizabeth Southbridge, aged thirty-eight, owned 20 per cent, and was listed as the company secretary. Jane Martin, aged forty-four, was a director and company accountant and Charles Adams, aged twenty-nine, was sales director. The company was formed in 2008 and was a distributor of Volkswagen and Skoda cars.

"Her previous history in Poole with her first husband proved Jane Martin was an ambitious lady and motivated by money," Bruno noted to Andy. "If she has anything to do with this vehicle sabotage, she would need an accomplice who is unlikely to be the owner of a successful business selling new cars, but someone working at Southbridge Motors might so we must check the employees and find out what Jane Martin does when she is not working.

The person to answer that question was George Martin. When Andy called him to arrange a visit he received a friendly response and he arranged a convenient time for Bruno and him to visit.

❖

George Martin's office was in Ryde, within walking distance from the Hovercraft passenger terminal to Portsmouth.

He had bought a detached Victorian residence with a rear garden that led down to the sea, with views across the Solent to Portsmouth, the naval dockyard and the Spinnaker Tower. One could sit at George Martin's desk facing the sea and imagine the history of the navy through centuries and through binoculars see Nelson's flagship, HMS *Victory*, and the first metal bottomed ship, HMS *Warrior*, lying berthed in front of the permanent museum housing Henry VIII's flagship, the *Mary Rose*, now fully dried out after years of chemical treatment required to preserve the hull after 400 years on the Solent seabed. One could also see today's modern Royal Navy ships including the flagship aircraft carrier, the *Queen Elizabeth*, arriving in its home port, and departing for missions in distant ports.

George Martin was happy to see Detectives Bruno Peach and Andy Bowen at his business premises. Any visitor would have enjoyed the welcome to a friendly and professionally-run office, with tea, coffee, biscuits in a comfortable environment with panoramic views of the Solent.

George Martin was a quiet professional businessman,

skilled in the field of insurance. "How can I be of help?" he said in a friendly introduction.

Bruno outlined the police interest in health and safety, and their as yet unconfirmed suspicions about the condition of the Carnival Queen's low-loader transport. "We understand that your vote was key to selecting Gillian ahead of your daughter as this year's Carnival Queen?"

"If I can clarify a small point, Inspector, before we continue. Elizabeth is my step-daughter. She is a lovely young lady and I love her very much. Her father lives in Bournemouth, where I met Jane. I wouldn't say that my vote at the PCC was key. We each had a vote, and Jane, for reasons only known to her, did not want Elizabeth to be this year's Shanklin Carnival Queen. I didn't withdraw her name, as she suggested. I voted for Gillian, same thing, but no fuss and as Fran wanted Gillian to be the 2022 Carnival Queen. I voted for her which satisfied both of them."

"Are you very friendly with Frances Napier?"

"Very friendly. That's a loaded question, Inspector. If you mean what I think you mean, no, I am not in a relationship with Frances Napier."

"I'm sorry sir, that question came out the wrong way. Someone implied that might be the case," said Andy.

"Would that be Mrs Bots, a fellow member of the PCC?"

"Unwilling to break a confidence," Andy Bowen said. "I'm sorry, I can't divulge the name, sir."

"Mrs Bots is elderly, with a Mills and Boon imagination, who no one takes seriously."

"Do you know of anyone who might want to wreck the Shanklin Carnival?"

"It's an absurd idea, isn't it?" he said. "Everyone looks forward to Carnival night, it's the highlight of Shanklin's summer. I believe the driver lost consciousness coming down the hill, probably a heart attack. Have you pursued that possibility?"

"We have medical reports on the deceased driver, no signs in the post-mortem of that."

"Then I'd say he lost control, going too fast, isn't the speed limit for those vehicles between 5 and 10 miles per hour?"

"That's a valid observation," said Andy. "Because we've recorded the speed at the time of the crash at 40 miles per hour."

"So, he lost control careering down the hill?" said Martin. "If it wasn't a heart attack, it must have been another medical condition?"

"Or a person sabotaged the vehicle," said Bruno.

"Did someone tamper with the vehicle?"

"Our police expert discovered that the hydraulic brake system had been made unserviceable."

Martin sat thoughtfully staring out of the window, thinking.

"You mean someone wanted to kill the driver or the girl?"

"We are assuming that Mick McClusky, the driver, was the target and the Carnival Queen was an innocent casualty," said Bruno.

"It's a frightening thought that he had enemies who would kill for no personal gain, if the intention was to kill the driver?"

"I don't know the McCluskys," he said. "But I am sure you gentlemen will get to the bottom of it. It's a terrible accident to have been caused deliberately."

"The defect on the braking system on the vehicle could only have been done by an experienced motor engineer," said Andy.

"There are plenty of those around," said George. "Not that I know any."

"Could you talk us through the insurance implications?"

"There are several. The damaged wall and forecourt to the Crab will be rebuilt, the vehicle is a write-off. Both were fully insured."

"Shanklin Carnival will be insured for public and private liability, and for losses on charity collections. There were two casualties and the Shanklin Carnival has public liability insurance. As a member of the PCC I wasn't consulted by the Carnival organisers about insurance. I am willing to advise in a personal capacity if asked," he said, "to ensure fair recompense."

It was obvious that Martin had no involvement with any activities connected with the accident or wished them to think his relationship with Frances Napier was anything different to what he had said.

"We spoke to Mrs Martin."

"She told me."

"She couldn't help us. Said she'd had never met McClusky. Do you know if his life was insured?" asked Andy.

"His employer might have taken out key man and death-in-service policies, if he was an important employee. It's worth you checking. I'll gladly look at any policy for you," Martin offered.

"Thank you, sir. If we run into that we will come back to you," said Andy.

"Thank you for your time today. I envy you the lovely property you have here," said Bruno, moving the conversation on.

"We haven't been here long, but we are very pleased with everything," said Martin.

"Is this a good spot for insurance broking, sir?" said Andy.

"We are not insurance brokers. I am a civil engineer and Fellow of the Institute of Insurance Assessors; we act for insurance companies in assessing claims. Yes, it is an excellent place to work, no distractions and there is always something going on, on the water. We are paid by the insurance companies to be completely fair in assessing claims. More often than not, we find ourselves deciding in favour of the claimant, persuading the insurers to pay the claim in full. There is nothing the insurers like more than a disaster, flood, tornado, oil tanker leak – they provide the perfect reason for increasing premiums for everyone."

"Interesting," said Andy. "Thank you for your time, sir, if you can think of anything give us a call."

With a friendly goodbye they left.

◈

"Let's speak to Linda Peploe," Bruno said on their way back to the station. "She might shed light on a dark corner. He handled your enquiry well, no sense of guilt or malice, just humour that an old woman is spreading a tale. However, Linda Peploe is a magistrate who listens to people telling lies all the time. She is on the bench and she must have an opinion about these two, and there are other things she can shine a light on. We would be wrong to ignore her."

She sat in court on Thursdays so was able to meet them on a Wednesday in Newport in the Medina café garden on the bank of the river Medina.

"Tell us what you think about this accident, Linda," said Bruno showing her the utmost courtesy any policeman would show a magistrate sitting on the local bench in the hope of gaining favour. However, her reputation suggested nothing positive ever resulted for the police on the Island from her judgements.

"Can you be specific with what you want to know, Inspector?"

"The voting by the PCC for the honour of being the 2022 Carnival Queen is a good place to start."

"What I know about the voting is this. Before the vote George Martin told Father Peter that he was going to vote for Gillian because Jane Martin did not want her daughter to be the Queen. Peter understood, and when he was asked to vote, he voted for Gillian too."

"Why did Jane change her mind?"

"She is a very difficult woman in every way."

"How do you know that?"

"She has a history and is a story in herself. What you see is not what you get. She is the opposite to George."

"We understand from George that he is Elizabeth's stepfather."

"That is correct," said Linda. "They've been married for five or six years."

"When Jane thought seriously about being the Carnival Queen's mother, she knew it might result in the press having a field day at her expense. She has many skeletons in the cupboard."

"Tell us more," said Bruno.

"Have you ever heard of the Poole Harbour explosion?"

"When was that?"

Neither Bruno or Andy could recollect the event.

Linda Peploe explained, "Jane Martin used to be married to Jim Ridgeway, who is the father of Elizabeth. He had a business in the harbour area in Poole. They lived in a swanky part of Bournemouth, the Hinton Firs district. Jim Ridgeway is a glass-blower of high artistic merit. Some of his work is magnificent and fetches decent prices. You might say he is the Clarice Cliff of glass-blowers. An original Clarice Cliff teapot can sell for thousands. One day a Jim Ridgeway might be of equal value. I have two pieces.

"When I visited his studio a few years ago, his building was divided into office area, showroom and the glass foundry. Jane worked in the factory as the office manager and did the accounts. Jim borrowed from banks to fund stock and expansion, yet it struggled to be profitable. However, Ridgeway owned the freehold of the factory premises, so he was able to work without financial pressure – liberating for an artist.

"Seven years ago, on a cold windy night the building caught fire, everything was burnt to a cinder. They were totally wiped out of business. It should not have been a total disaster because the business and the freehold building was properly insured. However, his wife had insured the business assets including the property in the name of Jane Ridgway. It had been their agreement when they started the business as a limited company to put all their assets in her name, so that should he go bust they would have protected their joint wealth.

"This was when Jim Ridgeway's problems started. George Martin came onto the scene as the insurance companies' assessor. It was his task to calculate the value of the claim and get both parties to agree. George Martin, in his late thirties, was a handsome, well-heeled bachelor, living in a nice house in a good class area of Bournemouth with his widowed mother, who looked after him and the family home. Jane charmed the pants off him, literally, and he responded by settling the best claim he could agree with the insurers in her favour. She kept the lot, several hundred thousand pounds, and ran off with George to the Isle of Wight. They bought a nice house in Shanklin and sent Elizabeth to Ryde Grammar School. George could carry on his business from anywhere. That's their story, Inspector."

"You said Jane Martin is a very difficult woman?"

"Yes, but difficult is the wrong word. She is a ruthless, greedy woman and by all accounts, from anyone who's ever had any contact with her, jealous and vindictive. Jim Ridgeway lost his wife, his daughter, the capital he had built up in the business, and had to begin again. George was in love with her and blind to her faults, in spite of having intimate knowledge of her treatment of Ridgway. She would have spun him a different story. As long as he is building a good business on the Island, she is happy, because he will be one of her next targets. Don't believe Sally Bots when she says he is having an affair with Fran, neither of them is that way inclined."

"How do you know that, Linda?" said Andy.

"Because, young man, I am a magistrate. Anything else, Inspector?" she asked bluntly, anxious to return to the hustle and bustle of the Newport Magistrates' Court, and some more sentencing.

Bruno thanked her and decided that she was probably a good magistrate and a million laughs. "You've shone a light into a dark tunnel, which gives us more to work on," he said.

CHAPTER 16

THERE WAS NO DOUBT she had opened up another avenue of investigation and that Linda Peploe was directing their investigation towards Jane Martin.

"She gave us an honest opinion, different to Sally Bots. Her attitude towards George Martin and that towards Jim Ridgeway, is leopards don't change their spots. Is there any reason why we shouldn't talk to Jim Ridgeway?" said Bruno.

"I can't think of one," said Andy. "We don't yet have a reason to speak to Jane Martin again about the accident, and he might give us an insight into her behaviour, like how could he have let her take all the money from the insurance pay-out? It wasn't an impetuous act at seeing the cash. She had planned it for years, putting everything in her name."

First they wanted to speak to Middleton about his two stay over visits to the Island, just prior to the Carnival, of which Matchett had no record.

"We cannot see him until Friday, so call Eileen McClusky and ask her if she could remember anything he, she, or they did on those two days or evenings. It may help us. And how can we contact Jim Ridgeway? Get the police in Bournemouth to do that for us."

⸭

Within twenty-four hours desk Sergeant Collins of Bournemouth City police called Bruno.

"I remember Jim Ridgeway, a co-operative and helpful gentleman," he said.

"We found no evidence to indicate that the fire that destroyed his business had been started deliberately. No arson. The insurer's conclusion was that wind swirled around the glass smelter and spread hot ash from the furnace tray, which ignited some waste material and spread too quickly to be quenched by the fire engines which arrived when the blaze was too fierce and dangerous to control. That's the story. We interviewed key members of staff who confirmed the accidental nature of the fire. It was properly insured. I know because we were contacted by the insurers for a copy of the report of our findings."

"I understand they were paid in full."

"What surprised me was that they did not rebuild the business on the site. It was probably a gold mine."

"Thank you, Sergeant, you have been helpful."

Jim Ridgeway had managed to hang on to the marital home after the divorce by re-mortgaging it to pay off Jane Martin's claim for 50 per cent, which was in addition to the insurance payment.

He was happy to meet Bruno and Andy if they wanted to discuss the Carnival accident. Elizabeth had explained the tragedy to him and how fortunate she had been.

"We speak at least once a week, so I know what goes on over on the Island. I see her quite often, but not on the Island," he said. "Jane does not want me hanging around to disrupt her school life, more likely her own personal goings on."

"We are talking to every parent who had a child participating in the Shanklin Carnival, and Elizabeth was one of several girls competing to be the 2022 Shanklin Carnival Queen," said Andy.

"She is a pretty girl," he said.

"Yes, she is," said Andy. "We have a number of suspicions regarding the accident, so we are speaking to as many people who had even the remotest contact with the main participants."

"Is my ex-wife involved?" he said.

"Only in so far as she is the spouse of a member of the group that selected the girl who lost her life."

"That would be George Martin," said Jim.

"You know him?"

"Vaguely, nothing wrong with George Martin. He ran off with my wife, who took and all my money and my daughter. I can't forgive her."

Jim Ridgeway was a man with a grudge, but he'd accepted the situation and continued his life.

"Tell us what you know about George Martin," said Bruno.

"Very little. He came to see me the morning after the fire, professional gentleman, polite, respectful, well-off, a bachelor, lived with his mother in Bournemouth. I never handled the office business, banking, insurance, the retail shop, I left it all to Jane, she ran the business while I concentrated on my work. I was happy with that. What I didn't realise was that from the beginning she had seen that everything of value was in her sole name. I wasn't working for us, I was working for her.

"The fire was the opportunity she wanted to cash in and jump ship, leaving me with nothing. She even took 50 per cent of my family home, that my parents had saved for all their lives. So, she received the insurance company payment for the full sum assured in which George Martin was very helpful. She then told me she was leaving me, and taking all the money and my daughter, and ran off to where she had been brought up on the Isle of Wight with George Martin, who she married once we were divorced a few months later. I had to pay her half of the value of the house and, until she married Martin, maintenance for my daughter."

"Did you suspect that she was capable of such behaviour during your marriage?"

"We were married for six years, although we had been together for five years before we married. It was when my work was being recognised, the shop was going very well and I was getting commissions from companies for glass sculptures. If you visit Barclays Centre between Bournemouth and

Poole, in their reception they have one of my glass sculptures. It was a £5,000 commission.

"When I think back, it was when I was becoming recognised that we married and she set about taking control of everything. She built up a social network of art lovers who bought things from her. It was as if she was the creative person who instructed the men who worked in the glass foundry. She would often bring me drawings and get me to quote for making the objects, but I never spoke to any client.

"Then I thought she was up to something, but not stealing the business. She is a strikingly attractive lady and I thought these commissions were coming from a male collector who fancied her. She is a sociable person, and I thought this was her way of contributing. I think she is the same with Martin. She sees a husband as providing security that allows her freedom to roam, and when the time is right, she moves on.

"With my business she was jealous of my work and tried to present herself as the creative spirit. When the fire destroyed the business she would not help me to re-create a new business, which was a pity because the insurance payout would have paid for a modern glass foundry with the latest equipment. So that was that, Inspector. She took the lot."

"Are you bitter?" said Bruno.

"I am wiser," he said. "And Elizabeth will help me rebuild my life, Jane Martin won't stop her," he added with determination. "She is aware of her mother's jealous, controlling behaviour and will leave the Island at the end of her final school year. After my experience with Jane, my business is now thriving again."

"I won't deny that it came as a bombshell to me when the cheque from the insurance company was addressed to her. I didn't know she had banked it into her personal account until she said to me, she was leaving. I was devastated, and it has taken me several years to recover. And she stole my beloved Elizabeth. I didn't care about the money, but

Elizabeth was my life. I'm sure she will go to art college here in Bournemouth, and I will look after her. That is my gloomy story, Inspector, but you didn't come here to hear that, so how can I be of help to you?"

"We need to understand the people connected with the two casualties of this accident. You have told us a lot about Jane Martin, and been helpful. Thank you."

◆

Their journey to visit Jim Ridgeway had been worthwhile and what he revealed about Jane Martin enlightening. They were dealing with a different personality to the one she had presented at their meeting. Although they could not yet connect Ridgeway's description of Jane Martin's character to this crime, there was enough to make her a person of interest. Her ruthless streak made her capable of extreme acts.

Linda Peploe and Jim Ridgeway had a frighteningly bad opinion of her because she had taken all of Ridgeway's money and livelihood, but most divorcing women in those situations advised by a sharp divorce lawyer, would have behaved the same way. It was expected of them in today's world and in the process, they became stronger and more self-assured. Some however become overconfident and are unable to conceal the worst aspects of their personalities.

It was her meticulous planning throughout her marriage and her behaviour towards him that set her apart. Jane Martin needed to be tested – but for what? They had to find out more about what she was up to with Charlie Adams.

The outstanding matter of importance that had to be investigated was Tom Middleton's visits to the Island that were not connected to his business in Newport. As he was due to meet Matchett the following day in Newport, that presented an opportunity to ask him about these visits.

In advance of that meeting Andy Bowen spoke to Eileen McClusky. Did she recall Mick's movements on these days?

Understandably she had no knowledge of his whereabouts

during the days in question. However, she was clear about the evenings of both days. The first evening she was certain that he was home all evening, because they regularly watched a television series together. The next evening, the night before the Shanklin Carnival, she was helping Mick in the garden with last minute decorating of the float that he drove to Popham Road at 5.30 the following morning.

Matchett had already told Andy that Middleton had not appeared in the Newport office on each of the two days he had journeyed to the Island, so it would be interesting to hear from Middleton his reason for these secret visits to the Island.

When Andy spoke to him and asked him to call in after seeing Matchett, he was on the Red Funnel ferry, a foot passenger being met by Matchett in Cowes.

He behaved in a confident manner, and even if the police were probing into his business affairs they would take a biased view, which he could refute. As a friendly, co-operative, helpful person, he was happy to call in for a coffee after lunch with Matchett, "to catch up", as he put it.

Having digested the information Andy Bowen had gleaned from Caroline Shuttleworth, the local director of the Southern regional branch of the National Trust, Bruno understood that the money the Middletons had creamed off from the sale of surplus parcels of pasture and woodland would have provided a lucrative second income to the Middletons. It would have eased the financial pressure of having to rely on the Newport estate agency to fund their lifestyle, to avoid living as bankrupts, while it lasted. But now both sources of income were threatened. In fact, one had already ceased.

Tom Middleton was clearly the frontman for his wife in their venture, known as FLA. Because of its reported success by the National Trust, Bruno doubted that he could be responsible for the vehicle crash, because he had options and he and his wife's lifestyle to protect. But his secret visits to the Island put him into a position of interest to the police.

CHAPTER 17

A S AGREED at 2.30 p.m., after a good lunch with Matchett, Middleton breezed into the Newport police to meet Bruno and Andy in interview room one, where a flask of coffee awaited them.

"Tell us about your showdown with Matchett?" said Bruno, using his friendly, put-him-at-ease manner.

"It went very well and I am pleased to say he is up for it. With that attitude I see no reason for him not to do well. I had to make adjustments, such as paying him more, not as much as McClusky to start with. But if the business does well, so will he. He couldn't take Mick's job on as well as his own, so I agreed that he could employ an experienced person, either to do what he does and run the office leaving him to build the business, like Mick, or vice versa. He could employ and manage an experienced negotiator. He said he'd already spoken to one or two candidates and he'd tell me when he'd had an acceptance. Subject to my meeting the person and agreeing, we'd employ him. So mission accomplished, Inspector."

"We are trying to fill in some gaps from the people we have interviewed in our investigation," said Bruno. "There are two journeys made by you to the Island on separate dates immediately prior to the Carnival accident. Can you tell us the reason for these visits?"

Middleton remained calm at Bruno's change of tone, and showed no disquiet at being asked this question.

"Inspector, there are matters concerning the Island that I don't always share with the Newport office, because I don't want to share them. I came to look at two parcels of land for sale by the National Trust, eleven acres of woodland in Whitwell, and three acres on the left as you drive towards Ryde. I don't work for the Trust. I was getting information for Sonia, who asked me to negotiate the sales. There have also been a couple of purchases I have done for the Trust."

Bruno did not tell Middleton that they knew that his wife did not work for the Trust or that they were aware of his interest in land sales on their behalf. It was not an unexpected answer from him, and it did not further their investigation into what he could otherwise have been doing on the Island on those days, and the fact that he found it necessary to stay over on his second visit meant he could have another reason.

"On the night before the Carnival, you stayed on the Island?"

"I met the tenant of the Whitwell parcel in the White Horse in Whitwell. He draws an allowance from the Forestry Commission for maintaining his own four acres of woodland, and I wanted to sound him out as a potential purchaser, to offer him the financial options. Tenants are our first port of call, because if one can persuade them to buy the land then it doesn't go for auction. Dennis is the name of the tenant and he was only available after work and in the evenings, so I stayed over. I had to."

"Where did you stay?"

"In The White Horse in Whitwell. Does that answer your question, Inspector?"

"It fills in some gaps," said Bruno. "Are there many of these land sales that you have been involved in?"

"Inspector, the Trust likes to deal with people known to it, so yes, several in various parts of South Hampshire. The Trust has no idea what a parcel of land or permission for access is worth. Why should it? The directors of the Trust are not property professionals, they are mostly volunteers."

"Can you give us the contact details of Mr Dennis, just for confirmation?" said Andy.

Middleton took out a pocket diary and gave him the address and phone number of Mr Dennis. Bruno knew that

Sonia Middleton would confirm that the woodland for sale existed, but it was not necessary to involve her at this stage, as a word with Dennis should confirm his story.

◆

Bruno was anxious to make progress and needed an opening or a lead to work on, so he and Andy trawled through and examined the notes they had compiled so far and the relationships amongst those that made it onto the list of persons of interest. Some had motives, but in none of which could he recognise murder.

While they were analysing their progress, Bruno received a call from Jim Ridgeway who wanted to discuss a matter of some importance, but not on the phone. All he would say was it concerned someone the police were investigating. As the Island was currently out of bounds to him, could he meet him on the mainland?

"No problem," said Bruno, and suggested meeting early the following morning off the Yarmouth to Lymington ferry. Ridgway was up for that and Bruno agreed to collect him off the 8 a.m. ferry and take him to breakfast at Fat Boy's by Shrimtons Boatyard, a few hundred metres from the ferry terminal.

They tucked into a traditional Fat Boy's breakfast. Only in a greasy spoon could you enjoy a properly cooked fry-up. No hotel or restaurant ever came near it.

Jim Ridgeway's artistic skills were not limited to making glass sculptures. He carved in wood, and sculpted in plaster, clay and carved stone, selling his work to shops in holiday towns along the South Coast, where he was known.

"There are a dozen shops along the South Coast from Weymouth to Southampton that sell my work. My difficulty is satisfying the demand. I can only produce so many original pieces and run the business."

"Do you have an apprentice?"

"I have two. Both are studying art at Bournemouth

University and I am hoping that my daughter will join me. She is interested."

"It is Elizabeth that I want to speak to you about," he continued. "Now the school summer holidays have started she has come to Bournemouth for two weeks, and is staying with me and seeing her friends from Talbot Heath, the girl's school in the town she attended and has kept in touch with her friends there.

"She reports that the relationship between her mother and stepfather is very bad and that Jane has accused him of an affair with Frances Napier, which she says he denies. Elizabeth believes he is telling the truth. She says that apart from the regular PCC meetings in Shanklin Theatre, he does not go out in the evenings, apart from church meetings and not at the weekends. She says he is very busy at his office his business is growing and many evenings he works late. When he does, she spies on him by sitting in her car and checking on what time he leaves. She doesn't cook for him and says 'the atmosphere is unbearable'. She mentions Mrs Napier all the time and not a civil word passes between them.

"Also, she is seldom at home when Elizabeth and her stepfather are home. She's at the Ventnor Tennis Club playing in club tournaments. At weekends she plays matches against other clubs, some on the mainland, with a business colleague, Charlie Adams.

"When they play on the mainland they stay together in an hotel. Elizabeth is convinced that her mother is in a relationship with Adams. I am thinking of sending her back to Talbot Heath for her final year at school in spite of the opposition I would get from Jane."

"Why are you telling me this?" said Bruno.

"Because of the proximity of these people to your investigation. I know my former wife will stop at nothing to avenge a perceived wrong against her. She is creating a situation that will end her relationship with George Martin. By inventing a grudge against Frances Napier, which will develop into a major incident in which Frances Napier will be hurt."

"Are you suggesting that she could have targeted her daughter to gain revenge?"

"Maybe it is part of her plan to get rid of her husband and take whatever support add-ons, the family wealth, now his business is flourishing, the court would give her," said Ridgeway. "Whatever the reason, it is affecting my daughter's life and I don't want her to continue living with Jane in these circumstances. She could study for her A levels at her old school and live with me."

"Can't you negotiate that with your ex-wife?"

"She is possessive, jealous and she would block it, because it would weaken her case for support with a divorce judge."

"When she is eighteen, Elizabeth can make her own decision," said Bruno.

"By then she could have suffered harm." Jim was clearly frightened of his former wife and frightened for his daughter.

Bruno thought Ridgeway's description of Jane Martin confirmed what others were saying about her. However, he was trying to use the police to pursue a marital issue, which was not what Bruno wanted to get involved in.

"When you called you said there was something I should know about those people I am investigating. Is that it?"

"Inspector, Jane Martin is capable of anything, even murder, and I am frightened for my daughter, so I'd like your help."

"You will understand that I can't take sides in a marital dispute."

"I am talking about protecting my daughter to see she comes to no harm."

"We shall do that as part of our routine duties. Why don't you go to the Island and speak to her face to face?"

"You don't understand, Inspector."

"I don't know if she had anything to do with the Carnival Queen murders. There is a lot to the story that we don't yet know about."

"Can you speak to George Martin again? He might be able to help me prise Elizabeth from her clutches," said Jim.

"I will think about it, Jim, and I will help you if I can. Make sure your daughter makes you aware of everything that happens to her on the Island."

Bruno returned to the Island with a better understanding of the type of woman Jane Martin is. She had cleaned Jim Ridgeway out and taken his daughter with her, the thing that he most treasured from their marriage. The sooner his daughter finished her final year at school and escaped, the better. Now he intended to reclaim her and protect her from the nastiness that would ensue as a result of Jane Martin's intention to extricate herself from her marriage to George Martin.

From what he had learned from Ridgeway she was not the type of woman who wanted to live alone. She wanted control, and that meant that she had probably already lined up her next conquest. Could that be Charlie Adams?

CHAPTER 18

Bruno arrived back at Newport Police Station at the same time as Andy Bowen returned from Southampton. Andy Bowen believed he'd been extraordinarily lucky in meeting Sonia Middleton, who was home alone when he was driven up the drive of number 15 Shirley Wood Avenue by PC Wendy Crane in an unmarked police car from the Southampton Police Force.

"Oh, hello," Sonia Middleton said, not seeming overly surprised at seeing him.

"Detective Sergeant Andy Bowen from the Isle of Wight."

"I remember you; you came here before."

"I called early hoping I'd catch you. Can we discuss certain of your business activities? Shouldn't take long," said Andy.

"He's not here."

"There is one particular matter that you can help us with."

At this she asked him to step inside and they sat in a front lounge room – no coffee this time.

When he sat in the upright chair she offered him, it signalled to him a formidable woman. At first he didn't speak.

"How can I be of help to the Isle of Wight Police Force, Inspector?"

"Four weeks ago there was a terrible accident in Shanklin when the brakes in a Carnival float failed and the driver lost control and he and the young lady were killed."

"I know all about it. Our man, McClusky, was the driver and he was killed. As our employee he is insured on our death-in-service policy, so when everything is sorted out, we shall see his wife is okay," she said in a manner that suggested she had rehearsed it.

"Yes, we would like a copy of the death-in-service policy."

"Why do you want that?"

"Standard police practice, Mrs Middleton, life insurance policy linked to an as yet unexplained death."

Her silence indicated that she had no intention of voluntarily giving a copy of the policy to the police.

"Mrs Middleton, the brakes on the vehicle failed because somebody cut the cables of the hydraulic cylinder, so we are looking for a murderer."

"What has that got to do with me or my husband?"

"You were McClusky's employer and he was your right-hand man running Middleton's in Newport. It is conceivable that he was murdered because of something to do with business. On two occasions in the fortnight before the accident your husband visited the Island and stayed overnight, and on each occasion, he did not pay a visit to your Newport business."

"That is correct. Detective Bowen we have other business activities as well as the Middleton office on the Island and my husband had several people to see about land sales."

"Can you tell us about the land deals he was working on?"

"He can give you the locations and the persons were are dealing with if you ask him. I deal with the paperwork of the business, the accounting, paying the expenses and the salaries of the staff, I leave the rest to my husband."

"The land sales were on behalf of the National Trust, is that correct?"

"Correct," she said.

"Are they happy with the service you provide?"

"Not entirely, but we get along. In fact we did, but we have stopped working for them now. Those awful Isle of Wight land deals were too much. We had to offer incentives to the farmers to buy them."

"But the Trust paid those incentives?"

"Of course," she said. "The people who work for the Trust

are a type, do-gooders, holier than thou, who think they are a cut above the rest of us. But they are not and they have no professional experience in land sales, even though they are always trying to sell off parts of their estates. So we tried to help them until they became greedy. They couldn't accept that without my husband they'd have never sold anything, and he had to work bloody hard to sell any of the parcels of land they put up for sale. Now he has to concentrate on the Newport office, that has to continue to make money now McClusky has gone. That's Tom's job. I've tried to get him to be more visible there, but he says that isn't the way to run it. I think he hates going there really, but we need the income."

"Why doesn't your husband pick up the threads from McClusky and do it himself? You can get to the Newport office quite easily on a daily basis."

"My husband is not an estate agent, Detective; he is a chartered surveyor."

"What else does he do apart from a monthly visit to Newport?"

"He advises private clients of development opportunities."

"On the Island?"

"No, in East Hampshire and West Sussex."

It was obvious she was making that up.

"I believe that McClusky's wife and his son are going to continue with Mick's contacts and set up their own office. Are you happy with that?"

"That's for Tom to deal with. He'll twist her arm in some way, there is the death-in-service payment to persuade her not to do that."

"Really?" said Andy.

"She won't see a penny if she tries to steal our business."

"Is that legal to stop paying a death-in-service benefit to a widow?"

"It depends on how the policy is written, and remember key man insurance is part of our claim."

"Perhaps you should check with your insurance company, that murder is not an exclusion on the policy you have," said Andy.

"I shall do that," she said. "The payment is discretionary."

"By the insurance company?"

"Yes, and by ourselves."

"Was stealing your business Mick McClusky's intention?"

"Definitely," she said.

"You didn't like him?"

"He was always after more out of the business than we gave him. Tom would have made him partner, but I stopped that."

"Don't you think he earned a partnership?"

"Middleton's are the most successful estate agent on the Island at the moment."

"So, if he had started his own business, it would have been because of you?"

"I would have stopped him; I will stop him."

"He is dead Mrs Middleton."

"I meant, I will stop his family opening up."

"How would you do that?"

"Perhaps you've heard of contracts in restraint of trade," she said. "We had one with McClusky."

"Are there any more National Trust land sales coming your way?"

"We've finished with them," she added. "So, Tom can concentrate on his other work."

"Who are his clients in East Hampshire and West Sussex?"

"He is a qualified surveyor and he can work as a freelance for any number of companies."

Andy knew that without a practising certificate he could not do that, but resisted an urge to tell her as she may not have known that his ability to practice as a surveyor had been cancelled by the Royal Institute of Chartered Surveyors.

"So, you cannot help me with details of his movements on the Island, the people he visited or the locations of the land deals?"

"I know that he stayed in a pub in Whitwell one night to meet a purchaser, but you'd have to ask him for the details."

"Mrs Middleton, we can call him if we need to know that."

"I cannot think that our business on the Island could have anything to do with the terrible accident," she said.

She obviously didn't get it, and by declaring her utter dislike of Mick McClusky, had talked herself into being of police interest.

"It's little things that help you see the whole picture Mrs Middleton, and it's just one piece of the jigsaw. Thank you for your help," and with that he left the precious house, climbed back into his unmarked police car and let PC Wendy Crane drive him back to the Red Funnel ferry terminal.

◆

His conclusion to Bruno was that she ran the Middleton business, knew precisely what her husband was doing every minute of the day, but sabotaging the Carnival low-loader might have been a step too far for both of them.

"I am not convinced that McClusky's departure from Middleton's in Newport was a real threat to their life-style. As long as Matchett can do it," Andy suggested. "The Middletons are an unprincipled pair who don't give a damn about anybody. One day they will chance their arm and come a cropper."

Having reported his meeting with Jim Ridgeway they agreed to speak to Jane Martin once more to try and expose her true character.

"Before we see her, I want another meeting with George Martin to check Jim Ridgeway's story. If it rings true, then apart from his successful business life the rest is pretty miserable. He might also tell us more about his wife and if she really has it in for Frances Napier."

CHAPTER 19

THE BEST TIME to interview professional men is at the close of a working day when they relax after a day making decisions for clients on which their reputation depends. So, his suggestion to George Martin that they meet in the pub a short walk from his office in Ryde after closing the office, was taken up in an enthusiastic manner.

"I had the pleasure of meeting your stepdaughter and her father yesterday, and what a delightful young lady she is," said Bruno, although he did not meet her personally, it introduced her to their conversation.

"How is she?" he asked, as if concerned about her. "She is on her summer holiday working for Jim, who is busy at this time of the year. I miss her, she is a bright spark," he said. "In fact I offered her to come and work for me, but her mother wouldn't allow it."

"Any particular reason?" said Bruno.

"Jealously," said Martin. "She can fly into a rage and the slightest hint of something she doesn't like or is not in control of, or can't have. She behaves that way to both of us, although to a lesser extent to Elizabeth. I think at the moment I am her prime target. It's a terrible, evil jealousy and destructive to yourself principally and everyone around you. We've only been married a few years but when I look back it was the same problem with Jim. She wanted everything he had, even pretending that the brilliant artwork he produced was her own work. She eventually took everything when his business burned down.

"That's when I met her. I should have known better when the insurers paid their claim, which I had signed off, to her. The property was registered in her name. She kept it, Jim got nothing. And using her considerable feminine charm, I fell for her. I was a bachelor and overwhelmed. She was a completely new experience. I should not have married her. Now it's my turn to be turfed out and I know she will take me for as much as she can. It's one reason she keeps Elizabeth with us, as I support her, and all her claims will be for the two of them."

Obviously a confirmed bachelor had been charmed into marriage by a woman he did not understand. He now found himself lonely without friends – except, perhaps, Frances Napier?

They listened to an unhappy man describe his living hell with Jane Martin.

"There is a view among some of the members of the PCC that you are in a relationship with Mrs Napier," said Andy.

"I'm not surprised, we come and go together because we travel in my car, but we are not having an affair. Far from it, she is very worried about her husband, who has taken Gillian's death badly. Neither can understand why it happened, that two people, neither of whom would harm a fly, were killed so brutally.

"I would not intrude in any marriage; I respect both of them. Before the accident she listened to my story, which helped me, and now I try to comfort her, but there is nothing of a relationship between us. As far as Jane is concerned, I saw what she did with Jim, and I have protected myself financially. She is reasonably well-off and with Jim's money she bought a house in Bembridge, which she lets for a good rental. The house we live in is mortgaged, I put all my cash into Ryde. I can live upstairs if I want to or need to. It has two bedrooms, two bathrooms, a large sea-facing lounge on the second floor.

"I am only waiting for Elizabeth to move away to Bournemouth, then I'll divorce her mother. Whenever she is away on these tennis weekends with Charlie Adams, I have her followed by a reputable agency, so I have all the evidence I need for a clean break.

"Frances knows Jane well because they went to the same primary school as little girls. She wasn't popular then because she was a bully. She remembered a sweet little girl called Lucy, who Jane used to torment in the playground. Lucy was too frightened of her to report her, but it had a damaging effect on her growing up."

Aware that the interview was straying from the subject, Bruno interjected: "So far we are making very little progress finding the person who sabotaged the Carnival float, so we are talking to anyone who is even remotely connected with the victims, hoping for a meaningful lead."

"I can't see any connection. Jane has a ruthlessly unpleasant streak, but a murderer? I don't think so. Go and speak to her. She works for Southbridge Motor Company, they are on the Ryde to Sandown Road, a couple of miles from here."

"Should we call her at work?"

"I don't see why not, you came to see me in my office, and she is not at home much now. Elizabeth is in Bournemouth so it's the only place you'll catch her, because she never appears home until late in the summer. She's at the tennis club."

While George Martin was getting more drinks, Andy said to Bruno, "They both paint Jane Martin in a bad light."

"There are two sides to a marriage and we've only heard his," said Bruno. "George and Jim tell the same story convincingly, but what is her side going to tell us?"

George returned with the drinks and was enjoying the chance to relax and share his woes.

"We hope she might help us as she is well-known and someone might have let slip something to her."

"Good luck," said George. "You're right, she is well-known."

❦

The following morning Andy phoned Jane Martin in her office. Although she did not want police visiting her at work, neither did she see any reason for them to see her at all.

"I wasn't involved in the Carnival. I have told you everything I know when we met."

"Just little things can point us in the right direction," said Andy.

Her reluctance to help or shed light on any aspect of the Carnival inspired a determination in Andy to find out why although, as he said to Bruno, "I find it hard to deal with a difficult woman."

"Who doesn't?" said Bruno.

"It's time for me to show you how it's done," he said to Andy.

"Genuinely, I'd be delighted sir."

Reluctantly she agreed to visit Newport police during her lunch hour, after what had been a disagreeable conversation in which Andy had intimated that they could compel her to see them by arresting her if they had to.

"What do you want to see me about? I cannot help you at all," she said the moment she set eyes on the two detectives.

Her manner had changed from that of hospitable housewife she had shown them when they had last met to a frightening adversary.

"Amongst your circle of friends and acquaintances are there any who held a grudge against Mick McClusky?"

"How would I know? To my knowledge, none of my friends have ever heard of Mick McClusky."

"How about yourself? Did you know him?"

"Although we both live in Shanklin, I can't remember meeting him."

"Would you remember if you had?"

"Yes, Inspector. I don't forget a face," she replied with a hint if sarcasm.

"Can you tell us about the men and women you spoke to about the Carnival on the week before the event?"

"What the hell, Inspector? I wanted nothing to do with it.

I keep away from that lot."

"So, you can't think of anybody who could have wanted to disrupt the Carnival?"

"I cannot think of anyone," she said. "It is a big event in Shanklin and raises money for local charities. I think the crash was an accident. Perhaps the driver had a medical condition that caused him to lose consciousness?"

"That would be an obvious explanation."

"What about Frances Napier?"

"I know her, but she has never been a friend. It's sad the loss of her daughter."

Her response gave no hint of her true feelings.

"A lucky escape for Elizabeth," said Andy, which elicited a glare from her.

"Shanklin is your home town, Mrs Martin?"

"I was born and bred in Shanklin. I feel like a change. We shall be moving as soon as this academic school year is over."

"Where to?" said Andy.

"Bembridge."

"Does your husband know of these plans?"

"He does what I want, so I don't burden him with loads of crap from estate agents."

"So, you'll be buying a house in Bembridge?"

"Yes," she said.

"What about your husband's thriving business in Ryde?"

"He works for major insurers and travels all over the South of England and a drive from Bembridge to Ryde is no further than it is from Shanklin."

"How would a move to Bembridge affect your work?"

"Bembridge is nearer to where I work. If that is it, Inspector, I have to get back to work," she said.

"What do think caused the crash?"

"I've told you. The driver had a heart attack. That's all there is to it."

Bruno hadn't learned anything from Jane Martin that aided their investigation, but she had revealed a side to her personality consistent with the view of others.

"Mrs Martin, thanks for coming over."

"I know I haven't been any help, but I tried to tell you that on the phone. Good luck with your investigation," she said, and left in a hurry to get back to Southbridge Motors.

"What do you think, boss?" said Andy.

"At this moment, I'm disappointed."

"Are we barking up the wrong tree with her?" suggested Andy.

"Are we? I think I disagree. But I don't know why. I wanted to believe we'd get something from her or her husband and former husband. They might have been exposing their own insecurities when they spoke to us about her."

"Did you like her?"

"No," said Bruno. "I disliked her."

"That's because you paid her no attention as a woman," said Andy.

"Are you an authority on women?" said Bruno.

"Not yet," said Andy. "But I am learning for you, sir."

"There is something ruthless about her, but I can't put my finger on it. Her relationship with her husband is cold, possibly cruel. Her daughter doesn't want to live with her. Yet she is capable of charm and warmth to men – some men, that is."

"To achieve her ill-gotten gains," said Andy.

"Yes, but its not just that. Her need to be in control and right all the time is hiding something."

"Perhaps the Shanklin gossip can tell us more?"

"Let's invite Mrs Bots for coffee and chat through some of the things we've found out," said Bruno. "She might embellish or contradict some of our assumptions or lead us in a different direction. If there is anything going on in Jane Martin's life, she might know about it."

When Andy called her, she was delighted to meet them in the Lookout Café on the Shanklin seafront for coffee in the morning.

CHAPTER 21

IT WAS A SUNNY MORNING at a table for four under a shade on the broad Shanklin beach promenade. The season was in full swing and the Lookout Café had been serving full English breakfasts since 7 o'clock. Their clientele, in shorts and T-shirts, were suntanned and happy, eating breakfast and drinking steaming mugs of tea.

Before the pier caught fire and collapsed into the sea one windy November night twenty years ago, comedians appeared at the Pier Theatre. In town, the Shanklin Theatre played to full houses during a twelve-week season, polishing their acts before embarking for Blackpool and an elongated season under the lights that Blackpool is famous for. Sadly, nowadays the Shanklin Theatre only features tribute bands and famous, nearly forgotten ex-footballers talking up their former exploits on the pitch.

The safe sand beaches attract families with young children, retiring to the rides in the Pirates' Kingdom and the slots in the Arcade, when the rain or hot sun drove them from the sand. Shanklin had its heyday in the twenty years after the Second World war, before cheap flights to Spain took over, but Covid and the airline crisis threatened to restore some of its former splendour.

Sally Bots had selected a table out of earshot and was about to start on a toasted buttered teacake and coffee when her new friends Bruno and Andy joined her. She was over the moon to see them, as Andy remarked at the end of their previous meeting of an hour during which she revealed more local gossip and opinions on the crash that had ruined Shanklin's summer Carnival.

The popular view was that the crash was an accident and the police were wasting their time searching for a needle in a haystack trying to find someone to pin the blame on, to escape criticism of the Carnival's health and safety regulations.

"What is your take on the accident, Mrs Bots?" said Bruno.

"Well," she said. "Brake cables do snap when applied fiercely, and in a crash bolts do drop out if carelessly assembled. Faults on heavy commercial trucks can happen without human interference, was the commonly held view," said Sally Bots, who had gathered opinions from various people in the town, and botched servicing was a possible hazard and considered a likely cause. "Are there health and safety checks on all the floats before they begin the procession?" she asked.

"We've done those," said Andy. "They don't check the function of the vehicles, they assume an MOT covers that."

During a pause for breath Andy was able to put the question to her: "Did you know Jane Martin?"

Her reply was immediate and exhaustive. Her opinion poured out of the snooty old witch like venom from an adder.

"Know her? Everybody knows Jane Martin! But what they know of her they keep to themselves, for fear of reprisals if she hears of people gossiping about her."

"Can you give us an example of the gossip, and these reprisals?"

"She is an attractive lady with the physique to complement her looks. She keeps that way because she is a very good tennis player, the star of the Ventnor Club. When I was young, I used to play tennis," she said. "Not at the Ventnor Club. I used to play at Bembridge. They were very selective with membership. It wasn't a question of how good a player you were, it was whether you fit socially. Of course, I had no problem there."

"It's the same with all tennis clubs, I've been turned down because I was a policeman," said Bruno.

"Yes, Inspector, it's a social game. To be a good player you must have the personality traits that she has. Apart from your tennis skills, you dominate your opponent from the baseline, in that you would be willing to literally murder him or her to win the point. When both players have the same approach, that's what makes for an exciting match. I did not have those qualities, so I was an average player."

"But you wouldn't be so inhibited nowadays Mrs Bots?" said Andy.

"You're dead right Detective Andy, and please call me Sally. The other reason people join tennis clubs is for sex. Singles, doubles, and mixed doubles. All types."

"No threesomes?" said Andy.

She replied with a broad silent grin and Andy imagined a young, not so prudish Miss Bots at the Bembridge Lawn Tennis club.

"Jane Martin plays doubles with Charlie Adams, who is the general manager at Southbridge Motors, a young-looking, athletic man, and using the expression 'playing away', they do at weekends at tennis clubs all over the Island and they go to the mainland. Playing alongside her immediate boss at Southbridge as her regular tennis partner, she has license to behave as she likes in the workplace. And Charlie Adams is unmarried, so he is at her beck and call 24/7. She also has control of the company finances. I'm not suggesting there is any monkey business there but, she has form in that department, as you police officers would say, and a check on her adding-up might be worth doing. She is not working at Southbridge Motors for wages! Think about it: you have owners, the Southbridges, who don't seem hands-on. They trust Charlie, who is controlled by Jane Martin, who is in charge of the company's money. One way or another, there must be an angle, Inspector?"

"Can you find out more Mrs Bots?" were Andy's thoughts, which he voiced.

"I will try, Inspector. I know everybody in Shanklin worth knowing, and they all know my friendly manner. So if I can help, I will be happy to try."

"Mrs Bots, thank you for your help. We know where to come when we need it," said Bruno.

Bruno accepted Sally Bots' character assassination of Jane Martin in the friendliest manner, paid the bill and they left her sitting in the sun with more tea, basking in a cloud of self-righteous satisfaction knowing that, with better game skills, she could have been a brilliant tennis player.

"We know who we are dealing with," said Bruno. "But the more we know about Jane Martin, the less we think she is in involved in the crash."

"Is there something staring us in the face?" said Andy.

"Sally Bots could be onto something when she pointed us in the direction of Southbridge. She works in a garage and has a young manager who is besotted with her, and vice versa, according to Mrs Bots," said Bruno. "But it doesn't suggest a motive for ruining the Shanklin Carnival, or why would she be involved in a murder."

"It may not have been intended to be a murder, but it seems that the opportunity is with her," said Andy.

※

Back at the station was a message for Bruno to call Matchett, which he did.

"Inspector Peach, I have something which I think will interest you and I'd like to bring it round."

"I'm here for another hour, so come now," said Bruno sounding enthusiastic at what could be a breakthrough clue for them.

"I think this could be important, Inspector," he said as he sat down in front of the two detectives and began to explain.

"Mick's desk in the office had several drawers, one of which he kept locked. I moved into his office and called Eileen McClusky to ask if she had any keys that might fit his desk.

Of course, I said that anything personal to Mick she could take. She was round like a shot, and together we opened the drawer. There was nothing personal in the desk, everything was to do with something in the business and there was a book in which he had his personal business contacts.

"She wanted to take it, but I pointed out his hardbacked diaries had MIDDLETON's embossed on the front cover, and all the entries related to business contacts. She fought hard to take it but I knew she wanted it for her new business venture, so I didn't let her have it.

"There was also a bank paying-in book. The paying-in book has several credit payments starting in January 2022, one each month approximately. The account is with NatWest in Newport. On each counterfoil were two capital letters, but no other details. The four counterfoils had the following eight letters, NW, BG, WH, SS and the total paid into the account amounted to £56,000."

"Can we find out who this money came from?" asked Bruno.

"Very difficult," said Matchett.

"Could it have been stolen from the business?"

"Not that I can tell."

"I have checked each invoice raised by the company this year for our fees due on completions, which are paid to us by the solicitors acting, and everything is in order. No amounts due remain unpaid and all receipts due have been received into the company bank account. This amount of money, if it had been due to Middleton's, would have been picked up by me immediately," said Matchett. "I've called NatWest and they will not disclose any details of the account."

"It's a private current account? Maybe its his monthly savings account?"

"At approximately £6,000 a month, not from what he makes at Middleton's," said Matchett.

"Leave the paying-in book with us and we will see if we

can find out more about it, I will come back to you," said Bruno.

Matchett was relieved to hand over the book to Bruno, and the responsibility for it.

"Can we see the diary of his business appointments?"

This Bruno realised could be important. They needed to crack this case, which was starting to drift and looked as if it might be running out of road. They could only spend so much time on one case before time pressures force them onto other things. Soon that could happen to this case.

The police have good relationships with local banks in a small town. Bank staff are as helpful as they can be within their discretion and the data protection laws. This account was in the name of Eileen McClusky, Mick's wife, and other than provide the name of the account holder they would give no details about the account and referred the detectives to the account holder.

When Bruno and Andy contacted Mrs McClusky to set up a meeting, she was full of whys and what-fors, and only reluctantly agreed to meet them.

The reception they got to their question about her NatWest bank account was hostile.

"How can my savings account have any bearing on my husband's death?" she asked.

"A lot of money went into this account, your savings account, regularly paid in by your husband, so can you explain the source of these funds?"

"Do I have to?"

"Yes," said Bruno.

"Well, I don't know, I assumed it was sales commission."

"From Middleton's?"

"Yes."

"Middleton's have no record of making these payments," said Bruno.

"Then I can't help you, Inspector, because I don't know

where this money came from. All I know is that Mick said it was saving for a rainy day."

"Mrs McClusky, this money was a regular cash payment to your husband for which no proper record exists, nor tax was paid."

"So, was it a gift, or payment for services rendered?" she suggested.

"In view of the circumstances surrounding his death I'm sure that you understand why we need to find out where these payments come from. Who paid them, and what were they for? This is a very important exhibit and could lead us to finding your husband's killer."

"I don't know anything about it, other than what I've already told you. What I can say is that Mick would never have stolen it."

"This money was paid to him as cheques. Some banks, not the NatWest in Newport, record the name of payees on cheques, but no bank that we know of record signatories. They are payments from a person he was seeing or working for regularly. Is there a name you recall that he might have mentioned casually?"

She looked at Bruno as intensely as if she could see right through him.

"There was somebody he saw often, but he never suggested it wasn't on Middleton's business. He said this person wanted to build a marina in Bembridge, but he needed waterfront properties in a particular place. He didn't want to advertise his ambitions, but he was certain he would get planning approval, if he could acquire the right water frontages."

"Can you remember who this person was?"

"I can't recall a name, but they always met in the evenings or at weekends. I am sure someone will know if a person is buying up harbour frontages to build a marina complex. They are a close-knit bunch in Bembridge and think they are a cut above the rest of us Islanders."

"Mrs McClusky, thank you. You have been helpful. If we get to the bottom of it, we'll let you know."

"You won't tell the tax man, will you?"

"Of course not."

Bruno was pleased. This was the first indication that McClusky was up to something with somebody with plenty of money who was paying him on the side to find people in Bembridge who wanted to sell their property.

"The Land Registry will tell us about recent property deals in Bembridge, so it shouldn't be difficult to find out who," said Andy. "If we examine the buildings that are suitable for creating a marina, it should be obvious."

Bruno thought Matchett's revelation about the monies paid to Mick were game-changing and created a platform on which to rethink their lines of enquiry. It was the first clear-cut indication that McClusky could have been involved in something that had turned sour.

CHAPTER 21

A VISIT TO the nearby Isle of Wight County Press archive library in Newport, revealed a great deal about the Bembridge Harbour owners, of whom there were several, involved in a long running legal battle with the Bembridge Harbour Trust. Harbour owners, Samuel and Susan Graham, had obtained a planning approval to build thirteen new homes on the harbour-side in order to finance improvement to the harbour facilities and were involved in defending an appeal by the Bembridge Harbour Trust, who for undeclared reasons, disapproved of the development. The Graham's claimed the development would enable them to provide improved facilities with a new admin complex for residents and visiting boats at the Duver Marina and the visitors' pontoon.

The Trust claimed their objective was to protect the as yet undisclosed interests of the harbour. The County Press reporter had written that there was a great deal of animosity between all parties with the Trust financed by the local authority spending large sums on legal action against the Graham interest.

A trip by inexperienced detectives to Bembridge Harbour highlighted the need for investment into the harbour facilities, which were unattractive, sparse and run-down. It seemed to Bruno that the harbour was ripe for development and several keen-eyed developers could at this very moment be looking at potential schemes. To redevelop the harbour, they needed to buy sites with potential. As Eileen McClusky had indicated, it was likely that Mick had been working for one of these developers, finding sites on potential knockdowns, and that these were being bought secretly by a wealthy purchaser, known only to Mick. In return for his efforts he was being paid handsomely with incentives

down the line which would set his new business off to a flying start.

Secrecy would have been essential. Putting that line of
business through Middleton's in Newport could have risked
it becoming public knowledge in no time, possibly destroy-
ing the plan.

Mick McClusky's secret dealings had to be investigated to
see if they could be connected with the accident that led to
his death. To establish that, they had to find out for whom
he was working.

The cash banked by him in the name of his wife proved
that he had been successful since the start of the year in
acquiring, from his patron, regular cash payments into her
"rainy day" NatWest bank account.

Matchett had brought the bank paying-in book to the
police, assuming the cash had come from McClusky's
Middleton-related business. But he confirmed to Bruno
every enquiry during the current year had been traced, leading to the conclusion that they had offered no opportunity
to Mick to make the substantial cash amounts credited to
the NatWest account. It seemed there was evidence that
McClusky was secretly working for a person or persons to
acquire suitable properties for development, and it was possible that someone else wanted to stop him. To find who
these people were was their task.

When he revealed their progress so far to Janet, she offered
a different take on his discovery: that they should not assume
that Matchett knew nothing about Mick's sideline, and that
he wasn't part of it. She said that the solution lay with the
alphabetic letters on the paying-in slips. If the letters on the
slips meant anything, it was a code for deals completed and
suggested payments against deals possibly completed.

"You mean, the initials are properties?" asked Bruno.

"They might be place names," suggested Janet. "It's a
simple code known to Mick for his personal records. Sniff

around the Bembridge property market, to find out from the agents what deals had been done since January. If these letters were short for names or addresses of properties, finding one should reveal enough to find moneybags who was financing the purchases. There is no doubt that Bembridge has a picturesque natural harbour in a perfect South Coast location, which, with some proper dredging towards the harbour entrance, could be made to take larger vessels and earn massive increases in revenue for the harbour owners."

◈

Bruno wondered how she saw so clearly the solution to puzzles, because the following day, Andy Bowen made a search of completed land and property deals in Bembridge since the start of the year, and quickly discovered two interesting new registrations. A detached four-bedroom Victorian house facing the harbour with water frontage, called Waterwheel House, had been sold in April for £1,300,000. The second sale was of the Bembridge Garage, a plot stretching back 100 metres to the road adjoining Waterwheel House in the same section of a parade of 100-year-old Victorian Buildings. Bembridge Garage, which had once been a select house facing the harbour, became a garage fifty years ago.

The harbour frontage of these two properties was a total of 600 yards, substantial and significant for a development. With a little imagination, whoever undertakes this project could make a lot of money, was their conclusion.

The purchaser shown on Land Registry documentation was the Parker Street Property Company, with a registered office address in Southampton city centre. The shareholders were a nominee lawyer with offices at the same address.

"The value of the second sale was £1,100,000 – less than Waterwheel House. The total of these sales was £2,400,000," said Andy. "Who would have that kind of money on the Island?"

"It need not be cash," said Bruno. "And the sum is not

so large that banks wouldn't lend against premium property investments in an area with the potential of Bembridge. It has a small airfield, it's close to Ryde and Fishbourne for car ferries to Portsmouth, which has excellent road and rail links to London. These two properties identified as WH for Waterwheel House and BG for Bembridge Garage, confirmed McClusky's involvement and his fees could be related to the property values and the fact it was a secret assignment. He'd have agreed a confidentiality deal because once their plan surfaces, prices of property in the area will rise. We need to know who owns Parker Street Property Company Ltd and what their other initials in the bank paying-in book, namely NW and SS stand for."

"Are there other properties in the Bembridge area?" asked Andy.

"If we can bottom out Parker Street, we'll find that out."

The directors of the Parker Street Property Company were not listed in the register at Companies House. The nominee shareholders were Gillespie & Co., Chartered Accountants in Southampton.

"Let's visit Gillespie's. We know they are the registered office for the Parker Street Company, and they will tell us who owns it."

"I wouldn't be so sure of that," said Bruno.

"Do you think Matchett has worked this out?" said Andy.

"Probably," said Bruno. "And wants us to investigate it. Something tells me that this could be a diversion and Matchett wants to take our eye off the ball. I don't think that any of this is connected to McClusky's murder. He is still a mystery to me and he has an angle I haven't yet worked out, He is a clever bugger, but even if he has, what use is it to him?"

"If he sabotaged the float, and with his motor engineering knowledge he'd be capable of doing it. We haven't found a motive for him," noted Andy.

"Although he is a suspect there's nothing about this

murder that suggests he is capable of this crime, and working for McClusky was an easy ride compared to running the show which he has now taken on. We will see how he performs now that the buck stops with him," said Bruno.

Bruno wanted to visit Bembridge and identify NW and SS, denominated in McClusky's bank paying-in book.

◈

Bembridge from Newport was a pleasant journey via Lake and Sandown, turning right off the Sandown to Ryde B3055, travelling east along a winding road. After a mile there was a turning to the right across the downs to Culver Cliff and the monument that stared out across the Solent. After another three miles, they passed the airport littered with small aircraft. It was always busy in the summer with planes arriving from various mainland locations throughout the day and thirty-minute holiday flights around the Island, taking off and landing all day.

At the crossroads before entering the outskirts of Bembridge on the left they passed the working National Trust-operated windmill.

"At the moment Bembridge is a downmarket Lymington," said Andy during their drive. "Lymington is full of boats, but they don't call it a harbour. They call Bembridge a harbour, but there aren't any boats and the coastline is nose to tail with decrepit houseboats."

The harbour was a barren sloping area situated to the north of the village, but the village catered for all, with small shops, a café, a restaurant, artisan bakers, an excellent fish shop, an upmarket Co-op food store and a smart chemist supplying essentials to the elderly.

"A perfect place for the well-healed, toffee-nosed middle-class yachtee," said Andy, intending to categorise all the residents of Bembridge.

From the village, a winding speedy road led to Bembridge Harbour and the Bembridge Yacht Club, facing the sea, situated in a prominent place at the start of Embankment Road, which bordered the harbour. It was busy in summer and deserted in winter.

On the land side of Embankment Road, a terrace of cheaply constructed holiday dwellings with balconies facing the water providing a sea view, which would be lost to them if comprehensive development went ahead. In the distance Portsmouth Harbour, the Spinnaker Tower and the ugly thirty-storey glass apartment block known as No. 1 Gunwharf Quays could be seen from the jetties.

Past the Bembridge Yacht Club was Red Wing Quay and Selwyn Marina, both with undeveloped water frontage. A quarter of a mile further, one arrived at Waterwheel House, an impressive Victorian villa with the best view of the harbour. Alongside with similar views of the water was the long-closed Bembridge Garage. On the land side of the road for a distance were businesses that served the yachting community and the residents of the waterside houseboats, none of which had ever been to sea.

For those with boats, repairs and maintenance was a perpetual activity. Chandlers and boat builders looked busy and both sides of Embankment Road offered development opportunities to any entrepreneur who could satisfy the scrutiny of the Isle of Wight planning officers.

During their visit they did not identify a site or business that the remaining codes in the bank paying-in book could be set against. There was no NW or SS, although there were several stretches of grass verge set back from Embankment Road that could be built on, as could Jacob's Yard letting vacant units, small areas of a three-acre field for boat building or storage. Telephone enquiries were invited by the Bembridge Harbour Authority whose roadside sign showed an Island number to call, which Andy noted.

An anonymous enquiry at Hose Rhodes, Dixon, the Bembridge Village Estate Office, revealed nothing. There were no industrial or sites with development potential for sale in the harbour area, or likely to come onto the market soon.

Even to an inexperienced eye, Bembridge Harbour seemed to have potential, and McClusky had been rewarded for two other unidentified transactions, which were connected with Bembridge Harbour.

◈

Having confirmed the existence of the two locations in Bembridge, Bruno decided they should visit Gillespie's in Southampton and see if they would reveal the names of the owners.

Bruno knew there was a balance to maintain when trying to obtain confidential information. As a police officer it was in your power to appear firm, direct, threatening, or soft, friendly and persuasive. Two plainclothesmen arriving unannounced, presenting their identity, was intimidating and frequently effective. The latter was the approach Bruno used with Gillespie's.

They arrived at 2 Landport Gardens, situated near to Southampton's main shopping centre mid-afternoon. Gillespie's occupied ground floor offices in a well-preserved Victorian terrace. It was a long-established legal firm, with a handful of partners of highly respected middle-class men and women. When the two detectives presented their identities to the receptionist, after a brief wait in reception, they were shown into the office of a lady solicitor.

She studied their business cards and introduced herself.

"Gentlemen, my name is Abigail Atkin, I am a solicitor here at Gillespie's. How can I help you?" She was young, pretty and from her professional manner, she would go far in her chosen profession.

Bruno explained that they were investigating a murder that had taken place on the Isle of Wight, and during their investigation had come across certain property dealings involving the victim and the Parker Street Property Company, whose registered office was at their office; and as no names of directors were shown in the Companies House search, perhaps they could help with the identities of the owners of the property company who they needed to interview.

"We are bound by rules of confidentiality with respect to our clients, so I could not provide you with any information unless you give me a specific reason, Inspector," she said.

Bruno explained the payments received by the murder victim from an unknown principal involved in the purchases of the Bembridge Garage site and Waterwheel House. Explaining that if the police applied to the court, they would give her a directive to provide the information to assist the police in their investigation.

"I am sure you are right, Inspector. I wasn't saying that we would not give you the information you need, only that we did not readily provide confidential information to anyone without an exceptional reason. A murder enquiry would provide sufficient reason. So, what do you want from us, Inspector?"

"We need the names of the directors of the Parker Street Property Company, which bought the properties, and where they can be contacted."

"I need a few minutes, Inspector, while I find out who is handling this matter and pick up the file. Meanwhile, I will arrange coffee or tea for you," she said as she left her office.

The coffee came quickly with biscuits and they enjoyed the calm and quiet of a lawyer's office, surrounded on three sides with legal books dating back to the 1960s, dark leather-bound copies with an unread look about them.

"They don't read them. They are for reference," said Bruno.

Abigail Atkin returned after ten minutes with a brown folder and a single sheet of Gillespie's headed notepaper which had been prepared for her.

"Gentleman, I have the file for your examination, but I must ask you sign a confidentiality letter confirming that the information given by us is for the sole purpose of your investigation and not to be divulged to any party whatsoever, including the names of the Parker Street Property Company."

It was single paragraph stating what she had read to them, timed and dated with space for three signatures, Bruno, Andy and the solicitor.

There was no problem for the detectives signing a confidentiality agreement, after which she took out several pages from the file, placed the copies on the desk and briefly explained them. The address of the company's registered address was Gillespie's, 2 Landport Gardens, Southampton. The names of the two nominee directors were partners at Gillespie's and worked with dozens of individuals who do not wish their identity to become public knowledge, yet wanted the protection offered by limited liability.

It was not a great surprise to both detectives to learn that the 100 shares in the Parker Street Property Company were divided equally between Mr & Mrs Alan Southbridge residing at The Withers, Sea Cliff Road, Sea View, Isle of Wight.

"The shareholders in this company are long standing clients of Gillespie's. There is nothing suspicious about them. We checked the source of funds at purchase, everything was above board. Legally we have to check on sources of funds to prevent money laundering through us."

"Do you know what their intentions are in buying these properties?" asked Bruno.

"No, but I expect we shall be employed in any legalities if and when," she said.

"Miss Atkin, you've been helpful and we shall maintain complete secrecy about the information you have disclosed to us."

They departed in the same courteous manner they had arrived.

◈

"So, what does that tell us about the murder of Mick McClusky?" said Andy over coffee in The Leafy Bean, a coffee house in the shopping mall near to Gillespie's offices.

"Nothing," said Bruno. "It tells us the Southbridges are embarking on a property venture, but what and when we don't know, or if the murder of McClusky is connected. It's obvious that McClusky was developing his private client list while still working for Middleton's."

"Wouldn't you have expected him to do that if the opportunity arose?"

"Of course, but why would that make him a target?"

"Don't know?" said Andy.

"The Island has a close-knit protective business community. They will try anything to prevent outsiders from doing something they could or might want to do themselves. The Southbridges would have known that, hence the secrecy."

"It is a coincidence that we are being drawn back to Southbridge Motors, where Jane Martin works?"

"No," said Bruno. "I don't believe in coincidence, but their property purchases could be connected to their motor business. What they are doing falls into that category. They are not property developers or builders, they run a car sales business. So they'd be seen as opportunistic outsiders, and someone might want to stop them."

"Shall we see the Southbridges?" said Andy.

"Not until we look at their accounts, and where we get to with Jane Martin."

"I'll get the accounts in the morning, sir," said Andy.

Bruno was concerned that whatever the Southbridge's were up to, it was unconnected with the Carnival deaths, and they were wasting valuable time. He considered the suspects on their radar.

Matchett seemed happy without McClusky. He was sure he could continue, even improve his lot without him.

Middleton was a 'fly-by-night', only interested in reaping

the rewards from a profitable business he didn't want to run himself. But if profits in Newport were to fall and it was not self-sufficient, then it would fold. The Middletons would not prop it up for even one day with a cash injection. The creditors would knock and it would be all over.

At present Jane Martin was a person of interest, nothing more, and if the Southbridges were paying Mick for his property experience, they wouldn't have anything to do with his murder. So, what next?

The Southbridges could provide them something to work on, so they would have a friendly chat with them.

CHAPTER 22

WHEN BRUNO STUDIED the report in the accounts of Southbridge Motors, he read about a well-run successful business making substantial annual profits paid out in dividends to the directors, Alan and Elizabeth Southbridge. These people were ambitious, hardworking and, from what they seemed to be planning, up for it. They were aware of the attitudes from the local community regarding the development of Bembridge Harbour. Alan Southbridge was amenable and friendly and agreed to meet Andy Bowen and Bruno Peach in Bembridge that afternoon for the reason that Bruno wanted to explore the connection between the Southbridges and Mick McClusky, if any.

"Sir," said Bruno, "we are trying to understand certain business activities of Mick McClusky, a Newport estate agent, who died recently in a catastrophic road accident."

"A very nice man, Mick. Elizabeth and I knew him well," said Southbridge. "What a tragic accident that was, and for the poor girl also. How did it happen?"

"During the police analysis, we have discovered that the vehicle driven by Mick had been deliberately sabotaged by someone with knowledge of this type of commercial vehicle. The hydraulic braking system had been made inoperable."

"And you think I might help you find this person?"

"That thought had not crossed my mind, Mr Southbridge, but your connection with Mick McClusky might help us find who did this."

Bruno carried on: "During the early months of this year Mick was involved in the purchase of certain Bembridge properties, not in the regular course of his business working for Middleton's in Newport. We know that these properties were purchased by Parker Street Property Company, of which you and your wife are directors and owners. We believe that Mick was working as your agent because payments were made to him personally. These were relatively large sums of money, and we need to be sure that this money was not connected in any way with his death."

Southbridge replied, "Inspector; we did employ Mick to act as our agent in the purchase of several properties in the Bembridge Harbour Estate. We employed him because we knew him and we wanted complete secrecy with these deals. Mick was not your normal run-of-the-mill estate agent; he was at a level where he could negotiate constructively the detailed requirements of our big scheme. He was professionally qualified to do that.

"Bembridge Harbour offers enormous potential to anyone who has the imagination, the money and the backing from the banks and financiers. It will cost tens of millions to do it properly, but we have the required resources to do it. Hundreds of years ago the harbour was much larger and deeper, and continued inland as far as Brading. We don't intend that, but we will dredge and enlarge the basin and provide moorings for bigger yachts. We will transform Bembridge. Not everyone is in favour of a scheme that develops the harbour. Someone might want to stop us before we get too far with our grand ideas."

"Is there anyone you know of sufficiently opposed to your plan, that they might want to stop you?"

"That we know of is difficult to answer, Inspector. Elizabeth and I have watched the Bembridge Local Authority and the Island County Council reject every scheme that has been put forward in the past fifteen years. Most of them were awful, with locals doing botched jobs that would see them making profits, but no overall plan. We know what is required and are working with a marine architect to deepen the harbour and to build a new marina and a first-class hotel, which will attract yacht brokers with an international following to bring in the rich yacht owners. We'd attract one of the boat builders from Southampton, either Sunseeker or a similar world-renowned company, to build in Bembridge. To get our plan moving we need to own the right harbour front-age, so we employed Mick to seek out owners with freehold property in these important parts of the harbour and negotiate a purchase, and until the accident he'd been successful."

"Who would have known of your plans?"

"I would be naïve to think that we had been able to keep what we are doing a secret, too many people were involved. We expected that, nevertheless, Mick was successful in acquiring four adjoining properties with the best south-facing harbour frontage from which we can begin the project. Without Mick's skilful persuasion of owners to sell, we'd have given up on our idea."

"So, Mick was seen as the driving force behind your scheme because he has been visible and up-front with a host of sellers and potential sellers?"

"Yes, Inspector," said Southbridge.

"Would you say that because of his involvement he could have been a target?"

"As an agent I would not think so. But now you put it that way, possibly, yes."

"Who might that be?"

"I can't help with that, Inspector. Elizabeth and I have kept our distance in each of the purchases, allowing Mick total freedom. All we have done is make the payments to our lawyers for the properties bought through Parker Street Properties, and of course we've seen inside of the properties usually after dark so prying eyes did not spot us."

"Who might be your competitors for the Bembridge scheme?"

"There are two or three Island developers who would want to be involved, but they don't have a track record with a big scheme."

"Would they try to stop you with your plans?"

"No, in fact the opposite, they would expect to be invited to participate. The local authority and the Bembridge Trust are always at loggerheads, so you are never going to please them both, and without their co-operation you won't succeed, but you can appeal all local authority refusals, and with the right experts you can win. We've already employed the best people to design the scheme. Have you heard of Fester Freeman, or 'FF' for short?"

Bruno and Andy admitted their ignorance of the world's foremost marine civil engineers.

"They've re-planned the whole harbour, incorporating a five-star hotel built on stilts over the water with a helicopter landing area. A development of luxury apartments, retail units, restaurants and a hovercraft terminal to Portsmouth. Bembridge Harbour is a straight line to Portsmouth. Acquiring the harbour frontage that we have, provides a kilometre of the deepest water at high tide. FF have already presented the scheme outline unofficially to the Trust and the local authority, who will benefit substantially from the scheme with increased revenue. So, at the moment we are confident that we shall start the project in the spring."

"So, if the two difficult people are onside, there is nothing to stop your scheme from being approved?"

"Theoretically nothing," said Southbridge. "However, stopping it going ahead is important for several local businesses, the premises of which are owned, or on short leases, by the Sharp family, who have been described as barrow boys from the East End of London. Which is a false perception. That may have been where they originated forty years ago. Since coming to live on the Island, where they had holiday homes in St Helens, they have built a substantial property empire, in the beginning buying short leases which they converted to ownership of freeholds. Bear in mind that St Helens, with its quaint little terrace houses, is less than three miles from Bembridge, hence their interest in owning leases in Bembridge. They believe they own the harbour."

"But your buying one kilometre of water frontage suggests they don't?" said Bruno.

"We don't want a battle with the Sharp family. We would give up our idea if that was even a remote possibility," said Alan Southbridge.

"Even though you have invested an enormous amount of time and money?"

"We know Billy Sharp and his wife Betty, and Charlie his son-in-law runs our garage business so we will resolve any differences when and if they arise. Billy Sharp is an honest businessman, and I like him."

"Why do you think somebody might want to kill Mick?"

"In your position, Inspector, I would think it was connected with our plans to develop Bembridge Harbour, but I don't."

"His death doesn't affect anyone's plans?"

"Not ours, because we are far enough ahead and we can find another agent."

"One final question, sir. We were given Mick's bank paying-in book, into which he paid the fees you paid him, did you record these payments anywhere?"

"They were paid by Southbridge Motors to Parker Street who paid Mick, through our professional and legal expenses account. All quite above-board, Inspector."

"That's it," said Bruno. "Thank you for your time and the best of luck to you and your wife with your grand scheme."

The payment of fees to Mick from Parker Street, and the Southbridge payment to Gillespie's opened a new avenue of investigation to Bruno. It posed the question, could McClusky have been murdered because of his involvement in some other venture?

"If Southbridge has already acquired the harbour frontage

he needs to succeed with the planners, then the feud must be over," ventured Bruno.

"It could be just the beginning if he gets his plans through the Local Authority," said Andy.

"But that wouldn't be a reason for anyone murdering Mick, would it?" said Bruno.

"There seems to be no connection between the property acquisitions, engineered by Mick, and the Carnival Queen's accident?" said Andy.

"Except that the Southbridge garage is a common thread," said Bruno.

"His relationship with Mick was amicable and business had been concluded successfully with the acquisition of the four buildings. I feel there is something missing from what we learned and he is pushing us towards the Sharps who are an important player in the development of the harbour. As a partner or a as a competitor," said Andy.

"Let's assume that if Mick was paid by the Parker Street Company under the guise of professional fees that the accountant at Southbridge would know about it. The book entries would not just show professional fees to Parker Street Properties. The Southbridge accountant would have asked for details, and we know who runs the accounts at Southbridge. There is a person at the centre of our investigation that we have not yet spoken to, Charlie Adams," said Bruno. "If we suspect Jane Martin, then we should speak to her boyfriend, the tennis partner she spends a lot of time with. He might offer us something to work on."

◆

It was Charlie Adams who met them, having seen the two detectives arrive at Southbridge Motors reception area.

Sally Bots, who had described him to Andy perfectly. Late twenties, single, handsome, ambitious and athletic, and the tennis playing partner of Jane Martin. Her other comments that they were in a relationship was unconfirmed gossip.

Jane Martin was probably twenty years older than him but one could imagine the instant attraction between them. "'Toy boys', they call them," said Andy, sometime later that day.

"Mr Adams, we are investigating the murder of Mick McClusky, the driver of the low-loader that crashed at the Shanklin Carnival."

"Call me Charlie by the way," he said. "I never knew him."

"Can you enlighten us concerning cheque payments made by Southbridge Motors to Gillespie's, a solicitor in Southampton?"

"I can't help you, Inspector, as the accounts are done by our accountant, Jane Martin."

"We thought you might cast some light on these payments. For example, what precisely they were for, and why did Southbridge made these payments?"

"Even if I had knowledge of these payments, I am not sure that I can tell you without permission from the directors."

"We are not questioning the legality of these payments. We are interested in the reactions of people like you, in senior positions, to these transactions?"

"I'll have to speak to the person who paid them, which would be our accountant, Jane Martin."

Painting a picture for Charlie of what Bruno thought had happened was pointless because if Jane Martin had pursued the destination of these payments, she hadn't shared it with him. Bruno then asked if Jane Martin could explain how she obtains authorisation to make substantial payments.

"Let's ask her," said Charlie, who picked up the internal phone and asked her to pop in.

A serious, sour-faced Jane Martin came in, in less than one minute.

"You know these gentlemen, Jane? They are investigating the murder of Mick McClusky and if there is any connection between him and the payments to Gillespie's in Southampton. They are interested in who authorised the payments."

"Alan Southbridge signed Gillespie's fee notes," she said. "Their notes did not itemise the work done or by whom, they just had a code number."

"Were you happy with that?" said Bruno.

"I don't own the business, Inspector. Alan Southbridge does."

"Any idea what these payments were for?"

"You'll have to ask him, Inspector."

"Okay," said Bruno, "I will."

"How many motor engineers do you employ?" asked Andy.

"Jane can probably answer that better than me. I do the sales."

She didn't answer his question. Instead she changed the subject.

"Have you spoken to Avana?" said Jane Martin. "They service commercial vehicles on the Island."

"The Avana Service Centre, I'll look them up," said Andy.

"Have you or anyone on your staff ever worked for Avana?"

"No," said Jane abruptly and irritated. "We have nothing to do with commercial vehicles."

"Do you have a commercial vehicle for work in your business?"

"No, Inspector, we do not."

"We have two vehicles that we use to collect and deliver cars," said Charlie.

She sat stone-faced at Charlie's intervention.

"Is that it, Inspector? Can I get back to work?" she asked.

"Yes, as far as we are concerned," said Bruno.

"Avana, you said. Can you tell us where they are?"

"They are in Ventnor at the top of the hill."

"Okay, you have both been very helpful. Don't show us out. We'd like to look at your cars."

◆

"There has got to be more to these two than we've found out so far," said Bruno on their way back to the station. "Southbridge must have more to tell us about these property deals. He must have spent five or six million pounds on those four buildings and the up-front costs for FF and the surveys and design is up-front cash, which is more than his motor business can fund. Charlie runs the business and she does the accounts, so they both know about the payments to McClusky."

"You're suggesting they're up to something?"

"Yes," said Bruno, "but I don't yet understand their connection with McClusky?"

"Let's assume that Adams is involved in McClusky's murder. How, we don't know. Let's look at his relationship with Jane Martin. Who is driving it? She is a woman who is flattered by the attention she is getting from him, whilst he may be using her for something. It seems that she is content to allow any rumours that George Martin was in a relationship with Frances Napier to fester. She wants the world at large to believe that she is an innocent bystander suffering her husband's infidelity, seeking solace in the company of Charlie Adams and the tennis fraternity and soon the divorce court. The fact that they know about Alan Southbridge's property plan is no motive in itself for them to murder McClusky, unless there are other matters."

"My guess is the opposite," said Bruno.

"Apart from tennis, what are his other interests?"

"They play together a couple of times a week and at weekends. The rest of the time he lives a single man's life while she plays housewife to George and her daughter."

"We need to know more about Adams. Start at the tennis club. How long has he been a member? Find out where he lives."

Andy Bowen took note of his boss's instructions, but decided first to see what Sally Bots could contribute about Jane and Charlie. The kind of snippet of gossip that she might contribute could lead him in the right direction, avoiding boring legwork.

CHAPTER 23

SALLY BOTS was excited to hear from Andy and agreed to sound out her gossip pals for anything about Charlie Adams. She believed that without the Miss Marples of this world, the police might fail to solve lots of serious crimes. Andy knew that Agatha Christie's elderly detective retired in 1974.

Producing the NatWest bank paying-in stubs to the police showing McClusky's out-of-office earnings did not release Matchett from suspicion. Discovering the truth about McClusky in the presence of Eileen McClusky must have been infuriating. What had possessed him to disclose the contents of the desk in the first place puzzled Bruno. He considered several questions:

Is it part of a picture he is trying to paint?

He could have opened the desk easily, so why bring in McClusky's widow?

Is there something in his behaviour that is incriminating?

Matchett's keenness to deflect attention from himself might have been the reason for him delivering so promptly the information that Bruno did not consider evidence, or at this moment even connected to the crashed vehicle. There was no doubt the money belonged to McClusky – and now to Eileen McClusky, as the NatWest account was in her name.

Its discovery was a reason for a closer look at Matchett. In Bruno's experience his behaviour suggested he was hiding something, and by keeping as close to the police as possible, he could track developments.

Having Matchett as the manager of the Newport office, Tom Middleton was reliant on him for his monthly income. Whereas McClusky's monthly reporting produced by Matchett, was accurate and punctually delivered, now it was less detailed. Matchett put this down to increased workload, but Middleton interpreted it as an unwillingness to reveal a negative picture.

Having discovered that McClusky was running his own sideline, alongside his job at Middleton's, Matchett too wanted to make money for himself. Unlike McClusky he did not have the personality to develop a sideline or the professional qualifications to offer to potential clients.

His plan in building a personal nest-egg was to steal from the day-to-day business, by omitting sales from the monthly figures. This would lead to trouble unless he proved to be a highly efficient manager. Instead of continuing with the accurate monthly returns promptly delivered by McClusky, Matchett chose to deliver a broad-brush report without forecasts of what sales would lead to exchange of contracts and completion dates, when commission is confirmed and subsequently paid to estate agents by solicitors.

This lack of the monthly reporting invited from Middleton a more detailed scrutiny, which started from the beginning of Matchett's promotion to manager, and was increasingly troubling him.

Bruno decided that Andy should develop his relationship with Matchett through an interest in vintage and veteran vehicles by seeking advice from him, hoping he was able to provide a useful checklist of what to look for when purchasing a vintage or classic car. As Matchett's office was a walking distance from the station, Andy called in when he could not see him at his desk through the shop window. They knew who he was, but he didn't announce himself by name, although he did take the opportunity to sit down and ask Brenda how everything was going without Mick at the helm.

"Okay," she said.

"Just, okay?" said Andy.

"It was a great shock. We haven't got over it. We loved Mick! He was so good to all of us, and he was a great salesman," Brenda said.

"I'll give your new boss a call," said Andy and left.

Matchett's obfuscation prompted Middleton to make the occasional surprise visit to the Newport office, using the pretence of land sales as his reason for showing up unexpectedly, but these visits had so far revealed just a general reluctance to share details about the business performance. This worried Middleton who, despite his chequered business career, was shrewd enough the detect weaknesses in the way Matchett was performing. So, he changed Matchett's method of reporting, insisting on him completing a detailed report with additional columns and figures on a bi-weekly basis.

Andy gleaned from a meeting with Matchett, that he had not changed the business methods of Middleton's, but what he had done in changing the fee structure was to level Middleton's down, instead of copying McClusky's working methods. He was cunning and greedy, but lacked the streetwise cred that enabled McClusky to prosper. So, it would only be a matter of time before Tom Middleton uncovered deficiencies that would lead to a fight and to Matchett's departure. Matchett had no professional skills to offer to the people who approached him in the Newport office. Very soon he had to get on making money for Middleton's, at least until everyone accepted him as the face of the business, and then he'd have options. However, it was not that simple, because Middleton had already detected a reduction in instructions from vendors of quality property.

Matchett had reduced the fee structure in an attempt to attract a broader base to the business, which found him operating more as joint agents, sharing commission on sales – something that Mick, who insisted on sole agency, would never have entertained.

Andy had a hunch that Matchett's hobby with the Vectis 33 antique bus meant that he possessed the knowledge of a skilled motor mechanic, capable of wrecking the Carnival float, so he'd not ruled him out of suspicion.

At the end of Matchett's first month running the business he broke even, leaving Middleton with nothing. Then the shit hit the fan, resulting in a major row with Middleton demanding a weekly meeting outside of office hours.

If Matchett had sabotaged the float to get rid of McClusky in order to gain control of the business, then he had succeeded. However, he had put Middleton's into a position where in the immediate future the business would need cash support, which Tom Middleton would not or could not provide.

Bruno felt certain that there was a link between Charlie, Jane and Mick McClusky, because they knew that he was instrumental in enabling the Southbridges to develop Parker Street Properties in Bembridge Harbour.

They had dismissed Barney Puff from the investigation. He was a busy blacksmith in a convenient location and his wife's roadside fruit and vegetable sales were booming year-round.

The location of their smallholding on a main road and parking frontage was proving a blessing. Mrs Puff had taken on a labourer to do the heavy lifting and, with selective buying, she was developing a successful small garden centre. They had ample parking for fifty cars and with their enthusiastic, dedicated work ethic, the potential was clear to anyone, and in a couple of seasons it could become a goldmine for the Puffs.

◆

It took Sally Bots two days to come back to Andy with her life history of Charlie Adams and his stepfather Billy Sharp. She prefaced her report to him in the most intimate way, inviting Andy to meet in Yelf's Hotel lunch bar in Ryde at noon, where Andy would pay for her scampi and chips, and a lemonade shandy.

Yelf's was a shabby, old-fashioned hotel that hadn't been redesigned or redecorated for decades. It dated from the time when Queen Victoria lived at Osborne House and people flocked to the Island on paddle steamers from Portsmouth and Southampton, and in the 1920s took charabanc rides to Sandown beach and Shanklin Chine.

She had dressed for the occasion in a 1960s style neat two-piece and a soft floppy felt hat, nylon stockings and leather flat soled shoes. It was the kind of outfit you might find in any charity shop from which nowadays many people dressed and styled themselves. She looked as professional as she could have contrived to be and might have been cast as Miss Marple in an Isle of Wight production of an Agatha Christie whodunit.

After pleasantries and she had given Andy time to admire her outfit, lowering her voice she said, "Inspector, I want you to listen carefully, and please note down what I shall tell you." At which she produced a black Moleskine notebook, specially purchased for her police assignment.

"Charlie Adams is the stepson of Billy Sharp, whose family own property in various parts on the Island. Sharp owns a substantial portfolio in Bembridge, some of it fronting the harbour. He began working for his stepfather about ten years ago at the Newport Car Centre, selling good quality second-hand cars, all makes. The Centre maintained all the cars sold and did the servicing and issued MOT certificates.

"So he is an experienced mechanic?" Andy asked.

Sally passed over this question and continued with her narrative: "When Skoda Autos was for sale about eight years ago, Billy Sharp tried to buy it, because he wanted a new car franchise, but he was outbid by Alan Southbridge, who appointed Charlie as his general manager about six years ago. I think he knew he was the stepson of Billy Sharp, and hired him for his connections.

"He is a very bright young man and has vast experience in the motor trade. He has the right Island connections and one must assume that he has his eye on acquiring the business one day should the Southbridges decide to sell. Hence, he works

for them and not for some business owned by Billy Sharp –
who is *not* an uneducated boy from Essex, as he is sometimes
portrayed by certain snooty residents of the Island.

"Billy Sharp started in London working for Jack Barclay
in Berkeley Square as an apprentice and spent two years
at the Rolls-Royce factory in Crewe, before working in the
London showroom in Berkeley Square selling Rolls-Royce
and Bentley cars. This enabled him to develop contacts with
expensive car buyers from London and other parts of the
world. Once he had learned the business thoroughly, he set
up on his own in Essex as a Bentley distributor and flour-
ished. He copied the Jack Barclay business model and succeeded. So much so, that when he decided to move and live
on the Isle of Wight, they bought his business from him for
several million pounds. On the Island he moved into property, with a long-term plan to develop Bembridge Harbour.
Billy's main interest is sailing.

"He was only thirty-two when he came to the Island and
married an Island divorcee who owned the Seaview Grange
Hotel. She still owns it, and it's let on a lease to the former
head waiter at the hotel. Billy and Betty Sharp are both sixty
years of age and have three children of their own besides
Charlie, from Betty's first marriage.

"Billy owns two yachts which he sails regularly. One is
berthed in Bembridge Harbour and, as you already know,
Inspector, he owns many of the buildings fronting Bembridge
Harbour.

"Charlie is not married but has an on/off partner, with
whom he does not cohabit, hence he is able to have an intimate relationship with Jane Martin."

"There is a big age difference between Charlie and Jane
Martin?" asked Andy.

"Yes, but Jane Martin has a way with men. I believe they
are up to something with Southbridge."

"What makes you convinced of that?" said Andy.

"She may not be a qualified accountant but she understands business, and that means balance sheets. There she controls the accounts, just like she did in the pottery business, and hires and fires the staff. What their angle is I don't know, but it is possible to lose a distributorship and Charlie would be in a prime position to win it, using Billy Sharp to front it. The Southbridge's have been buying water frontages in Bembridge for several months, but the properties they have acquired will not give them what they need to develop an up-market resort. They would need several more stretches of frontage to make what they want. Anything less would not attract wealthy boat owners into a new marina."

"Are you saying that they have invested unwisely with what they have bought so far?"

"The point in what they are doing is to redevelop Bembridge Harbour, and if they need to acquire a lot more frontage, they have to deal with Billy Sharp."

"So, why are they not doing that?"

"Maybe they are?" said Mrs Bots. "Inspector, you have the authority to find out. Go see Billy Sharp and get his take on what is going on."

◆

Sally Bots had provided what he'd asked her for: the inside information on Charlie Adams, who had no obvious connection with Mick McClusky's murder, except that he worked for Alan Southbridge.

When Bruno listened to Andy's report on Charlie Adams, he was sure that he'd kept Billy up to date with whatever business the Southbridges were up to and vice versa. Charlie would know about Alan Southbridge's property plans. In view of Billy Sharp's connection with Bembridge and McClusky's activities, Bruno called and arranged to meet him with Andy Bowen at his office above a yacht chandlers' business in Bembridge High Street.

Billy Sharp was a handsome sixty-year-old, with a sailor's

rugged, weather-beaten complexion. One would never have placed him as a motor engineer on Rolls-Royce cars. He began by explaining his reason for having his office in Bembridge Village.

"I like it in the village because I can walk to the beach in five minutes. There are two tea shops I can visit mid-morning, and the village is never overcrowded. I am only ten minutes from my sailing boat, which is moored in the harbour, and I live ten minutes' walk away."

The walls of his office were decorated with pictures of sailing regattas and Billy with famous yachting personalities, Sir Ben Ainslie and others that he had met at the Americas Cup venues in Australia and New Zealand. He'd agreed to see them to help the detectives understand how the Bembridge Harbour community got on.

After Bruno painted a picture of the police investigation into McClusky's death, Billy Sharp confessed to never having heard of Mick McClusky, neither could he remember the Shanklin Carnival crash.

"I may have read about it in the local paper, Inspector, but I don't remember it now," he said. "We get the County Press at home, but I don't often read it, unless it's about something going on that I am involved with on the Island."

Bruno went on to explain that McClusky had acted as a go-between, helping Alan Southbridge buy harbour-side properties in Bembridge.

"Yes, I know Alan and Elizabeth have bought Waterwheel House and two or three other properties in Embankment Road. The old Bembridge Garage was one of them. I know what the Southbridges are doing, and we've agreed we'll work together on one or two things."

"We thought as your stepson worked for Southbridge he might have mentioned it to you."

"I don't see Charlie often, he calls in to see his mother, my wife, when I am not there, he's always been like that, he's very close to her. But we get on, don't misunderstand me, and he calls me occasionally about cars, which used to be my main business, Inspector."

"Alan Southbridge is investing money in Bembridge property and I'm pleased someone is, because for anyone to do anything revolutionary in Bembridge Harbour with waterside property, they have to deal with me. I bought up concessions for almost everything surrounding the harbour years ago, but I've never been brave enough to go the whole hog, borrow a fortune and gamble on making Bembridge the sailing mecca of the South Coast. Also, I don't want the hassle of running a big development project, and I like to go sailing. I really am retired, Inspector. Only a person or business with capital north of fifty million could do it, when and if it failed it would just be only a dent in the balance sheet. It could wipe me out and I'd end up in an early grave. So, I'll be pleased to listen to what Southbridge is planning when he gets round to speaking to me, which he will have to do before he starts on his grand scheme.

"You see Inspector Peach, I own the shore rights and wayleaves for most of the harbour frontages which he will need permission to cross to put a boat into the water from a private dwelling. I know Alan, and I like the way he is going about things. He will call me when he is ready, and we will do a deal.

"Now, Inspector, I must go. Good luck with your investigation. I am sorry I haven't given you that important clue that would help you find the killer."

Bruno wasn't sure about that.

He liked Billy Sharp, and he didn't see him as the type of person who would get involved in a murder plot. He held the aces to any grand scheme and regardless of Southbridge's plans, he believed they would never raise the finance.

❖

McClusky's killer had a more personal reason for murdering

him, which brought him back to what Jane Martin and Charlie Adams were up to in the garage. She is a lady with a purpose and Charlie is a player.

"They are in a relationship, for sure," said Andy.

"Very likely," said Bruno. "But it's not the main reason for their attachment. We've seen she uses her sex appeal to achieve something she wants, and it's not the odd night in a hotel bed. I am sure they are both flattered by their sexual indulgences, she with a man nearly twenty years younger, and he enjoying the attention of an experienced lover."

"And they play tennis together," said Andy.

"Ventnor Lawn Tennis club is west out of Ventnor, up the hill next to the Botanic Gardens," said Bruno. "Go along when she is working in the garage and look at the tennis club noticeboard, see if she features on the club tournaments. There is always a list of members at the reception desk. Get hold of a copy. I want to build a clearer picture of what this woman does and who her friends are. From what we know of her so far, she is not the kind of woman to have many female friends, but if she was involved in this murder she would not be tinkering around the truck. Someone else would do the dirty work.

"Try and get in to see them play somewhere," continued Bruno. "The fixtures will be on the Ventnor Tennis Club website. Go to an away match where they stay over and see what you can find out. They are both working on something to do with Southbridge Motors, which we might find out if we keep talking to the Southbridges. I will ask Jim Duncan, our local accountant, to analyse their latest accounts to see if the garage is connected to these property purchases."

That did not take long, because the accounts were up to date and company year-end was just a few months previous. They showed a very profitable year. The profit was substantially higher than the previous year, also a record year and in the notes there was no mention of property acquisitions. The chairman's statement from Alan Southbridge implied that these profits would be maintained and there were exciting developments ahead, an optimistic forecast for the future, what every employee in any business wants to hear from the boss.

In order to fully understand Southbridge Motors, Bruno wanted to hear from the horse's mouth and to put more flesh on the bones regarding their plans for the harbour development. He had started to believe that McClusky's murder was connected to the Southbridge's alternative business ambitions in the property field, and he wanted to establish the precise time line of their business relationship with McClusky.

CHAPTER 24

WHEN BRUNO CALLED Alan Southbridge to arrange a meeting, he requested that Mrs Southbridge attend, to which there was no objection. Bruno was pleased that Alan suggested they meet at the business premises, as it might unnerve any of his employees who had something to hide. The presence of the police always aroused the curiosity of the innocent and the fear of the guilty. This sometimes led to unusual reactions.

The Southbridges were an attractive couple, on the young side of middle age, handsome and feminine respectively. They were community-conscious and helped the less well-off wherever possible. Elizabeth was chair of the Church of England foodbank volunteers and gave Saturday mornings to distributing food essentials to needy people who lived in and around Bembridge and St Helens over a five-mile radius. Alan helped whenever volunteers could not show up at the Church Hall, and from a prescribed list filled cardboard boxes with the essentials and loaded these carefully into Elizabeth's car. He greeted the needy young mothers with babes in arms who could not afford the baby products to make their children dry and comfortable. The Southbridges were a caring couple, who sought ways to give to the poor and distressed.

"Inspector you've come to see us because you think we can help you find Mick's killer, and if we can I assure you that we will," said Alan.

"Thank you," said Bruno. "Perhaps you can help us with the timeline in your dealings with Mick McClusky. We'd particularly like to return to the time when you stopped using his consultancy services. Why was that?"

"We did not stop using Mick's services, Inspector. He decided in late spring that he was leaving Middleton's, where he had worked for many years, and was going to establish his own business in Ryde. It needed a few weeks, possibly three months, to get going, so we agreed to continue our relationship and he would not invoice us for work done, which was always against results, until his business was up and running. We have other purchases that Mick negotiated going through at the moment, for which Mick is due his commission payment, and when these are concluded we shall settle up with Eileen McClusky in a generous way. It's a great loss to us because Mick was a shrewd operator and we regarded his contribution to our venture as vital. We shall now deal with his son, David, whom we have met."

"We spoke to Billy Sharp to see if he'd had contact with Mick at any time, and apparently he hasn't, but he was quite pessimistic about your plans and claimed that you would have to accommodate his demands in order to proceed," said Bruno. "Of course Billy would say that. Have you never met a motor dealer? They are always right on the button, and miss nothing."

"You don't think I would proceed or even start on my plan without ensuring there were no obstacles in my way, do you, Inspector? From day one I have worked with Billy. We all had lunch, me, Billy and the girls last week, and he's on board with the whole scheme."

It was a revelation to the detectives, who on reflection now realised that Billy Sharp was sending them up when he played the martyr at their meeting, or at least maintaining secrecy that was common with Island businessmen.

"Here you are Inspector," said Alan Southbridge, who took a file from a desk drawer entitled Billy Sharp and revealed two signatures on a legally drawn-up agreement, with two pages of clauses that Bruno did not read, but it was signed and dated in February that year.

"So, Billy Sharp has known about your plans since the start?"

"Yes, I wouldn't have signed up for Waterwheel House before getting Billy's okay."

"Who might Billy have told about your plans?"

"Nobody. Except Betty, of course. Billy isn't interested in being a partner in the overall scheme, I don't think he believes in it. However, our agreement states that he will grant all the permission we need in return for new leases at an agreed market rent to be determined by the RICS where appropriate. So, he will benefit from the anticipated uplift in values. He is very happy, and Elizabeth and Betty are great pals, so their input will be valuable.

"There is only one other thing that Billy wants from me, and that is Southbridge Motors, and Elizabeth and I have agreed to sell it to him. We've just signed off on last year's accounts, so he can begin due diligence whenever he wants and we shall agree a price. It gives him a main dealership on the Island, which he has always wanted. And Betty's son Charlie will continue to run the business, if he wants to work for Billy. Those are our plans, Inspector. They unfortunately shed no light on who murdered Mick."

"Sometimes the more irrelevant things do," said Bruno. "I feel privileged that you've shared your plans with us."

"On the basis of confidentiality," said Elizabeth, who would not have been so forthcoming with confidential information as her husband had been.

"I give you my word that nothing you've disclosed to us today will go beyond this room," said Bruno. "Does anyone else have know your intention to sell Southbridge Motors?"

"Only Billy, and he will conduct his business through his main auditors who will handle the due diligence."

"And this was part of your agreement from day one?" said Andy.

"Of course," said Alan Southbridge. "Inspector, we hope, you find Mick's killer. It's left a hole in our plans and we do feel a little bit responsible for his death."

"I wouldn't think that, we don't think he was murdered because of his work for you," said Andy.

◆

Debriefing back at the station what they had learned from the meeting with the Southbridges enabled them to focus on the individuals remaining on their persons of interest file, namely Jane Martin, Charlie Adams and Terry Matchett, who they had not heard from recently.

"So, the Southbridges and Billy Sharp are good friends," said Andy.

"Definitely business partners, friends maybe," said Bruno. "If you had believed Billy, you'd have thought they had never met."

"Well, don't tell two men from the Force what's going on if you don't have to."

"I think it's a shrewd partnership. Billy is sixty and wouldn't risk his wealth, lifestyle or health on his own. But Alan is forty-five, he will do all the heavy lifting, raise all the cash, and Billy will get Southbridge Motors as part of the deal."

"Where will that leave Jane and Charlie?"

"Charlie will be fine; Jane will not last out a day."

"It's a good business as the accounts show, and it seems to be run by two trusty lieutenants, one of whom is his stepson. So Billy will let him continue, I think?"

"You've got to wonder why he left him before . . . Do you think Charlie has known about Billy's plans from the start of February?" said Bruno.

"Yes, but not from Billy. Billy would have told no one," said Andy.

"But his wife, Betty, who sees her son regularly, would have told him. After all, her son's position at Southbridge Motors could rest on the success of Alan's property venture. My bet is she would have whispered to her son what was going on. I'd imagine she will like the idea of Charlie working for Billy.

Billy would regard Charlie as valuable. And I am sure if there is anything that a purchaser should know about the business, Charlie will tell him. By now whoever is responsible for McClusky's murder will be beginning to feel safe that they have gotten away with it," said Bruno. "Although the Southbridges had been open about their future plans, nothing changed concerning the motor company, in that no one was yet aware that it was to be sold. I would be surprised if the Southbridges' behaviour regarding these property purchases had gone entirely unnoticed by Jane and Charlie since the start of the year. Let's assume that Jane and Charlie have known what's going on for some time."

"How would it affect them?"

"It would only be important if they were hatching something between them, which you might find out by going to the tennis club," said Bruno in a light-hearted manner. "If this couple were up to something in connection with the business, in addition to their romantic liaison, it could surface in conversation together during a weekend." In Bruno's opinion there had to be some other reason for their relationship.

◈

McClusky had been close to Alan and Elizabeth Southbridge. With their agreement to make further commission payments to his newly-formed company, it could have had important ramifications to a third party's plans, as could a whiff that the business was for sale. He needed to know the locations of the other deals that McClusky had already completed in respect of which Alan Southbridge intended the fees to he paid into his new business account. There might be something suspicious, even illegal, about those deals that created danger for McClusky.

A call to Alan Southbridge confirmed the addresses' locations, the names of the vendors, and the price negotiated. All bought in the name of the Parker Street Property Company.

Bruno instructed Helen, a member of the office staff, to

create a map of Bembridge Harbour, showing the ownership of all the properties with harbour frontage. Her task included head leaseholders who controlled access through covenants to the water line. He wanted to see if there were other persons with a vested interest in the Southbridges' Bembridge Harbour development.

CHAPTER 25

THAT EVENING Bruno attended a dinner with Janet at the Luccombe Grange Hotel in Shanklin. It was an annual end-of-year gathering of the South Island head teachers, arranged to renew old acquaintances and meet new teachers. The hotel was situated on the corner of Popham Road in which the Shanklin Carnival floats had gathered on the evening of the crash. Had Bruno realised its location early enough he might have excused himself and not attended. Now that he was aware of the parking arrangements for the Carnival floats on the day of the Carnival, a closer look at Popham Road might reveal something relevant to help this investigation.

Luccombe Grange was a comfortable, family hotel with a well recommended licensed restaurant open to non-residents throughout the year. The banqueting suite was a feature room situated on the first floor at the front of the hotel with a full view of the car park. The east side of the hotel faced the bandstand in Rylstone Gardens, visible through giant one-hundred-year-old oak trees, on the other side of which lay Shanklin Chine. In summer the Island brass bands played regularly in the gardens, raising money with a bucket collection for Island charities.

The award-winning tea gardens had mini golf, with afternoon cream teas for spectators. One could picnic, relax and from high on the cliff watch the breakers lap against Shanklin seashore.

From Bruno's seat, at the end of the long table, opposite Janet, next to the Brading Primary school head teacher, he could see a part of both sides of Popham Road where the display vehicles set up to be decorated with bunting before the start of the annual Carnival. The now-empty road took his attention for long enough for Janet to notice and bring him back from his thoughts. She had not told any of her

174

professional colleagues that he was a detective, so he was able to join in conversations as the partner or escort, whichever Janet chose as appropriate for the occasion. Being introduced as a policeman in any company always took him down a pathway of conversation that did not end. Bembridge Harbour had been uppermost in his mind throughout the day and it surprised him when one of the guests mentioned it, and how everybody had a view on the Bembridge development, a subject he avoided.

"There's nothing there except the windmill before you hit the town," said Karl Roberts, seated diagonally opposite Bruno, who admitted to visiting once and, after one circuit of the town, had left.

Thankfully the conversation moved on from Bembridge to more interesting subjects and no one mentioned the accident at the Carnival. It was a pleasant evening in good company. Sensitively, Janet did not return to what had been occupying him during the early part of the evening.

❁

The next morning curiosity took him back to the evening's dinner location at the Luccombe Grange, where he had met Steve King, who with his wife, owned and ran the hotel.

To Steve King, Bruno introduced himself as the Detective Inspector responsible for investigating the accident and expressed his interest in the view of Popham Road. From the banqueting suite in front of the hotel entrance was a marked-out car park for thirty cars, lit at night and protected by CCTV cameras fixed to the front of the hotel, one camera pointing towards Rylstone Gardens, and another pointing along the whole length of Popham Road. The cameras, visible high up, were identified with notices which read:-

HOTEL CAR PARK PROTECTED BY CCTV CAMERAS

Apart from their value as a deterrent, they could be used to identify thieves and vandals committing offences in the hotel car park.

Steve King regularly changed the cassette tapes in these age-ing cameras and kept them to reuse if he ran out of cassettes.

"Anything more than a year old I throw out," said Steve. "The cameras have been a success and in this quiet part of the road, we've had no thefts or vandalism."

"What have you got covering the past few weeks that you could show me?" said Bruno.

"Is it important?" said Steve.

"Very," said Bruno. "On the day of the Carnival someone vandalised one of the vehicle floats while it was parked up in Popham Road. We've no idea who it was or even if it was vandalised whilst it was parked that day, but your camera might show us something."

"What was the date of the show?" said Steve. "Leave it with me, I will need to find that day on the tape and if I do, I'll call you, Inspector. It will take me too long to set it up and do it now."

"Thank you, Steve," said Bruno.

Bruno believed he might get something from the camera and he could wait a couple of days to find out.

◈

That morning Andy Bowen had pursued the instruction to visit to the Ventnor Lawn Tennis Club. The noticeboard fixture list displayed in the reception showed an away match against Emsworth Lawn Tennis Club, scheduled for the coming weekend, beginning with a ladies' singles tournament on Saturday at 2 p.m.

The weekend program consisted of men's and ladies' singles and a mixed doubles match between Jane Martin and Charlie Adams, who were the club champions, and the Emsworth club champions. On day two a men's singles and men's doubles tournament was scheduled.

"The club secretary said the club plays Emsworth every year, and this year it's away, so we can assume they will stay in a local hotel on Saturday."

"So how do we find out what they are up to?" said Bruno.

"I am not sure they are up to anything connected with McClusky," said Andy.

Bruno could not accept that what they knew already about them was the whole story.

"Car showrooms are busy at the weekends. People come and view cars, some take test drives, some are just tyre kickers. But weekends are not the best time for the chief salesman to go off playing tennis. In fact, they may hire extra staff for weekends. Let's visit Southbridge's showroom on Saturday morning. We know Charlie and Jane are not going to be there, so we can talk to whoever is there about cars. We might find out something useful."

◆

After a morning catching up at his desk, Bruno left Andy to dot the i's and cross the t's, and took the afternoon off to go walking with Janet across Tennyson Down. When the great poet walked the Down it was to study geology or for bird-watching at dawn, or for dusk astronomy. Tennyson was inspired to write some of his greatest poems while walking the Down. Then Tennyson Down was called High Down. The Charge of the Light Brigade was one of those great poems. What Englishman can't quote a few lines from that famous poem? Bruno believed that during a several-mile walk across Tennyson Down, it might inspire him to alight on a clue that could help him find McClusky's killer. The truth is it was Janet who was his inspiration.

Tennyson spent a significant part of his life on the Island and walked this Down regularly, backwards and forwards to his home at Farringford in Freshwater, past St Catherine's Oratory, on to Chale, where Bruno led Janet to the White Horse Pub and Restaurant for a pint of Island bitter and freshly cooked fish and chips for supper, sitting at a table in the sunshine.

The weather was glorious high summer and in truth the

perfect opportunity to forget about the McClusky case. If something didn't turn up soon, he would have to downgrade its importance in favour of more pressing, immediate and urgent cases.

They talked about how relaxing the Island could be and how the pandemic had had a positive impact on the Island. A huge increase in visitors and property purchases had occurred, and with Wight Fibres broadband rollout it was possible to live and work on the Island or travel to the mainland daily, even to London.

It was a beautiful, long summer's evening, the day still an hour before sunset, when they drove home to Newport.

◈

Bruno was convinced that Southbridge Motors held the clues to the entire case, and with a clear mind he was ready to explore the probabilities with Andy Bowen the next morning.

Janet's view was that if Jane and Charlie had murdered McClusky it was to prevent more of Alan and Elizabeth's property acquisitions, which they had discovered by virtue of the payments to Gillespie's from Southbridge Motors company accounts.

Billy Sharp had said that Charlie frequently visited his mother, usually when he was out. Janet was confident that Betty Sharp would tell her son of any developments in her husband's business that might have relevance to him, and a quiet word about the purchase of Southbridge Motors might have slipped out.

Their arrival in reception at Southbridge Motors to speak to Charlie Adams drew the response that Bruno had wanted from the young lady at the desk.

"He is not in today, sir. Can someone else help you?"

"He was going to show me the car range you sell."

"I'll get Eddie Compton, our sales executive, to do that, sir. Please take a seat."

The showroom was busy as you'd expect a car showroom to be at weekends, and Eddie Compton took a few minutes to greet their arrival.

"How can I help, gentlemen?"

Bruno did not introduce himself and Andy, but said they'd spoken to Charlie during the week and he'd agreed to take them for a test drive early on Saturday, but hadn't said he would not be in today.

"I can't take you for a test drive gentlemen. Those cars have to be reserved in advance, and we have to see your driving licence. But I will show you our stock."

After listening to twenty minutes of sales talk, in which Eddie convinced them both that the Skoda, which is a Volkswagen with a different badge, was a brilliant car, they moved to a comfortably furnished area with a coffee machine and biscuits served by Eddie to listen to him pitch the various purchasing options for them.

"Mr Compton, before we discuss a specific purchase, I should tell you that we are police officers from the Newport office and the purpose of our call today was twofold. We wanted to speak to Charlie Adams about a future business opportunity for Southbridge Motors, as well as cars."

"Inspector, Carol recognised you both and prompted me as to who you were."

It was no surprise to Bruno that they had been noticed by the young lady at reception and shifted their conversation away from cars.

"Tell us about the business, Eddie," said Andy. "It seems to be buoyant?"

"It is now! It wasn't like this a couple of months ago. Then we thought the owners were selling up and moving into the property business. They've made a fortune here, so why not?" he said. "It worried some people – Jane and Charlie particularly. They saw themselves out of a job, which would have affected them seriously. They behaved as if they owned the business, because Alan Southbridge has given them full control and they knew that a new owner would get rid of them. Then their property agent was killed in a car crash and that put an end to the idea that they were selling the garage, I think," he added.

"You are not sure?" said Andy.

"I am not certain," he said. "I think the Southbridges were already committed to various deals, and it is probably a good time to sell this very profitable business."

"Would it affect you?"

"Officer, two years ago I was top UK Skoda salesman. I can get a job anywhere. Peter Scott, the Island BMW distributor, would hire me tomorrow."

At that moment Carol knocked and opened the glass-fronted door to the sales office and said, "Eddie, Mr James Fleming from Scottish National has called in to see Charlie. I said he is not in today, then he asked for the accountant, and I said Jane wasn't in. Can you have a quick word? It seems important."

"Will you excuse me, gentlemen, for just a minute?"

Bruno and Andy were all ears to Eddie Compton and happy to wait and see if more pearls of wisdom can be coaxed from him.

Within a couple of minutes, Eddie returned and tossed James Fleming's business card onto the desk.

"He called in to introduce himself as our new account manager. They are the company we use or we recommend to purchasers who lease or buy their car on hire-purchase."

"Do most buyers buy on HP?" said Andy.

"Almost all. We prefer that because we earn a commission on the finance. They also do 'stocking', which we don't use."

"I am not familiar with 'stocking'," said Bruno. "How does that work?"

"Most dealers finance the stock in their showrooms, which is then repaid when the car is sold. Scottish National are the biggest and best, part of NatWest bank. We don't do stocking because it can be expensive, the high interest rate that you pay cuts into your car sales margin. And if it's a model that is slow to sell you can find yourself out of pocket. With a big showroom it can run into millions and if the dealer doesn't have the capital to invest in the stock, it's straightforward industrial banking," said Eddie.

"How often do you see Alan Southbridge?"

"He comes most mornings. He deals with staff issues mostly. The business is run by Charlie, Jane does the accounts and my job is sales and seeing all pre-delivery work is done."

"How do you get on with them?" said Bruno.

"Inspector, I sell the cars. If you were really here to buy I'd have sorted a deal for you by now. They are too wrapped up in themselves. Off playing tennis together this weekend. But I am happy. The Skoda range is brilliant. With its massive TV advertising, my job is done for me. And buying a new car is an emotional experience. It's not about the car, really, its about satisfying a desire."

"Eddie, you've taught me a lot about the motor business and now I must let you get back to the serious punters." It was time to leave, so they thanked Eddie and promised to contact Charlie on his return.

"Nice to meet you Inspector," said Eddie. "I saw you visit Charlie a few days ago. I hope I behaved properly?"

Both detectives smiled and laughed.

"Perfectly Eddie," said Bruno, they shook hands and departed.

In the car park, on their way out, they saw one of the Southbridge Motors delivery vehicles capable of carrying two cars.

"It's not dissimilar to the Carnival float," said Andy.

"Let's visit Avana," said Bruno. "I think it's a red herring but we might learn something if it's only the reason why Charlie Adams sent us there."

CHAPTER 26

AVANA WAS VISIBLE just off the main Newport to Sandown Road near Rookwood. It was a series of workshops built of red brick in which were fixed hydraulic lifts capable of upending heavy vehicles or trucks for engineers to tackle their undersides.

Phil Foden, the general manager, was sitting at his desk when Bruno tapped at his office door, politely introduced himself and asked if he could have a word.

"Come in, Inspector. Sit down."

"This is my colleague Andy Bowen," said Bruno. Their business cards confirmed their identity.

Phil Foden was fiftyish, neatly dressed with rolled up shirtsleeves. He was handsome, with a full head of dark hair, and welcoming, with an immediate offer of tea or coffee refreshments.

"Forgive our unannounced visit Mr Foden, but in truth we were passing and hoped you might help us with a technical problem."

Andy then quoted the precise make and year of the Carnival float and explained the reason for the police interest. "We understand that to get at the cables in the hydraulic brakes would require an experienced motor engineer. Can you talk us through how someone could damage the brakes on this vehicle?"

"It's not difficult, gentlemen, but if you cut the hydraulic connection, you make the vehicle unroadworthy, because you have no control. Finish your coffee, gentlemen, and I will show you. We have one of these trucks in for service now."

Phil Foden escorted the two detectives to one of the repair workshops and showed them the panel that had to be opened to access the brake cable that connected the hydraulic system to the brake pads.

"The damage you've described could have been done in a matter of seconds, but only by a person who understood the system."

"All you have to do is loosen off the two Dzus fasteners, you could do it with a coin." He demonstrated. "A small screwdriver is better, and a pair of hand-held cutters to cut through the cables, then that's the brakes out. Have I been of help, gentlemen?"

"Very much so," said Bruno, who thanked Phil Foden for his help and headed back to the station in Newport.

✦

Back at his desk, Bruno received a disappointing call from Steve King at the Luccombe Grange Hotel in Shanklin, saying that he'd been unable to read the tapes on his machine. However, he had sent them to his local security contact to see if they were readable, and he'd call him if he was able to show him something.

Phil Foden had been helpful but it did not materially advance their investigation. The motive for McClusky's murder was still a mystery, certainly with the people of interest they were looking at. So who would most want the Southbridges to fail in their property venture and maintain the status quo at the car sales business? Charlie Adams and Jane Martin? Would they have murdered McClusky to achieve it?

"At present none of the evidence we have suggests that or that their murder was a mistake and that they were simply intending to wreck the Shanklin Carnival."

Middleton had nothing to gain from murdering his best employee and indeed, as events were proving with Matchett, had everything to lose. With the fall in the volume of completed deals, as a result of Matchett's changing of the fee structure, the business, after paying all expenses, including salaries, was just breaking even. Matchett's response was that he needed time to make his changes work, but Middleton didn't have time. He could not allow another month to go by and the Newport office only break even without taking action. Nevertheless, he had no option but to allow the business to continue.

To fire Matchett would cost him thousands in notice period and then redundancy and only then after formal notice and justifiable reasons for dismissing him had been discussed with him and put in writing. At break-even he had to let it continue and hope that Matchett succeeded, but a loss would be terminal because the Middletons wouldn't cover it. Eventually his only option would be to delay paying the salaries and stop paying the creditors for as long as possible, say two weeks, take whatever income Matchett could collect, and close the business down, putting it into administration in the name of his wife.

Bruno was disappointed with Steve King and wondered why he'd installed a camera security system if he couldn't backtrack instantly if a vehicle had been stolen. Instead he turned his attention to James Fleming of Scottish National, to see if he could find out more about the finances of Southbridge Motors, which were managed by Jane Martin.

"Do you remember what he said to Eddie Compton?"

"Remind me," said Andy.

"He said he called to introduce himself and to discuss the stocking facility. He remarked it was sufficient post-Covid, when the cars were flying out of the showroom."

"This is contrary to what we have been told that they don't use stocking finance. So let's go and see James Fleming and get the facts."

◆

Fleming's office was in Southampton and Andy discovered he was due to visit the Island in two days' time – the day after tomorrow. His biggest client was the BMW dealer, Peter Snow, located in Newport, so he agreed call in to the Police Station around lunchtime.

Good news came in a quick call from Steve King, whose recording engineer had transferred the contents of the tapes satisfactorily from Steve King's out-of-date equipment, onto a new system that he'd installed into the Luccombe Grange Hotel, and Steve could show him the results any time.

Bruno's hunch was that something would reveal itself from these two avenues of investigation and enable them to make progress. If nothing exposed Adams or Martin as murder suspects, then their investigation would grind to a halt.

Bruno had to ask all the right questions of James Fleming because rules of business confidentiality would restrict him providing confidential information. However Janet suggested, over evening supper, that a young man might be flattered to be involved in a murder enquiry. She suggested that Bruno start by explaining his reason for the meeting. That might draw him in, so that business confidentiality would not be a problem.

One advantage Bruno had was that Fleming had not met Charlie Adams or Jane Martin, so he might assume Bruno was investigating Southbridge Motors, having seen him through the glass-fronted office with Eddie Compton.

Andy Bowen had persuaded his wife Hilary, herself a tennis fan, to travel to Portsmouth on Sunday to visit Emsworth Lawn Tennis club to watch Jane Martin and Charlie Adams play. It was an impulsive decision by him, mainly because he felt that he and Bruno were clutching at straws and if they didn't make an arrest soon, their investigations would wither on the vine.

CHAPTER 27

D RESSED IN a short-sleeved white tennis shirt, tailored tennis shorts, and trainers, his eyes shielded by dark glasses, Andy looked every inch a tennis player. In a nondescript, back-to-front baseball cap and with a lady he was unrecognisable as the suited police officer Jane Martin met at Southbridge Motors. And he had no intention of getting anywhere near them himself. They went on Sunday to observe behaviour, aware that it was a men's single tournament scheduled to start at 2 p.m., but actually started at noon.

There wasn't a huge crowd in attendance, probably less than a hundred, of which most were competitors, club members and officials. There were two lawn tennis courts in play, and one semi-final underway, with Charlie Adams to play in the second semi-final. The men played one sudden death game to decide the winner. Andy judged that the tournament would finish late afternoon. At first they sat watching together, until Andy saw Jane Martin with Charlie on the far side of the court waiting for semi-final number one to finish, which it did quickly, leaving her to sit and watch him alone.

Andy persuaded Hilary to cross to the other side of the court and strike up a conversation with her, which enabled him to move to a less prominent seat where he could see them, but to them he was out of view.

Hilary understood police business and was as interested as Janet in their methods and the outcome of murder cases. As a nurse she had got to know the basics about patients by asking them. From a distance Andy could see they were getting on and at the end of the first set, which Charlie won, Hilary went to the club bar for tea and scones with cream.

Charlie won the first set six games to two in forty minutes and started the second against Mark Billings, who was

Emsworth's number-one, and again won easily six games to one, enabling Ventnor to retain the cup for another year.

Hilary had shared tea with Jane Martin and in a friendly manner discussed living on the Isle of Wight, until Charlie clinched his win and they said goodbye and Jane went to celebrate Charlie's win with him.

Andy did not reunite with Hilary until they met outside of the club to walk the quarter mile to Emsworth Southern Railway station car park.

"We had a friendly chat about tennis and she said that she and Charlie had won the mixed doubles yesterday and she expected him to win the singles, which he did. He is good enough to be a county player," she said. "But they don't choose Island players, too difficult to travel. He is a left-hander." This remark rang a bell with Andy, but he couldn't remember why.

"She referred to him as her partner and I wasn't sure what she meant, tennis I presumed. Because she is much older than he is, I could have been forgiven for thinking he was her son. Then she said they had come for the weekend and stayed in the Crown Hotel for two nights. When I asked where she lived, she said Shanklin, but we are moving to Bembridge, I said, 'You and Charlie?', and she said yes. There was no mention of her husband and daughter. She said Charlie was a director of a motor distributor but did not say where."

Andy struggled to see any connection between these two engaged in a clandestine love affair and McClusky's murder. However, he now recalled a conversation with someone that the saboteur of the Carnival vehicle would have been left-handed. When he relayed Hilary's conversation to Bruno, it gave him something to think about, it was a small thing but could be relevant.

"What did you think of her?" Andy said to Hilary on the drive back to Portsmouth. "Did you like her?"

"No," said Hilary. "She was pleasant, we had tea, but no."

"Why not?" said Andy.

"She must be late forties behaving as if she was in her twenties. Her clothes, her hair, make-up, it's all about me. I would say she has a grudge against men, all men, except Charlie of course, at least for now."

"Perhaps she was abused by a man when she was much younger?"

"Maybe," said Hilary. "For her age she is attractive. You said she had a teenage daughter? Poor girl. I'll bet she never speaks to her, never says she looks nice. She is interested in herself, not even in Charlie, just herself. Although they are enjoying the sex, she is not in love with him. Apart from sex and tennis their relationship is based on something else, probably to do with business, where they work together."

"That's where we have got to," said Andy. "And it's very helpful to have our suspicions confirmed."

They were driving down the Eastern Road towards Southsea, when Andy suggested they have a seafood supper in the Dolphin on the beach in Southsea, which was a reward for a successful day.

◆

Bruno's examination of the tapes showing the floats and vehicles parked in Popham Road were informative, helpful, but not conclusive, because the float being driven by McClusky was parked at the end of Popham Road beyond where the road bent in a dogleg and out of sight of Steve King's cameras. The cameras covered two-thirds of the Carnival procession vehicles but not McClusky's or the leading floats.

"They were hidden round the bend," he said to Andy after he'd listened to his report on his Sunday visit to the Emsworth Tennis Club with Hilary.

"All I could see of interest was the vehicle that drove past, carrying supporters to adorn the floats with flags and bunting. Members of the public were appearing throughout the day, bringing items to stand on the vehicles, chairs and benches, and some were decorating them with flags, balloons and paper streamers."

At the station Andy took a call from Sally Bots who'd spoken to Sam Levy, a Carnival committee member, who had some information he wanted to mention to the officer in charge of the police investigation into the accident. She behaved in her Miss Marple manner and left Sam's number with Andy.

When Andy eventually caught up with Sam Levy, he said that he was a member of the seven-person Carnival committee and had been in Popham Road for most of the Carnival day. Mostly his time was spent on the floats, helping to ensure that objects and furniture carried by the floats were properly fixed to bases. Although he was up and down Popham Road throughout the day, he noticed at about 1 p.m. a small orange saloon car. It was a Clio, with an Island registration number, driven by a person who was wearing dark clothing, a headscarf and sunglasses, who looked like a lady driver.

The car stopped in a gap behind the leading float, which was McClusky's. A man wearing dark overalls, dark glasses and a baseball cap climbed out of the passenger seat carrying a briefcase, canvas bag and jumped up onto the low-loader and did something behind the throne which Levy could not see.

Levy recognised every other person that came and went during the day, because he was on Christian-name terms with everyone. He was suspicious, so without staring or making his presence visible, he watched the float until, six or seven minutes later, the man stuffed into his bag things which he could not see. He then watched him jump from the back of the low-loader back into the orange Clio and drove away. From a position out of sight he took several pictures using his phone camera, which he sent to Andy from his smartphone.

He did not give it another thought at the time, because

almost exactly the same insignificant kind of incident was taking place throughout the day on all the parked vehicles. It was mainly the fact that he could not identify the two individuals that prompted him to watch them, take pictures, and inform the police.

As this information could be extremely valuable, Andy persuaded Sam Levy to meet them in Popham Road, where he indicated exactly the position the low-loader was kerbside, and where the small car stopped.

"They didn't hang around," said Sam Levy, "straight to the junction with Priory Road, took a right, and a right again, and the were off through the Old Village and away."

After Sam Levy described the orange saloon car as best he could, they all went to Steve King's cameras at the Luccombe Grange Hotel. Steve was happy to indulge the police and set up the screens so Bruno could view all the cars that entered Popham Road on Carnival Day.

It was a tedious way to spend an afternoon but an accelerator button reduced the time overall. There wasn't a huge amount of traffic in the morning, but before noon it increased considerably, fading away at about 12.45 p.m.

Levy had said 1 p.m. was the arrival time of a small orange car in Popham Road, and proof that he had remembered exactly was that at 1 p.m. camera time an orange Clio drove past the hotel cameras, on which were recorded the first three letters of the number plate: DLE. Fuzziness on the camera recording prevented complete visibility, but Sam found the full number plate on one of his photographs: MB16 DLE.

Bruno was convinced that the driver and passenger on the Clio were the saboteurs they were searching for.

"The driver and passenger had made themselves temporarily unrecognisable by what they were wearing, but we could get around this with our technology," said Bruno. "I think we could X-ray these photos and match with X-rays of our suspects."

Andy wasn't quite sure what Bruno meant, but it sounded like a good idea.

It was a fantastic positive referral by Sam Levy, and Andy was quick to thank him. They now had indisputable evidence of the persons responsible from which identification could be possible.

❖

James Fleming's appointed time to be interviewed by Bruno and Andy had arrived. As James had not so far met Charlie and Jane, it was the perfect opportunity to gain some knowledge about Southbridge Motors' dealership finance.

James had worked for a year for Scottish National, most of the time working in their Southampton office, learning the company methods. For three months he'd worked in their Bournemouth office as office manager, installing a new computerised company profiling system connected with risk avoidance. His job on the road was to sell vehicle stocking plans and to service clients who used their motor dealership financing.

James explained that dealers use their finance to pay for new cars in their showrooms. These cars are owned by the finance company, who allow the dealer to sell it on their behalf.

"So, the dealers never own the cars they sell?" said Bruno.

"Correct, Inspector," said James. "My job is to see the dealer is happy with the service we provide, like any bank, for a fee. The current interest rate for stocking finance is negotiable 3 per cent."

"Do Southbridge Motors use your money to buy their new cars?"

"Yes, we finance all of their new cars and finance to the purchaser if they pay on HP or lease."

"How much of your money has Southbridge used to finance their stock?"

"Confidentially, Inspector, their limit is £420,000, based

on their current turnover. Charlie Adams is the director who manages the stocking arrangements and it was him I was calling to see. He referred me to his Mrs Martin, who is the company accountant. In fact, I am going to see them on my way to the farm this afternoon."

"Please do not tell them about your visit here," said Andy Bowen.

"Nothing will pass my lips about our meeting," he said.

"Are they under investigation?"

"They are persons of interest, nothing more at present, but we are trying to establish the scale of the business," replied Bruno.

"Since Charlie Adams implemented our stocking plans, the records show substantial growth. They are selling very good, attractively priced cars. I hope I have been of help, gentlemen, and I would say that as far as I am aware it is a well-run business."

Principally through the efforts of Charlie Adams and Jane Martin; he, fronting the business, and she, controlling the business finance. But what do they make out of it?

Jane Martin always had a personal agenda above and beyond her wages, so what is it with Southbridge? Were they barking up the wrong tree? There was only one way to find out, and that was from Alan Southbridge. To progress his hunch Bruno made a mental note to set up a meeting with Alan Southbridge before the weekend.

Bruno recalled that Eddie Compton had mentioned that he had become aware that the business could be up for sale two months ago, which would predate the murder of McClusky. It could have been a rumour, invented by Eddie, who liked to be that person in a company known for knowing what is going on. How that would affect Charlie and Jane would depend on who the purchaser might be.

"It could be a status quo?" said Andy.

"Or the opening of a can of worms," said Bruno.

"What do you mean, sir?"

"Their joint dedication to Southbridge Motors doesn't make sense unless there is something in it for them."

"Finding the orange Clio should not be impossible on the Island," said Andy. "With the full registration number, the DVLA will tell us who the present owner is. I'll follow that up sir, and I will call Alan Southbridge about these for sale rumours."

CHAPTER 28

Too many visits to the business by the police and tongues start to wag, so Bruno decided that he could discuss vehicle financing with Alan Southbridge on the phone.

"Although it might not seem connected with McClusky's murder, did you know that the matter of your selling your motor business was openly discussed in your company three months before he was murdered? Would selling the business affect anyone in particular? Could there be a connection with McClusky?"

Alan thought about Bruno's question before answering, as if he was not aware how this rumour could have started.

"I am trying to think of a connection between what we were doing with Mick and selling the business. The only person who I share my thoughts with is Elizabeth, and she does not have much contact with the garage. My present position is I have made good progress buying harbour frontages. I have planning approval for the development subject to signing up wayleaves and access points with Billy Sharp. Part of our agreement is that he will buy the garage, and I think he will let Charlie continue to run it. Charlie has done a good job for me and there is no reason why he shouldn't continue with his father-in-law as the owner. I am just waiting for Billy to confirm the date that his advisors will start due diligence and then I'll tell my key staff if Billy wants me to. He would prefer not to make an announcement until we've signed the contract. Charlie will handle Billy's advisers. It shouldn't take more than a couple of days.

"I have agreed my line of credit with my bankers and my scheme architects are ready. The dirty work of demolition, underground road work, services, a new main sewerage pipe will be done in the autumn and winter. Come spring we shall be ready to start the main construction, and I hope for good

weather throughout the summer. Bembridge will be trans-
formed into a major south coast sailing venue with all the
benefits the Solent waters offer."

"Alan, it sounds exciting," said Bruno. "We haven't been
able to discover the source of the rumour of your intention to sell the garage earlier in the year and perhaps it is
not important anyway, but during the early part of this year
when your Bembridge plans were gestating your enthusiasm
was solely directed towards making the proper decisions for
this new venture."

"Correct Inspector, it is a challenging, time-consuming
project, so during this time I leave the running of Southbridge
in capable hands."

It had been a useful discussion with Alan Southbridge, as
far as facts were concerned. Bruno had planted in his mind
doubts that there lurked somewhere in the business a problem connected with his activities.

※

Whilst they were waiting to receive details of the owner of the
Renault Clio, Alan Southbridge called to say that at a dinner
party with the Sharps in April, Elizabeth had said to Betty
Sharp that when their harbour scheme took off, they would
not have time to continue to own and run the garage, so they
would sell it. Alan believed that her off the cuff, semi-con-
fidence to Betty, would have got back to Billy that evening,
and considering her close relationship with Charlie Adams,
he too would probably have been told.

Bruno was pleased to have learned this from Alan because
it was potentially an important piece in the jigsaw. So far,
they had discovered the source of the rumour that Alan
Southbridge's garage was possibly soon to be sold, and that
fitted with their suspicions that Charlie and Jane had a special interest in the business.

They were both surprised when they received the email
from the DVLA stating that the Clio with registration

MB16 DLE was owned by Southbridge Motors of Ryde, Isle of Wight. Now they had evidence that the orange colour car seen on Luccombe Grange Hotel's camera was at some time owned by Southbridge Motors, although no confirmation that it was still owned by them on Carnival Day. Even if it was, the driver and passenger could have been anybody.

They discovered through a quick call to Eddie Compton at Southbridge, another of Andy's new mates, that the car had been acquired from a Mrs Winter of Stenbury View in Wroxhall on the 1 July in part exchange for a Skoda saloon. It was a low-mileage clean car and had been bought by a member of the Southbridge staff by the name of George Foley. He took possession of the car on 20 July, which was some time after the Carnival. Southbridge Motors was still finalising the paperwork to complete the sale formalities and inform the DVLA of the name of the new owner.

"Where was the car between the lady in Wroxhall delivering it to you, and the new owner taking possession?"

"It was out front in the forecourt with the used cars for sale."

"Is it too early to reveal our interests? Until we can identify with certainty the driver and the passenger, let's wait. The driver and passenger of the orange Clio on Carnival Day have no idea that we believe the Carnival float was sabotaged by them, or that we have a witness that saw the saboteur climb onto the vehicle, spend several minutes interfering with the mechanics while the driver waited for him or her, then return to the car and drive off. They don't know we have timed photographs of the time they were on the float."

What they learned from Eddie confirmed their suspicions that the motive for McClusky's murder was connected to a reason they had not yet discovered involving the business of Alan Southbridge, and the perceptions of certain staff at the motor company that the company was being sold. Selling the motor business would prevent somebody at the motor company from achieving their objective. It could have exposed certain secret activities that might involve acquiring the business for themselves.

"You are suggesting that they killed McClusky to prevent him from continuing to build Alan Southbridge's property empire, so he would no longer need to sell Southbridge Motors?" said Andy.

"It's could be one reason," said Bruno. "But we don't know whose reason, do we?"

"They were not to know that McClusky's demise wouldn't have stopped Alan from continuing with his harbour plans, and that he's going to sell it to Billy Sharp anyway," said Andy.

"Coming back to McClusky, our conclusion is that it's too hypothetical, and the property deals had been done. Regarding the orange car, ask him to tell us the date the garage bought it, how long they had it and when they sold it."

"Can he do that without getting the garage staff involved?"

"Easily," said Bruno. "He can look up all the part-exchanges on cars for June. Give him Mrs Winter's part-exchange registration number. We just want dates. Then we will ask him to show us any diary entries relating to Charlie Adams' and Jane Martin's absence from the business on Carnival Day."

❦

Janet was always keen to listen to Bruno's progress in his investigations and understood his approach by not disclosing the orange car information. However, she suggested that if he planned on seeing Alan Southbridge it was an opportunity to delve further in the day-to-day running of the business. For example, what authority did Charlie Adams have to spend company money? Janet believed that his relationship with a woman that was probably old enough to be his mother was based on something other than sex and playing tennis together. As they spent every day together at Southbridge Motors, it was there that their mysterious business activity was taking place.

An in-depth discussion with Alan Southbridge about how the business is run, who does what, ahead of due diligence that Billy Sharp will shortly be engaging in, could be welcome and helpful to him.

CHAPTER 29

T
O KEEP ABREAST of developments in their investigation, Matchett at Middleton's had gone quiet. It was the
middle of the holiday season. Schools were closed, and people were not planning to sell their properties and move. The
legal profession was traditionally closed in August so completions, and therefore the payment of agent's fees due on
completion, were not taking place.

Tom Middleton was about to reach a crisis. His wife had
a bank facility of up to £20,000, which she was reluctant to
use. Forecasts coming from Matchett showed the level of
business had fallen dramatically, so to pay the August salaries that facility would have to be used, and continue to be
used unless a dramatic improvement took place in the first
part of September.

Middleton's in Newport was a limited company in which
she owned the entire share holdings. If it could be sold and
she broke even, she'd be relieved, but as things stood today,
she would be in for the £20,000 guaranteed to the bank.

If Matchett believed in his ability, now was his chance.
He had the security in his mortgage-free home and as the
likely only bidder he could apply pressure to the Middletons
to sell him the business, in exchange for taking on the
day-to-day running costs. There was nothing that Andy in
his ongoing discussions about buying a vintage commercial vehicle had made him a more likely suspect, although
because of what became a blind alley he had to remain a person of interest.

◈

After Bruno had arranged another visit to him, Alan
Southbridge talked at length to his wife Elizabeth about
Bruno's friendly approaches to him.

"What can I tell him about our business that will help him

find Mick's killer? It is obvious to me that he believes the killer is one of our employees," she said.

"Why do you think that is?"

"Because whoever committed this awful crime had to know how to render the Carnival Queen's vehicle inoperable. Any one of our motor engineers could have done that, even you, Alan."

"I don't think I would know where to start."

"The Inspector doesn't know that."

"So who do we employ that might have wanted to kill Mick?"

"I am surprised he hasn't dug deeper into Billy Sharp's activities," he said.

"We don't know that he hasn't," she said.

"Anyway, Billy is as straight as a die. It seems much more his scene than ours. You often see Betty. Is there anything you can remember that she has said that's connected?"

"I think you're confused, Alan. I'll see her on Friday at our PROBUS lunch, if you can prepare a couple of searching questions, I can ask her. I'll try to find out if they are up to something."

"But what about us? Not us, I mean our employees. And specifically, Charlie and Jane? That's who Peach is interested in."

"We've had no connection with anyone who might have wanted to kill Mick. Although many of our employees at Southbridge Motors could have committed this crime, none of the engineering staff had the slightest interest in it, no motive."

"But what about Charlie and Jane?"

"Can you think of a link? I can't. Our harbour project will disrupt their lives and what was a rumour, that we intend to sell Southbridge Motors, could affect their jobs. But is there a definite reason why those two might want to stop us doing anything?"

"That's for us to find out," said Alan.

"And Bruno Peach," Elizabeth added.

"Will he handle the questions to the staff? He is only interested in what Charlie and Jane are up to."

"You mean screwing around at the tennis club?"

"Yes, but he suspects that they are up to something else, feathering their own nest in some way from our business."

"I don't think that is possible."

"You are not there all the time, Alan. I don't know Jane very well but from what I've seen of her, my guess is she wouldn't do any job without an angle to it."

"So, what's the angle with Southbridge Motors?"

"That's what we have to find out."

◈

When Bruno and Andy turned up to meet Alan, he was friendly.

"Ask me anything you want, Inspector, and I will endeavour to help."

"Alan, talk us through the business. How do you make money?"

"There are five ways," he said. "New car sales, second-hand car sales, profit in service and maintenance, insurance repairs and finance commission from HP sales. We get a small percentage on all hire-purchase business on cars we sell. With new cars we have a target with the manufacturers, which we try to meet quarterly. If we reach our target our commission on sales increases. And we always meet our target.

"On second hand sales we do well, especially now when there are very few new cars available. Service, maintenance and insurance – repair business is the service manager's responsibility to make a profit and he is paid a bonus quarterly. Our manager is Jack Watson, he has been with us since we bought the dealership, good guy and does very well for us."

"Is Charlie responsible for all sales?"

"Yes, and he is a good buyer of the trade-ins. Charlie always meets our new sales targets and he doesn't buy and make a loss. All our second-hand deals make a profit, eventually."

"What about stocking?" said Andy, speaking as if he had knowledge of the motor trade.

"We don't finance our showroom stock, most dealers do but I use my bank overdraft to finance the cars we buy from VW. The manufacturers give us generous terms anyway, because we regularly meet our sales targets. My overdraft is one per cent above base rate, so it makes no sense to pay three per cent over base for stocking finance. I run a tight ship, our auditors are happy with the business, and now is the right time to sell, especially as Billy Sharp has always wanted to buy it. A willing buyer, a willing seller."

"Alan, I am very pleased that you have explained your business methods. In our business we learn something every day," said Bruno. "I don't think we are going to find our murderer in Southbridge Motors."

"I am happy to talk to you at any time, Inspector. It must be very interesting being a detective."

"The grass is not greener on our patch, Alan," said Bruno. "We have our moments, but not all the time, there's more plodding than you see to what we do."

◆

Back at the station in Newport, Andy Bowen was mulling over the information Alan Southbridge had communicated to them about his motor business and specifically his answer to his question about car showroom stocking finance. Didn't James Fleming of Scottish National, who they had met at the Southbridge Motors showroom, say that his company were providers of stocking finance to Southbridge?

"Yes, he did, said Bruno. "He gave us chapter and verse. He said he was calling to speak to Charlie about stocking finance, I took it he was looking for business."

"No, he was the new kid on the block. He called to

introduce himself as the man to talk to about stocking levels, and he told us what Southbridge's existing stocking borrowings are. The industrial bankers are looking for new business all the time, and by all accounts make good money out of car finance."

"But Alan did not want us to know that he has a large stocking loan."

"No, he didn't," said Bruno. "I wonder why?"

"So, where are we?" said Bruno.

"Matchett, as is proving to be that case, has more to lose from McClusky's murder than anyone, and we've not convincingly connected him with the accident. Neither have we connected Jane and Charlie to the murder.

But if Matchett can secure the business from Middleton he could be the big winner."

"I still don't think he could run it. There is something slimy about him that I can't quite put my finger on, Andy."

CHAPTER 30

THAT AFTERNOON Bruno received a telephone call from George Martin who claimed that he had information he'd like to share with the police, which he thought might be connected with Mick McClusky's murder.

"Yesterday I picked up a brown folder in the bag Jane carries to and from work. It contained a finance agreement for new cars between a company called Adams & Martin Ltd and Scottish National Banking in Bournemouth. It provided the Adams & Martin Limited company a £300,000 banking facility against the security of all new cars in the Southbridge Motors showroom, with the condition that all new cars delivered from the manufacturers replaced sold cars on a rolling basis, thereby maintaining the security of banking facility against the cars.

"The names of the directors of Adams & Martin Ltd are Charlie Adams and Jane Martin. The registered office of this company is our home address. No mention of Southbridge Motors appears anywhere in the file. This raised my suspicions because the directors of Adams and Martin could take the £300,000 at any time.

"I employed a local agency to investigate their relationship. They provided proof that Jane is in a relationship with Charlie Adams. I have the usual evidence – photographs, hotel bills, credit card receipts. So, as far as our marriage is concerned the ball is in my court but I don't want a fight, I would not know how to handle her. I would like one meeting and for it to be over.

"Adams & Martin Ltd requires some explanation, which I have no wish to explore. It may involve Alan Southbridge, but he is not an officer of Adams & Martin Ltd.

"And the reason I am involving you, Inspector, is because McClusky's dealings with Alan Southbridge could have exposed Adams & Martin Ltd by bringing uncalled-for exposure on the car business.

"Perhaps you will discover something that will unravel without my involvement that gives me a quiet exit from this marriage."

"You scratch my back and I'll scratch yours," said Bruno.

"Inspector," said George Martin, "I am going to send you a copy of the full company documentation and the transactions undertaken by the company." He then photographed each page and sent them to Bruno's smartphone.

"I'm not sure of the significance of all this to our investigation," said Bruno. "I will tell you what it means when we have looked at everything. Thank you for bringing this to us. It could prove to be important. We'll keep in touch, and good luck with your plans."

"Clever bugger, isn't he?" said Andy. "Bringing this to us!"

"He is sure we will dig up enough about them to give him solid grounds for an uncontested divorce, without an unpleasant confrontation and a fight. That would save him a fortune."

Bruno believed they should help him in return for giving them their first solid clue. They now had something to work with, whereas previously they had firm suspicions but no evidence to back it up. This could lead them towards discovering the identity of the visitors to the Carnival float.

"To avoid having the wool pulled over our eyes by Charlie and Jane, we have to begin with Alan Southbridge. Is he aware of this company Adams & Martin? If so, it means nothing to us. My hunch is that he doesn't. Create a file of the documents that we can show to him. His reaction will be interesting."

◆

Alan Southbridge was all ears when Bruno and Andy arrived for an early morning chat, as Andy had put it to him.

Being all over it and as a form of encouragement, Bruno let Andy present the printed copies of the documents George Martin had sent them the previous day. It was a simple question to Alan that Andy phrased in his opening words to him, to which the answer could make or break their investigation.

"Can you tell us about Adams & Martin Limited?" he said, not connecting the names Charlie and Jane.

"Gentlemen, I have never heard of Adams & Martin Limited. We have already discussed vehicle stocking, the last time we met. I explained to you that we have enough capital in the business to finance our showroom stock. I said financing our showroom stock could be quite expensive, do you remember?"

"I do," said Andy. "But I couldn't assume without checking with you that you were not aware of this company. Yesterday we obtained some new information, which I will explain to you with the aid of full company documentation. We have not shown or discussed it with anyone, waiting for your comments first.

"Adams and Martin is a limited company set up by Charlie Adams and Jane Martin, registered at her private address. Its memorandum states that it was set up to finance showroom stock sold by Southbridge Auto. It has a bank facility of £300,000 provided by Scottish National depending on the value of showroom stocks in you showroom.'"

Then Andy spent what seemed a long time, but was less than five minutes, presenting copies of everything George Martin had sent.

When he had finished, Alan Southbridge sat quietly for some time and then said,

"I presume you want me to handle this?" he said, which surprised them.

Bruno replied, "Alan, we are conducting a murder investigation into who killed Mick McClusky. Although Adams & Martin do not seem to be connected, there is a possibility that they are. So we do not want you to handle anything. This is police work."

"If Adams & Martin are stealing from me, that is up to me. And if I don't wish to press charges, that is up to me."

His unexpected response caused Bruno immediate concern. What or who was he trying to protect, and was he involved with the Adams & Martin company?"

"Alan, out of courtesy, before taking any action and speaking to Adams & Martin, we needed to be sure that you are not a party to this activity. We believe that this company was set up to defraud Southbridge Motors and you, for a purpose unknown to us. However, when it became company knowledge that you were planning to sell Southbridge Motors to concentrate on your Bembridge project, Adams & Martin had to accept that with a change of ownership their stock company would collapse. So, what could they do?"

"Front it out or stop the progress of your Bembridge Harbour development."

"What do you think they did?"

Alan did not answer.

Bruno continued, "If these two people are stealing from you, it is a sophisticated fraud. The lenders and the police shall come back to you with the full picture. It is correct that if someone is stealing from you personally, then in some circumstances if you do not wish to press charges the police will drop the case. But this is not a personal matter. A limited company has been formed for a specific reason, namely to borrow money against collateral it does not own. This is a company fraud perpetrated by two employees of Southbridge Motors acting as officers of the company, not as individuals. Our interest is based on the connection that Adams & Martin have to the murder victims. So for now, we must ask you to maintain confidentiality on what we have disclosed to you and allow us to continue with our murder investigation.

"We will keep you in the loop once we've bottomed this out," said Andy.

◆

As they left the building, Andy remarked, "Alan did not seem too happy that he was sworn to silence. Like most successful entrepreneurs he thought he could handle the situation best."

"Perhaps he could," said Bruno. "But he is not trying to find a murderer."

It was time to examine their position before setting up a confrontation with Adams & Martin. The fraud they were engaged in could only continue whilst Alan Southbridge maintained the status quo with the motor company, letting Charlie run the business and Jane do the accounts, and limit the auditor's participation.

Bruno decided it was essential to know the date they began their scheme, because it was the threats to their activities and the fear of being found out which would have caused them to react. The company had been established in 2021, and the contracts with Scottish National started in the autumn, on 1 October, and the credit limit of £300,000 had been reached by the end of February, and represented the value of eleven cars.

"I believe Alan Southbridge knows nothing about this stocking scam. The money is either in Adams & Martin Ltd waiting for them to use it, or it is squirrelled away into their own pockets, and they have bought something. Could be a business, anything. How does this help us to find McClusky's killer? From what we already know," said Bruno, "Adams & Martin, having formed the company on 1 October, by the end of February it had drawn down £300,000. We learned from Eddie Crompton, the salesman at Southbridge, that early in March a rumour had gone around that Alan was selling the company to concentrate on his Bembridge Harbour development.

"A sale of Southbridge Motors would have meant a discovery of the new company and the fact it had £300,000 against Southbridge Motors' showroom stock of unregistered vehicles. At that time there would be no way of checking a registration number to see if it were on HP. Between March and the end of May, Mick McClusky was firming up and completing the purchases of the Southbridge's new property empire. There is still no connection between the stocking scam and McClusky. The connection is Southbridge's decision to sell his car business and become a property developer.

"To prevent this happening, they had to stop him buying more of Bembridge Harbour properties and not sell the motor business until Adams and Martin had gotten clear with the stocking money."

Andy interrupted, "So, are you suggesting that their warped minds might have persuaded them to find a way of eliminating Mick McClusky?"

Bruno explained, "They might not have started with the idea of murdering him, just taking him out of the loop for a while, and at the same time knocking Alan Southbridge's property development plans for six and giving them the space to pursue their plans."

"How do we prove that sir?" said Andy.

"It's all going to come on top one day soon," said Bruno. "But don't bet on them not getting away with it. Perhaps if Billy Sharp buys Southbridge his stepson Charlie might find a loophole. Let's trace the Clio to its new owner."

CHAPTER 31

BRUNO DECIDED NOT to interview Charlie Adams or Jane Martin regarding Adams & Martin and the stocking finance business. He did not trust Alan Southbridge not to discuss the situation with them, and anticipated that their response to Alan Southbridge's approach might be more revealing than a police interview. From the information Bruno had given him he would know what they were up to. Knowing that sooner or later they would be found out, what was their endgame? That could answer some of Bruno's questions.

To Alan, who was about to sell Southbridge Motors to Billy Sharp, it was a serious matter. Due diligence by Billy's accountants would expose the loan and materially affect the consideration for the business. It would introduce an element of distrust at a time when a purchase price had not yet been discussed. It was part of a deal that included wayleaves, licences, and the leases and concessions that they would have to agree and incorporate into their final contract.

A critical issue for Alan to explain was why this liability did not appear in his recently finalised business accounts. The fact that he was not aware of it implied some kind of fraudulence that would put off most potential buyers.

Bruno's check with Southbridge part-exchange department had confirmed that the car caught on camera at lunchtime on Popham Road was owned, as part of their secondhand stock for sale, by Southbridge Motors on that day.

"That points the figure at Charlie and Jane," said Andy.

"Yes, it points to those two but it isn't conclusive," said Bruno. "Any person could have driven the car, picked up a lady passenger, cut the brake cable on the lorry while she hovered with the engine running for the few minutes he needed. We can't haul them in on that basis."

Was McClusky's success in building Alan Southbridge's property portfolio a threat to them? In the spring while he was enjoying success in building Alan's portfolio they obviously thought so, and then danger threatened their grand scheme.

Mick's success in acquiring freehold property on behalf of Alan Southbridge was the reason that he was switching his focus, energy and money on to the Bembridge Harbour development. This created uncertainty in the minds of the Southbridge employees back in March, particularly Charlie and Jane, which could cause them to panic. So, what might they do about it?

"I'm not sure murdering McClusky would change anything. The stocking loans would surface sooner or later. What do you think they are planning to do with, or have done with the money?"

"It's a lot of money, so it must be something major or expensive. I would like you to visit Southbridge and check the documentation related to the sale of the Clio. Their paperwork might show that on Carnival Day the car had already been sold to its new owner and the paperwork had not yet caught up with the sale. When a car dealer sells a second-hand car, if there is an outstanding hire-purchase liability they are obligated to settle with the HP company, but they won't do so until they sell it and probably not even immediately, so maybe they didn't own it on the day of the Carnival."

"I'll do that right away, sir," said Andy.

It was a straightforward routine enquiry for a police office to check on the change of ownership of a car that had passed through their hands recently. Maureen at Southbridge Motors was able to provide the information quickly and easily. It was good fortune that neither Charlie Adams and Jane Martin were seen by him when he called.

The information that he obtained provided the police with

an unexpected new line of enquiry that opened another window into the case. The Clio, which was in pristine condition with very low mileage for a six-year-old car, was bought by a member of Southbridge Motors' staff one week before the Shanklin Carnival.

He was an experienced motor mechanic by the name of George Foley, who had worked for Southbridge Motors for six years. He was in his mid-twenties, originally from Cork in the Republic of Ireland. He had gone to art college in Dublin after school. He was a single man who'd been attracted to the Isle of Wight by a lady in a relationship that had ended soon after his arrival. He loved the Island and with a secure job at Southbridge Motors he lived in a rented flat overlooking Sandown Bay in Shanklin. He was physically attractive to women, and it's true to say that Jane Martin had taken a shine to him since he joined the company. She always ensured that he was welcome at every company social function that took place on special occasions, a gesture he reciprocated when called upon to keep her personal car properly serviced.

It did not require an experienced pair of detectives to imagine that George Foley, an experienced motor engineer, could have been the man who jumped out of the Clio and sabotaged the Carnival float.

Andy Bowen had noted his home address from Southbridge Motors' sales records. Bruno thought it appropriate to visit him out of business hours in the privacy of his home.

◆

Flat 4, Eastcliff Court in Crescent Road in Shanklin, was a pleasant sea-facing two-bedroomed first floor dwelling. When they called before supper time at 6 o'clock George Foley was at home and had changed from his working clothes.

Bruno and Andy introduced themselves by showing their photo identification to a pleasant, youngish twenty-seven-year-old Irishman, drinking a glass of beer and sitting at an easel painting a portrait of a lady in her twenties. The flat was decorated with unframed oil paintings, not all complete, and there were various canvases dotted about leaning against the walls.

Bruno explained that the police were aware that he had acquired his car on a date a few days before the Shanklin Carnival parade, and that his car was seen in Popham Road, Shanklin at about 1 p.m. on Carnival Day.

"Could you tell us the reason for your visit on that day to Popham Road?"

After checking the day, date and time against his pocket diary, he said that he was working at Southbridge Motors all day.

"Inspector, I have no idea where Popham Road is in Shanklin. I only take half an hour for lunch, so I couldn't possibly make that kind of trip at that time of day."

"We have a photograph of your vehicle in Popham Road at lunchtime on that day."

George Foley did not immediately respond to Bruno's statement, but maintained a tight-lipped silence for a few moments, before continuing: "I don't think that is possible, Inspector. Check the clock in the workshop and you'll see I clocked out for thirty minutes and I sat in the canteen with a few of the other boys, as I do every day. We have options for lunch, we are allowed one hour, officially; but my deal is thirty minutes and I start at 8 a.m. and leave at 4 p.m. Does that answer your question, Inspector?"

"In part," said Bruno. "Can you explain how your car was seen in Shanklin at around 1 p.m. on Shanklin Carnival Day? Did you lend your car to anyone on that day?"

"I never lend my car to anyone on any day," he said.

"Perhaps if I showed you our recording of your car being driven along Popham Road on this particular day, you might be able to identify the driver and the passenger in your car?"

"I'll try," he said.

Bruno called Steve King at the Luccombe Grange Hotel, and asked if he would show the video to them. He agreed they could come over right away.

It was less than a mile from Eastcliff Court to Popham Road. On the journey to Luccombe Grange, Foley explained that he was a trained artist and advertised his portrait paint-ing skill in the County Press where he obtained commis-sions. He was on the Island Education's list for a vacancy as an art teacher, which he was qualified to take up. He also provided a useful piece of information about staff parking at the Southbridge Motors workshop.

"Because they use every square inch at the garage to dis-play cars for sale, there is very little parking for staff. So we park in the showroom car park, where customers park, but we have to leave our keys on a hook in reception, so that anyone can move your car if it turns out you are blocking car movements. When you knock off you collect your car key from reception. So reception can vouch my car key was there all day."

He showed the officers his car keys which had a plastic tag with his name and the registration number of the car.

Steve King was waiting for Bruno and was willing to show the three men the video showing the traffic flow along Popham Road on Carnival Day.

Bruno said to George, "I want you to study carefully the driver and passenger, you can't see their faces, but see if you can recognise any other physical characteristics in the body shapes of the two people in the car. As an artist trained in looking at body shapes, you might spot something."

Foley was surprised to see his newly-acquired Clio being driven by a person wearing a woolly hat pulled down over the ears. As far as the driver was concerned, he was certain it was a woman, her body shape confirmed it to him. She leant slightly forward, suggesting the vision of a mid-forties per-son not wearing spectacles. The width of her shoulders and

the position of her arms and elbows were distinctly feminine, but to an artist's eye her neck was the most convincing.
Foley said it was certainly Jane Martin's neck, which he had
studied often. As a portrait painter it becomes a permanent
habit, sometimes embarrassingly so, to look closely at the
facial construction of people generally, choosing the most
permanent features, as a cartoonist does in caricature form.
It could be regarded as staring and offensive.

The male passenger he could not determine, other than
his shoulders and neck were definitely male, "No one I have
seen," Foley said. The visible characters of the registration
plate proved it was his recently-acquired Clio.

"She must have taken my keys from reception and used
my car," he said, "assuming I'd never know, which without
this video of her I never would have," he said referring to
Jane Martin by name. "What are you going to do about it,
Inspector?"

"Well, the shape of her neck from the back is not evidence,
but it is very helpful information. We don't know who the
man sitting next to her is, so let's not guess. Can you give me
your guess as to how tall the man is?"

"I know that you sit tall in a car, but I don't think he is a
tall man. Five foot six?"

"Okay," said Bruno

"Is it someone from the garage?" said George.

"Not necessarily," said Bruno. "She could have picked
him up en route, and taken him back, so for the time being
we shall not speak to her. Please don't go back into work
tomorrow and ask the receptionist if anyone used your car
on Carnival Day. Let us do our job in our own time."

On their way back to Foley's flat they thanked him for
being so helpful.

◈

"That was an eye opener," said Andy on their way home.
"What do you think of his paintings?"

"I was impressed," said Bruno. "If he keeps at it, sometime soon he'll be able to make enough to live on."

"He said it was a short man in the passenger seat. Wouldn't you say Charlie Adams is over six foot?"

Bruno didn't answer directly, but replied, "If it was some- one from the garage he didn't work with George, or he'd have recognised something about him and probably remembered that he wasn't a thirty-minute lunch man. Anyway, men who clock in and out don't drive off during lunchtime on an assignment, they are working men paid by the hour. If she was the driver and the passenger was not Charlie, perhaps we should interview them both under caution. Charlie would have an alibi but she would not. That doesn't give us much, except her denial that she was driving and the picture of her neck in a security camera will not prove she was the driver. When we first met Jane Martin, she said she was moving to Bembridge. Don't you think it is a coincidence that she was, or is, planning to move to the place Alan Southbridge was buying up property?"

"It hadn't crossed my mind," said Andy, "but there could be something there. Do you think she spoke to any estate agents about her plans?"

"We could start with Middleton's, she may have spoken to someone there. There are seven reputable estate agents in Newport. Wander round one or two of them and see if they've sold any properties in Bembridge. Using your police charm, try to find out who bought them," said Bruno.

◈

It wasn't a difficult task to speak to agents and express an interest in property in Bembridge. Where better to start than Middletons and speak to Matchett?

Andy discovered Matchett was on holiday touring the Island, visiting country fayres and showing off his vintage bus. However, his absence proved to be a blessing in dis- guise, because the stand-in office manager, Beryl Brown, was considerably more forthcoming than Matchett would have been. Beryl knew there had been interest in several properties in Bembridge during the first part of the year.

One was an average property behind the High Street, suitable as a starter home. The second was a very desirable building in Harbour Lane, with sea views of Bembridge Harbour, but situated about one hundred metres back from the water.

"We had viewings and several offers below the asking price, which was a full price because of its location. The neighbouring properties were all desirable. In the end a Mrs Jane Martin agreed to pay the asking price of £750,000 cash, which was accepted. Matchett handled that sale because Mick was busy at the time and he liked to jump in on sales whenever he could while Mick was out. The sale was progressing well when the vendor suddenly withdrew, we were told by Mick. It was bought by Elizabeth Moss, which is the maiden name of Alan Southbridge's wife. Mick must have had a reason for ensuring 'Mrs Moss' got the property, but we didn't know what happened there," she said.

"Did Mrs Martin buy something else?"

"Not through us," said Beryl. "I recall there was a row because Mrs Martin had paid for a survey and incurred other expenses also. When she found out that Mick was involved, she accused him of double dealing. Maybe he was, but he did get the vendor another £25,000. Mrs Martin was fuming, and she told Mick here in the office."

"You have been very helpful, Beryl," said Andy.

"Try the other agents. Watson's have an office in Bembridge. I don't know what you are looking for, officer?" she said, anxious to hear something she could gossip about.

"We are trying to build a picture of property sales that took place in Bembridge this year, nothing more than that."

✦

Back at the station Andy's report excited Bruno. Not only because his hunch was leading somewhere, but it brought

Matchett, who he had never quite fathomed, back into the picture.

"Let's add to what you have learned with everything else we've got," said Bruno. "Sometime in the spring Jane Martin set about buying an expensive house in Harbour Lane in Bembridge, at the time their new company, Adams & Martin Ltd, was helping itself to cash against the security of Alan Southbridge's car stock. Was it as a love nest for the two of them?"

"If they were eighteen years old, maybe," said Bruno. "But not at forty-six," he said referring to Jane Martin.

"Let's ask Matchett what happened in the sale."

"He is on holiday this week, so we'll have to wait."

"In summary, if we go back to early spring the situation is as follows. Mick McClusky is building a useful portfolio for Southbridge, knowledge of which has spread in the Southbridge Motors. This rumour could possibly have come from Matchett, although his behaviour to us implies that he did not in fact know anything about Mick's work for Southbridge, until he found the bank paying-in book and brought it to our notice. Therefore I don't think it would be impossible for him to have found out what Mick was up to," said Bruno.

"It was common knowledge Mick was planning to leave after the two farms were sold to the London buyers. There was something fishy going on with those deals, which only the participants will know about. So, Alan Southbridge's wife gazumps Adams & Martin, who fail to buy in Bembridge. And a sale of Southbridge Motors would expose the stocking loans. Is that a motive for killing McClusky?"

"Not for most people," said Bruno. "But somewhere in this lies the answer and I suspect we are not going to get any nearer to finding out until we open up about the money from the stocking loans, but let's start with Matchett. He's back on Monday, to get his side of the Harbour Lane deal."

CHAPTER 32

W HEN ANDY BOWEN called Matchett and asked him about the negotiations for the sale of Harbour Lane, Bembridge, he said he didn't remember the transaction at all.

"It must have been one of Mick's deals," he said. "What do you want to know?"

"We are interested in who the purchaser was."

"Tom Middleton has taken the office copies of all Mick's deals, but I will ask him when I see him."

"So, you've no record of any of Mick's deals?"

"Not here. What was the property again?"

"Harbour Lane, Bembridge."

"I have made a note," said Matchett after a magnificent pause.

"So, you'll get back to me?" said Andy.

"Sure," he said.

"Can you do that today?"

"No, I won't be seeing him this week. Why, is it urgent?"

"It is routine police work. We like to dot all the i's and cross the t's."

"I'll come back to you if I find anything," he said. From his manner it was obvious that he had no intention of providing the police with any information about his handling of his failed attempt to sell Harbour Lane to Jane Martin.

◆

However, his tight-lipped response provided an opening to speak to her about the failed transaction and penetrate deeper into her relationship with Matchett. Her response to Bruno's call requesting a meeting was hostile and aggressive.

"Detective Peach, I think your time would be better employed finding the person responsible for the Carnival crash than with people who know nothing about it."

"Mrs Martin, I'd like you to arrange a convenient time to

meet today. Or I shall I call at a time of our convenience?"
suggested Bruno.

"Okay, lunchtime," she said, "but not at Southbridge
Motors."

"Let's say Newport Police Station, 1 p.m.," replied Bruno,
ending the call.

"What do you think, sir?" said Andy.

"I think she will be talking to Matchett now and they
will agree to put the deal on to Mick. But if it was an argument about the price that led her deal to fall through, call it
gazumping if you like, there is no reason for either Matchett
or Jane Martin to deny their involvement."

"Unless," said Bruno, "there is something else between
them."

"Let's find out," said Andy. "I think they are up to something and with the gazumping of Harbour Lane it all went
wrong."

◈

Jane Martin arrived promptly at 1 p.m. Her demeanour had
changed and she now presented herself in her best light.
She had not come from her office. Because Bruno wanted
a record of this meeting, they met in one of the properly
equipped police interview rooms.

"Mrs Martin, as part of our ongoing investigation into the
accident which resulted in the death of Mick McClusky and
Gillian Napier, we are looking at the sales he negotiated during the period prior to his death. Can you take us through
your attempted purchase of No. 9 Harbour Lane, Bembridge,
in the late spring?"

"I think you must be mistaking me for another person,
Inspector. I never attempted to purchase such a property."

"So, you didn't make an offer on that property?"

"It was not me," she said. "Inspector, if you had asked me
on the phone, I'd have told you then, and we wouldn't have
had this charade today. I am a busy lady."

"Our information differs Mrs Martin. Middleton's estate agents involved in the sale of 9 Harbour Lane have written records of your offer, your solicitor's details and the acceptance of your offer by the vendor. Yet you deny making an offer?"

"I think you are looking at incorrect reporting. Perhaps it was sold by Middleton's, but not to me, Inspector."

"It was sold by Middleton's to another person, but only after they increased their offer by £25,000 more than yours."

"Inspector, what has the sale of a house in Bembridge, that I have no knowledge of, to a person I don't know, got to do with me? For all concerned, it's a sale that did not go through, so of what interest is that to anyone?"

Under police persistence she was becoming unsure of how she was behaving, knowing they did not believe her lies.

For Bruno her denial that she had ever attempted to buy Harbour Street confirmed his belief that she was covering up something, as was Matchett by his evasive replies. Unless he could destroy all records of Jane Martin's attempt to purchase 9 Harbour Lane, they were in trouble.

For the time being Bruno decided to terminate their meeting, as if he was accepting her statement that she had never made an offer to buy Harbour Lane. Her denial had been revealing and it was now back to Matchett.

◆

First Bruno decided to return to the stocking company accounts and involve Alan Southbridge. This might lead to a major row where the leading characters' motives could be revealed. From what Bruno could tell when he had called him, he said he had not spoken to Charlie or Jane about the company Adams & Martin. He said that he had kept away from the showroom in the past week to decide how to handle the matter with two of his key workers, knowing that if the police were right, a major disruption would follow with possible criminal charges.

Bruno's police accountants had done a remarkable job of research into Adams & Martin Limited with the help of credit agencies and statutory information filed at Companies House. They had obtained the banking record of the company, detailing the individual cash drawdowns against the vehicles delivered to the car showroom. Bruno had to remind himself that he was on the hunt for the killer of Mick McClusky, not investigating an elaborate company fraud.

When he requested a meeting with the directors of Southbridge Motors, namely Alan and Elizabeth Southbridge, Charlie Adams, and Jane Martin, Alan agreed to 11 o'clock the following Monday morning.

Bruno was aware that this approach could get him nowhere if Alan Southbridge wanted to preserve the integrity of his company, namely that he had bigger fish to fry, especially that he was preparing to sell Southbridge Motors to Billy Sharp, Charlie's stepfather.

The police investigation had established that up to the end of February, Adams & Martin had borrowed or stolen against showroom stock £300,000. The cash had been released by the finance company by way of a bank transfer to a Lloyds Bank account in Shanklin in the name of Adams & Martin Limited against the security of the entire new vehicle showroom stock.

For Bruno the theft of £300,000 was not a crime until it was reported by its owner. Its significance lay in its loose connection of the perpetrators of this swindle with the Shanklin Carnival Queen's accident. Therefore whatever the outcome of the meeting with the directors, it would have no relevance unless it shone a light onto the killer. It was more important to explore the response of Matchett and his denial of any involvement with Jane Martin in the abortive purchase of Harbour Lane.

❖

In a message on Sunday, Alan Southbridge rearranged the

venue for the directors meeting to his home, suggesting that he was intent on avoiding a confrontation on business premises. And it came as no surprise to Bruno and Andy that the only two directors present at 11 o'clock were Alan Southbridge and his wife Elizabeth. Alan was casually dressed and gave the impression that they had enjoyed a relaxing weekend that had set them up for their normally busy working week, starting with this meeting with the police.

"Gentlemen, thank you for coming here instead of the garage. Once I explain why, I hope you will understand. I was grateful for the information you provided about Adams & Martin Limited, about which we were completely unaware. Although our Bembridge Harbour reconstruction and redevelopment project is not connected with Southbridge Motors, once the plans are made public, people will connect the two. I have seen this as a problem since the start of the year, and because my time will be fully taken up with the Bembridge project. I know I must sell Southbridge and concentrate on one thing only, and it would not take a genius to guess who I might approach to buy it.

"The Sharp family have been friends of mine and Elizabeth's for years, even decades. Billy has always wanted a main dealership to complement his used car business in Newport. I offered to sell the business to him in the spring and we have traded concessions. I needed to progress any development plans and we shortly sign the deal after Billy's advisers have completed their due diligence, which they will start very soon, probably next week. This brought your revelation into focus that Adams & Martin limited had borrowed money against our showroom stock. That was a hammer-blow to Elizabeth and me, so disturbing we had to tackle Charlie and Jane straight away.

"I know I said I'd maintain the confidentiality between ourselves, but we could not do that, because Charlie Adams is Billy Sharp's stepson. Making the revelation that he and

Jane Martin had successfully stolen £300,000 from my company would have killed my deal with Billy and ruined my plans for the Bembridge Harbour scheme. He could never have made the concessions I need to progress the scheme if we were engaged in a legal battle with Charlie. So, we called them together on Saturday to explain themselves and this was their explanation.

"Jane Martin gave us the following explanation, which Elizabeth had recorded on her iPhone."

Alan then summarised: "Their response was surprising, and obviously they had prepared for the inevitability that their scheme would be discovered. They began by reminding Elizabeth and I that as working directors of the company they were responsible for ensuring that the day-to-day business of the company was properly conducted. During the pandemic lockdown in 2021, when car sales slowed, they took the decision to protect the working capital in the business by raising additional finance, as a capital reserve to guarantee the continuity of Southbridge Motors. They chose to create a new company to conduct the stocking through. It was a protective business decision by them as directors of Southbridge Motors.

Elizabeth played the recoding back to them:

"It was never our intention to steal any money from Southbridge Motors, it was a management decision taken jointly to improve the profitability of the company. It was our intention to increase the stock level financed through the stocking loans and extend the range of models we sell. We were also aware that you might sell the company soon and Charlie and I wanted to be able to make an offer to buy it, and we have been promised by Lloyds Bank the facility to buy it, which has been offered because of the professional manner in which we have conducted our business with them."

Then they heard Alan interject, and Jane reply:

"Where is the money now?"

"I have proper accounting records of all the trans-actions and I will show you online the bank account balances."

Alan explained, "That is what Jane said, before she took out her computer, logged in to Adams & Martin Limited's current and deposit accounts, which showed a combined balance of £314,000. She then took from her bag a file in which was detailed each transaction, by type of vehicle, cost/value, selling value, 80 per cent of cost as a stocking facility with dates until the date of sale. Each loan was settled on the sale of the vehicle and the facility transferred to a new replacement. She delivered a complete record of all the business conducted by Adams & Martin Limited since its formation."

As Elizabeth played more of the recording, they heard Jane say:

"We apologise for not involving you in this company, but Alan has often given his views on stocking and is against it. We have disagreed and taken a different view that it was a business opportunity that should be explored to expand the business. However, here it is, an established company as you can see from the share register it is 100 per cent a subsidiary of your company, Southbridge Motors, which we pass over to yourself and Elizabeth, and if you require it, we shall resign as directors and employees of the company. We think the ability to raise capital on showroom stock enhances the value of Southbridge Motors, especially as you are preparing to sell it. It could be an attractive facility to a new owner."

That was the end of Jane Martin's defence of their stocking activities. She had convinced the Southbridges that they had all along been working in Southbridge Motors' best interests, with no criminal intent or personal gain, and as properly appointed officers of the company were obligated to act in the best interests of their employer. In court it would have been near impossible to prove otherwise.

Bruno understood that if the Southbridges accepted Jane Martin's explanation, that was the end of the matter, but given this opportunity of a face-to-face meeting with Elizabeth Southbridge he decided to ask her about the purchase of Harbour Lane in Bembridge.

"Mrs Southbridge, can you tell us about the purchase of 9 Harbour Lane in Bembridge? We are curious about Mick McClusky's involvement in your purchase?"

"It's a long story. But if it helps your investigation, okay," she said. "Harbour Street is a lovely house with glorious views of the harbour entrance, which is only a short walk from the sea. It was owned by Hilda Prescott, a marine artist, who had inherited it from her father. We have known her for years, and had we known she was selling we'd have done the deal with her and saved her agent's fees. Estate agents' boards are forbidden in Harbour Lane, by a covenant in the deeds of all houses on the street. A Bembridge friend who knew Hilda, casually mentioned to me one day that she had sold her house through Middleton's in Newport. When I asked Mick about it, he said he'd not been involved in that sale because it was done in the office and no one had mentioned it to him. When I asked him who had bought Harbour Lane, he gave me the name of Jane Martin.

"It is an extensive property, which needs completely modernising, new bathrooms, kitchen, heating, an electrical rewire and a new roof, it will take us a year and cost a fortune, and I didn't want her taking that opportunity ahead of us.

"Mick said that Jane's purchase was proceeding, but they had not yet exchanged contracts. So I spoke to Hilda and we offered her £25,000 more and persuaded her to withdraw from her sale to Jane and accept our offer. That caused some ructions at Middleton's, but Mick sorted that out."

"Did you ever discuss it with Jane Martin?"

"We had never mentioned it, but we know she had a fight with Mick over it, and threatened to sue Hilda Prescott for the costs of the survey and legal costs, but she never did when she found out it was us that bought it."

"Did Mick ever mention her to you?"

"No, but I know he put Hilda's mind at rest when Jane Martin paid her a threatening visit."

"What did she say to her?"

"When she wouldn't change her mind, she threatened to sue her for her expenses. Mick told Hilda to ignore the threats but make a note of time and place that Jane Martin spoke to her."

"Did Jane sue her?"

"No, gazumping is not against the law. Anyone can change their mind buying or selling, right up to exchange of contract."

"She never spoke to us about it because a purchaser's name is confidential. Because of the dispute we used our lawyers in Southampton as a nominee. There is something about Jane Martin that makes you not want to get on the wrong side of her," said Elizabeth.

"About this stocking company, Adams & Martin," said Alan. "If we had handled it differently, we could have got into a scrap with them. Make no mistake – had we accused them of wrongdoing, they would have sued us."

"Thankfully that matter is now resolved. We will continue our investigation into Mick McClusky's death elsewhere," said Bruno, knowing that Adams & Martin had been cunning enough to protect their backs and gotten away with it.

The Southbridges opinion of Jane Martin was helpful, adding to what they already knew about her. Matchett had lied to the police about his involvement in her failed purchase of Harbour Lane for a reason. It was Bruno's intention now to bring in Matchett and find out.

CHAPTER 33

As THEY DROVE BACK to the Police Station, Bruno said, "From what we know so far of our suspects, the solution to Mick's murder lies with the relationship between Terry Matchett and Jane Martin. The intervention by Mick in securing the purchase of 9 Harbour Lane for Elizabeth Southbridge would have enraged both Martin and Matchett. It cost her time and survey fees, and Matchett commission and office credibility. If we add McClusky's threat to the Southbridge's car sales business as a result of his purchases for their Bembridge Harbour scheme, he would appear as the obstacle to whatever Martin was trying to do."

"Enough to murder him?" replied Andy.

Bruno silently mulled this over. The Harbour Lane matter had become central to their investigation between two otherwise unconnected people: Beryl Brown, in the Middleton's office, and Elizabeth Southbridge, who had supplied the motive he had been searching for.

That Jane Martin had it in for Mick because of the Harbour Street gazumping was obvious from her reaction to Hilda Prescott when she learned she had lost the sale. Having concealed the identity of the purchaser, the Southbridges had escaped what might have descended upon their shoulders, had she discovered they were the purchaser. Her relationship with each of her husbands demonstrated personality traits capable of severe aggression against people close to her.

Before contacting Matchett, Bruno said to Andy, "I want you to contact George Foley, the buyer of Mrs Winter's Clio so we can be certain it was the car in Popham Road on Carnival Day and request if we can have possession of the Clio for a day. Lend him one of our cars while we have it. Give it to our print boys to inspect, take every hand and fingerprint visible in the cab. It's a long shot, but if a driver and passenger had journeyed in the car for an hour we might find a finger, thumb or handprint that we can match with a suspect."

◆

Bruno knew it would take a couple of days for Andy to sort that, so he took off with Janet to Bournemouth for two days to enjoy the luxury of the Cumberland Hotel, the clifftop Claridge's of the town, said to be like Claridge's in London because it too had been restored to its 1930s Art Deco elegance by the architect.

One of Janet's hobbies was collecting Art Deco by known artists in the 1920s and 30s and visiting signature buildings built during the Art Deco period. For Bruno mentally and physically, it was a break from being a detective, a job which Janet believed was as creative as artists of this period. Bruno accepted her flattery graciously. To complete their weekend, they attended the Poole Harbour car boot sale searching for Art Deco objects.

After just five minutes Janet was rewarded, discovering a cap and saucer of the 1930s which some detailed research might prove to be a Clarice Cliff piece.

For the entire weekend Bruno had resisted further analysis of the McClusky murder, knowing that on his return he would have to succeed with his final shot at solving the case or move on to something else.

◆

By the time they met on the following Monday morning, Andy had obtained the forensic results from their examination of the Clio.

"There were seven recognisable prints," said Andy. "The present and previous owners we eliminated yesterday. This leaves five unknown."

"Great," said Bruno. "We don't need to do anything except to obtain something from Matchett and Martin, and if we get a match, we will bring them in. Let us speak to Matchett again and see if he remembers Harbour Lane."

◈

Whereas previously Matchett had been eager to assist the police in their investigation, his response this time to Andy's invitation to call in was negative.

"I don't think I've anything more to add to what I've already told you," he said – until Andy reminded him that he was investigating a murder, and if he didn't walk in voluntarily before the end of the day, he could come and arrest him.

"All right, Detective Sergeant Bowen, I can make it after work at 5.30 this evening."

"We will see you then."

Andy arranged the police interview room to meet him. Previously they had met in the less formal cosy office of Bruno. But a record of this meeting would enable a more detailed scrutiny of him.

He arrived on time, exuding all the *bonhomie* he had displayed on his previous meetings with Bruno and Andy.

"Gentlemen, how can I help you?" he said with a smile.

"I expect you'd like some refreshment after a long day," said Andy. "Tea or coffee?"

"I'd prefer some water."

"Sparkling or still?"

"Sparkling."

Andy pushed a full glass of ice-cold sparkling water towards him and waited for him to drink it, which in the course of the interview he did.

"We'd like to come back to our discussion about the sale of 9 Harbour Lane in Bembridge. When we last spoke about the property you denied any knowledge of it. Can you confirm that statement to us?"

"Yes, I can," he said. "I made a mistake about that property. As your aware, gentlemen, I wasn't involved in sales when Mick ran the business. I have since checked our files and the company was involved in the sale of 9 Harbour

Lane. It was one of Mick's sales. The purchaser was a woman who paid cash up front, a clean sale as far as I know. It was a straightforward transaction as far as the business was concerned."

"And no one else was involved?" said Bruno.

"No, and there were no problems, unless something has come up since that I don't know about, but I'm sure there hasn't," he said. "Sorry again, Inspector, that I might have misled you."

"We had a report from our local police office in Bembridge that the vendor, Hilda Prescott, had been threatened and harassed by a woman who claimed she had been promised the property first. It was a person called Mrs Martin. Do you know anything about that?"

"No, that was in Mick's time. He always kept his cards close to his chest."

"Do you know Mrs Martin?"

"Never heard of her, Inspector."

"Attractive woman, mid-forties," said Andy.

"Mick did all the negotiations with the purchasers and he wouldn't let me near anyone like that."

"Well, you've cleared that little matter up," said Bruno. "So, we will let you go to enjoy your evening. Before you go can you sign this confidentiality report, it says simply that what you've said to us about the business of Middleton's is confidential, and we won't release anything to anyone."

"Okay," said Matchett and took out a pen and signed a police information sheet.

"That's it, thanks a lot," said Bruno. He offered his hand, to which Bruno and Andy responded, and he left.

"Left-handed people always look awkward when writing don't, they?" said Bruno, referring to Matchett signing the police confidentiality document that he'd invented in order to find out if he was left-handed. They left the interview room, locked to await the print expert's imminent arrival to check the glasses and other places Matchett might have touched during the interview.

"Matchett is lying. Undoubtedly, he was involved in brokering the sale to Jane Martin, showing Harbour Lane to her, and taking details of her lawyer and the surveyor, so their office records would show that, unless he has destroyed them. So what happened between these two while this was going on? He was flattered dealing with an attractive woman turning on the charm, and who knows what they got up to, until the sale collapsed, in an extraordinary way. Had Mick not intervened, Martin would have got it. We know from Elizabeth Southbridge what happened then. He doesn't know that went through his appointments logged with Beryl Brown, who must have kept quiet about our visit."

"Let's do the same with Jane Martin and see what she says," said Andy.

"She won't come into the station voluntarily," said Bruno.

"She might, if she thinks we want to talk about showroom stocks, which by the skin of her teeth, she has got away with, for the time being. She definitely put herself in a position to take the money. Now she will try something else. We have to prove who was driving the Clio on Carnival Day, and who sabotaged the Carnival Queen's float. At the moment we believe Matchett was the saboteur and Martin the driver. Proof that it was Matchett will come from the print analyst, which leaves Martin."

"Leave that to me, sir," said Andy, and he picked up the handset. "It's Monday morning she'll be at Southbridge," he remarked as the receptionist put him through to her.

"Mrs Martin?"

"Yes, can I help you?"

"Detective Sergeant Bowen from Newport Police. We'd like to ask you a few questions about withdrawing your daughter from the Carnival Queen contest."

"There's nothing more to tell you. I changed my mind and I am glad I did."

"We are interested in timing and we have no record of when you withdrew her candidature?"

"Her 'candidature?' That's a funny way of putting it," she said. "I don't recall any dates. My husband withdrew her name, not me. Why don't you ask him? Anything else, Detective Sergeant Bowen?"

"Yes, we believe that at some time in early spring you were negotiating the purchase of a property in Bembridge, but the sale fell through?"

"That's right, Middleton's chose to sell it to another purchaser."

"Can you give us your side of the story?"

"There's nothing to tell you. The lady chose to sell it to someone else."

"As you know, Middleton's in Newport are at the centre of our investigations and we'd like you to tell us your side of the story."

"I don't want to come to your Police Station, it makes me feel uncomfortable."

"We will make it easy for you. You can park in the Police compound and we will have coffee and biscuits ready. Shall we say when you finish work today?"

She didn't answer for a while, then asked, "Do I have an option?"

"We want to wrap up this investigation as soon as possible and we cannot leave questions unanswered."

"I'll be there at 5 o'clock," she said, and hung up.

Andy said to Bruno, "I am interested in the date she withdrew her daughter from the Carnival, because she could have planned this for some time. We have a witness that she was angry about Harbour Lane, and she is the kind of woman who does not forget an incident of being denied. So, we know who we are dealing with."

◈

Promptly at 5 p.m. she arrived, and passed the first test, a glass of sparkling water. She was relaxed and clean, not as if she had just finished a day's work.

"Did you speak to my husband? He would remember the date I asked him not to put my daughter's name forward."

"No, but I can if you can't remember," said Andy.

"It was at least two weeks before the Carnival."

"Can you run me through your attempted purchase of Harbour Lane, please?"

"There is nothing to say about it. I was outbid, and that was that."

"Can you talk us through the circumstances?"

"It's a situation I want to forget, if you don't mind, gentlemen."

"We understand the sale was brokered by Mr Matchett from Middleton's Estate Agents in Newport."

"He is not a person I have ever had any contact with."

"We were informed that he took you to view the property and to meet the vendor?"

"I have never met him," she said firmly.

"Who did you deal with at the estate agents?"

"I picked up a brochure and contacted the vendor direct, she spoke to the agents to tell them she had taken it off the market."

"That's pretty unusual," said Bruno.

"I didn't want to appear over-eager to buy it, and I thought I might save the vendor the agent's fees."

"I don't think she would have got away with that, do you?"

"Why not? I was giving her the option."

"Your solicitors, were they involved with the agent?"

"Yes."

"Who are your solicitors?"

"Jarvis Rolf in Shanklin."

"When somebody outbid you, what did you do?"

"Nothing, we hadn't signed a contract."

"Do you know who it was that bought it?"

"No one would tell me, even Middleton's didn't know the buyer's name."

"I think you have told us everything we need to know," said Bruno. "And thank you for clearing up these details for us,"

"Can I go now?"

"Of course."

With that she departed, hopefully leaving them with the evidence they needed.

CHAPTER 34

It took one more day to compare her finger and handprints on the water glass and chair, and for forensics to report their findings. The detectives concluded that Matchett and Martin had gotten wind of the police interest in her attempted purchase of Harbour Lane and agreed their replies, and Matchett had told Beryl Brown in the office she had got it muddled, so Andy concluded that the person who could confirm the situation was the person who sold Harbour Lane: Hilda Prescott.

A call to Elizabeth Moss provided them with Hilda Prescott's present address and phone number, and she willingly agreed to meet them the following morning for a short discussion in her new home.

"Elizabeth has just called me and said that you might call, so I know you are bona-fide. Let's make it 10 a.m., shall we?" she said.

She lived in a spacious newly-built apartment in the centre of Bembridge. She was elderly, in her early seventies, and after selling the only home she had ever lived at remained in the town she had been born in, near to her friends and relatives. She made them tea and sat with them to answer their questions.

"Can you talk us through the sale of Harbour Street to Mrs Moss?"

"Yes, she is not Mrs Moss, she is Elizabeth Moss, and her married name is Southbridge, but I haven't told a soul that, because they wanted to keep it secret."

"Tell us what happened when you instructed Middleton's to sell."

"When I called them, they sent a man to value the property and they agreed to place it on the market, and they sent me a copy of the details to approve, which I did. Four days later the man who valued it called and said he had a buyer who wanted to view the property, which I agreed to do the next day, after a frantic clean-up.

"He turned up with a well-dressed lady called Mrs Martin who liked the house and later that day his office called to say that she made an offer, which they said I should take. It was a few thousand less than the asking price, but they had put it up anyway, so I was happy, and I instructed my solicitors with my agreement to sell it to Mrs Martin, and to proceed with my purchase of an apartment in Bembridge. I wanted to stay near my friends.

"Then I had a call from a gentleman who said he was a director of Middleton's, and he had received a substantially better offer for my home, and that as I had not yet exchanged contracts, would I speak to her. Elizabeth Moss then came over with this gentleman. An increase of £25,000 was not to be sniffed at, so I agreed to withdraw from selling to Mrs Martin, who became very abusive and threatening. She came here on her own screaming and shouting. You would not believe such behaviour! I still have nightmares about her."

"Can you tell us the names of all the people you dealt with at the estate agents?"

"I can't remember offhand, but I will get my file, that will tell me," she said and left them to refill their cups with tea.

She returned with a brown folder in which was all the correspondence relating to the sale of 9 Harbour Lane and stapled to the cover were two business cards.

"That was the first gentleman," she said pointing to Matchett's card. "And that was the man who claimed to be a director of Middleton's." An identical card with the name of Michael McClusky.

"May I copy these?" said Andy, raising his mobile phone and without waiting for her answer, photographing the two business cards.

"Of course, Inspector," she eventually answered.

At that point they had confirmed what they already suspected and departed their host with grateful thanks.

They had proven Matchett and Martin had lied because of police interest in their activities before Mick McClusky's murder. What Bruno now needed was confirmation from forensics that their prints collected from their station interviews matched something on the Clio.

So, it was with great anticipation they arrived at 8 a.m. to meet two officers from the forensics team.

CHAPTER 35

W HEN TOMMY DODD, head of the Island forensic team, arrived he seemed pleased with himself. This irritated Bruno and Andy, because his manner implied, as always, that he, on his own, was going to solve the crime for them, and was looking forward to receiving the acclaim that he always considered he richly deserved. In the room that served as the meeting room for large groups of policemen, he started to display the results of his work on a laptop computer.

"The prints taken from the Clio I have arranged in groups. Group 1 is fingers and thumbs, totalling sixteen prints. Group 2 is palm and handprints, totalling seven prints. And Group 3 is miscellaneous prints from edges of seat, door handles and from function buttons that required pressing, twisting or pushing, pasted onto two A4 size sheets of paper," he explained.

He then produced finger and palm prints of Terry Matchett and Jane Martin from the glasses, table and chairs they had touched and occupied during their police interviews.

On the screen he overlaid the fingerprints from Matchett with the Group 1 prints and bingo, the two prints matched. Staying with Matchett's prints he'd obtained a match with a palm from Group 2 and an index finger on the passenger side window button.

Moving to Jane Martin, Bruno scored similar successes.

He then produced three additional fingerprints, and said, "Many of the prints taken from vehicles are smudges or are indistinct. What we can rely on, though, are fingerprints from the driving mirror which every driver adjusts when sitting in an unfamiliar car and I can confirm the finger and thumb prints on the rearview mirror match those of Jane Martin. The evidence from the matching prints implied that on Carnival Day these two could have driven in this car along

Popham Road at around lunchtime and were responsible for the damage to the Carnival Queen's float that resulted in the driver losing control on the downhill slope that led towards the chicane in the Old Village. Unable to use the brakes, the accelerating heavy vehicle crashed into the boundary wall of the famous Crab Inn, demolishing it and toppling into the thankfully unoccupied patio of the pub, bringing down the iron pole carrying the ancient sign, demolishing the steel structure in which sat Gillian Napier, this year's Carnival Queen."

Tommy Dodd had produced sufficient evidence for Bruno to make an arrest of Matchett and Martin, during which he hoped that their motive for the crime would be revealed.

◆

Nevertheless, before bringing them in and charging them with murder, he had to justify his actions against the suspects to Chief Inspector Barlow, who would challenge his evidence, although he believed the evidence was watertight. The absence of a conclusive motive was still a weakness in his case.

Matters relating to McClusky's relationship with the Southbridges and his relentless pursuit of property acquisitions in Bembridge did not seem to intrude into Jane Martin's life, except the Harbour Lane deal which cost her money, but not so much as to plan and execute a murder.

"It is not a crime to have an evil nature," said Barlow.

"But you need one to murder somebody," said Bruno.

"Accidents do happen," said Barlow.

"If you engage in an act of revenge and end up murdering someone, that is murder," said Bruno.

Barlow was not entirely convinced. He understood the need to prove an intention to kill was necessary to obtain a murder conviction.

"Yes," he said, somewhat sceptically. "Okay, go ahead. But I think you will need something else. Lock 'em up, keep them apart. Matchett's your best chance. Perhaps you should talk to his girlfriend first. He may have dropped something to her?"

Matchett's motive for participating in sabotaging that float was his involvement with Jane Martin. He had tried to exclude Mick from the sale of Harbour Lane to Jane Martin, because of her influence over him, and to show to the office that he could negotiate and complete a property sale without Mick's involvement – an attempt that failed.

At Middleton's his actions would have been seen as no more than office politics, behaviour of which Matchett might often be guilty, always working and lurking in the shadow of Mick McClusky.

Jane Martin was a different kettle of fish. Her reputation as an avaricious, selfish, ruthless, and immoral woman could be amply demonstrated from her relationship with her first husband. They say there is no smoke without fire, and her presence at the blaze that destroyed Ridgeway's business in Poole was never investigated because of her relationship with George Martin, who was the insurance assessor on the case, whose job it would have been to investigate anything suspicious and report to the police. This he did not do. Now her behaviour towards him and her relationship with Charlie Adams confirmed her unscrupulous and avaricious nature.

Apart from driving Matchett to sabotage the float, she'd had no personal confrontation with McClusky.

"Strange, don't you think," said Bruno, "planning to attack a man she had never met?"

"Her motive is connected with her perceived threat from the Southbridge plan," said Andy. "She has a substantial influence in Southbridge Motors. She was able to set up Adams & Martin Ltd under the nose of the Southbridges and almost get away with the stocking swindle, and McClusky's property wheeler-dealing in Bembridge on behalf of Alan Southbridge was a threat to the Southbridge Motors status quo, which threatened her position."

◆

While DI Bruno Peach had been updating Barlow with progress on the McClusky murder case, Andy Bowen received a call from Sally Bots.

"Good morning Inspector Bowen, how are you getting on with finding Mr McClusky's killer?"

"Slowly, Mrs Bots, but we shall get there I am sure."

"I have some very important information that could solve the murder for you."

"Can you tell me what it is over the phone?"

"I'd rather not, because I need to show you something. Can you meet me at the Ventnor Lawn Tennis Club this morning around 11 o'clock?"

"Is it just you?" said Andy thinking it might also be Jane Martin.

"Yes, I have just become a member. All your fault, Inspector. We talked about the old days when I last saw you when I belonged to Bembridge Tennis Club, so I thought, I am only seventy and they run a senior vets club twice a week, so I came to it. I have already got a tennis partner, he's a charming man called Brian."

"There aren't many of those left," said Andy. "They are like Michael's, they are very old-fashioned names. Okay, I will see you at 11 a.m."

"I look forward to it," she said.

He was intrigued by the venue and that she had something to tell him connected with Jane Martin.

"Okay, I'll bring my boss with me, Detective Inspector Bruno Peach."

"Of course, we all know each other," she said. "I will meet you in the reception."

When Bruno returned to his desk Andy reported the call from Mrs Bots to him.

"You should go alone," he said.

"I'd prefer you to come too, sir. This sounded important,

and we need to make sure we hear what she has to say properly."

When they arrived promptly she was waiting in the club reception, dressed in white tennis top and shorts.

"Come through to the restaurant gentlemen," she said, "And have a cup of coffee."

She led them through into a comfortable large sports club lounge with tables and cubicles seating four people. There were several members dotted around, all young females and a few pushchairs. It was busy and one could sit quietly unnoticed in one of the cubicles, which she led them to.

"It's important we sit here for what I am going to tell you. We can talk privately here," she said.

While Andy went to the counter and ordered coffee for three from a barista who was busy making lattes and capuccinos from a Gaggio coffee maker, Sally Bots was explaining recent developments in her social life to Bruno.

"Well, Inspector, this tennis thing all started from our chat about tennis clubs when we last met. I had such fun as a young girl at the Bembridge Tennis club, so I decided to go along and see what was happening there nowadays. It was worn out and tired, no pool, not that there was one in the old days, but it was uncomfortable and no age range, nothing to entice people my age. So I decided to look at this place, and it is completely different. Here they have groups of players and twice weekly for three hours over-seventies meet, so I joined the club.

"Now I know that Jane Martin and Charlie Adams are the club champions here, but I don't come when they do, except that one day last week I was sat here exactly where I am now, and Jane Martin with another man came and sat in the next cubicle with her back to me, as you can see."

Sally Bots demonstrated with her right hand, that she could physically touch someone seated back-to-back with her.

"I remained quietly out of sight while they drank coffee and engaged in an animated conversation, which I recorded on my iPhone, which we can play outside the club after we've finished our coffee and croissants. Aren't they delicious, Inspector? But the gist of the conversation went like this."

She took out a notepad in which she had transcribed the conversation between Jane Martin and the man, unknown to her.

"They spoke quietly at first but these seats are so close it is easy to hear a conversation in the adjoining space. Inspector, can I remind you this is not gossip that I am going to reveal to you, it is the result of proper detective surveillance." She looked Andy straight in the eye to emphasise the value of this evidence.

"We understand, Mrs Bots," said Andy, maintaining a serious expression.

She then began to read from her black Moleskine notebook the conversation between Jane Martin and a man she did not know, whom the police quickly believed to be Matchett.

She started with a barely audible whisper and occasionally looked up from her Moleskine to see if anyone was listening to her, but there was no one seated in the adjoining booths.

"'It's important that you don't admit any involvement in the Harbour Lane fiasco,' said Jane Martin. 'Step back from it, deny even going there. I'm behaving as it never happened, and it's not important to their investigation anyway.'

"'So why are they asking me all the time to explain what happened?' he said.

"'Because they want to connect us to the murder of McClusky.'

"'I never wanted to sabotage the Carnival float, that was your idea,' said the man.

"'But you did, and they know you've the mechanical skill to do it.'

"'Not without your help. You wanted to kill McClusky

for other reasons, you said, but you didn't tell me what they were.'

"'He was ruining my plan to take over Southbridge Motors with Charlie Adams. We had everything lined up and McClusky's property acquisitions for Southbridge meant he had to set up a deal with Billy Sharp, which included selling him Southbridge Motors. McClusky was still working on a number of deals when he died. I had to get him out of the picture to try to save my plan to take over Southbridge," she said. "He's paid for his bloodymindedness with his life, that was what I wanted.'

"'Yea, don't mess with Jane Martin, eh?' he said. 'I would never have cut those brake cables if I'd known that it would kill two people.'

"'If you wreck the brake system of course you are going to kill someone when it crashes. Remember you don't know me, you can't remember having met me,' she repeated. 'No one saw you wreck the low-loader, and there were crowds of people in and out of that road during that day, so we've never met okay?' she said.

"'You'd better stop calling me at home then. It's irritating Deb,' he said.

"'What does she know about me?'

"'Only that you are buying a property through Middleton's, that's all.'

"'Does she know my name?'

"'No,' he said.

"'Did you tell her I was buying a property through Middleton's?'

"'I had to tell her something or she'd have thought you were a girlfriend.'

"'You could have said anything, but not that. I don't think we should speak again on the phone,' she said.

"'Is that it?' he said.

"'Yes, I am leaving too, I'll show you the way out.'

Sally Bots broke off from reading her transcript, and added, "With that, they left, and I watched her drive away."

"How did you know it was Jane Martin?" said Andy.

"I sometimes see her when I take my car for a service at Southbridge Motors."

"But she didn't see you?"

"Not in this get-up with a sun visor shading my face. Now gentlemen, I don't expect you to take my notes as gospel, so I am going to lend you my phone so you can download what I've just told you. I will use another phone until you return it to me."

"Mrs Bots, how can I thank you for bringing this to us? I think you have obtained a confession and identified the murderers," said Bruno.

"It's a pleasure not to be treated as an old gossip," she said with a huge dose of job-done satisfaction. "Can you see yourselves out gentlemen? I can see Brian waiting for me," she said.

CHAPTER 36

M ORE NEW EVIDENCE came that afternoon in an unjexpected phone call from George Foley, who in his lunch break called the station to speak to Inspector Peach.

"Inspector, I was cleaning the inside of the Clio yesterday, and under the passenger seat I found something which I'd like you to have."

"Okay," said Bruno. "Come to the desk and we will take a look at what you've got."

"It could be anything," said Andy after the phone call ended.

"It won't be anything," said Bruno. "Foley knows what we are trying to do, so it will be something important to us."

And so it proved to be.

◈

"I've left my car in your compound because I want you to see what I found and how I came upon it. I have put it back where I found it, so you can see why the person who left it did not take it when they left the car."

In the compound Foley allowed the detective to retrieve what he had found down the side of the driver's seat. Andy bent over and could not get his hand into the gap between the seat and the central tranmission tunnel, so he twisted his head to peer under the seat from the front and spotted a small piece of paper and retrieved it. It was a till receipt for the purchase of petrol at Wilson's Garage in Shanklin by credit card on Tuesday 12 July at 12.55 p.m. It was a small slither of paper, almost weightless, lying on edge between the seat and the central transmission tunnel, nearly invisible.

"I thought you would like that Inspector," said George Foley.

Andy could see immediately it was an important clue.

"My car was running low on petrol when I arrived for

work on the morning of the day of the Shanklin Carnival, so before I left at 4.30 p.m., I put twenty quid into the car from the Southbridge garage pump. But as you can see, the person who bought these five litres, just about the minimum you can buy at a pump, did so at lunchtime on 12 July, because the tank was very low when I came to work."

"Thank you, George," said Bruno. "It could be the most valuable piece of information we've gathered so far."

A very satisfied George Foley drove off to Shanklin, followed by Bruno and Andy to visit Wilson's Garage to see if their forecourt had any CCTV coverage.

Although Wilson's sold petrol to the public, it was an engineering business, so did not advertise fuel sales. Their business was second-user car sales and car maintenance.

Harry Wilson, the owner of Wilson's garage, was able to present the detectives with their second win of the day by showing them a CCTV recording of the Clio's visit to the garage on the day and the person who put five litres of unleaded petrol into the car at 12.55 p.m. on 12 July, minutes before it was captured on the Luccombe Hall Hotel's CCTV camera driving down Popham Road.

The photograph of the person putting the petrol into the Clio was Jane Martin. She was wearing a coloured headscarf, sunglasses and a white sunhat, her hands displayed two distinctive rings on the wedding finger hand. The owner of the credit card could be identified and Harry Wilson promised to send through those details by mid-morning the following day.

While Bruno drove home to relax knowing that the next day he could be in a position to charge Terry Matchett and Jane Martin with the murder of Mick McClusky and Miss Napier, he was convinced they now had a cast-iron case against them.

Sally Bots had tipped the scales distinctly in their favour and George Foley had provided the icing on their case.

Barlow was happy with the evidence his detectives had gathered so far as sufficient to arrest them on suspicion of causing the death of Mick McClusky and Gillian Martin, by inflicting criminal damage to the low-loader transporting the Shanklin Carnival Queen.

◆

The secret of success in police investigations is the element of surprise, so warrants for both suspects were obtained, effective from midnight, although Bruno instructed the uniform squad to make the arrests at their homes at 7 o'clock the following morning.

The warrants stated they were wanted for questioning concerning the crash of the Carnival Queen's float in the Shanklin Old Village, which resulted in the death of Mick McClusky and Gillian Napier.

Neither pair of uniformed police officers experienced physical resistance from either party to their arrest. The suspects' reaction was more their frustration at being prevented from going to work and being called into the station once again.

"Not again!" said Jane Martin.

Both interview rooms were set aside for Matchett and Martin, arriving at different times to be unaware of each other's simultaneous presence at the station.

Having noted Barlow's comment before beginning their separate interviews, Bruno decided to visit Matchett's home after he had been successfully detained in Newport police station and speak to his lady, and if she was not there to visit her in her own home.

Newport Football club ground was a fifteen-minute walk from Newport Police Station, opposite Terry Matchett's three-bedroomed bungalow, behind which was located the home of his lady, Debra, where she lived caring for her elderly mother.

Presuming she'd be at Terry's, Bruno and Andy rang

Matchett's doorbell. They were right. A concerned Debra opened the door.

"No, Mr Matchett isn't here," she said.

"Debra, we met here a few weeks ago. We wondered if we could ask you a few questions concerning Mr Matchett?" said Andy, and they introduced themselves and showed her their police identification.

"I said he's not here," she replied.

"We know, we want to speak to you."

She didn't speak, but she opened the door to let them in.

"Shall we sit down?" said Bruno, in a quiet friendly manner. "We don't know your surname?" he said.

"It's Weller," she said. "Miss Deborah Weller."

"Miss Weller, have you ever heard of Mrs Jane Martin?"

"That's the woman who keeps calling Terry about some house in Bembridge? I think that was her name. She still calls him. She terrifies my Terry a lot."

"What does she say to him?"

"Oh I don't know. Basically, she seems to be telling him what to say all the time."

"Have you met her?"

"No, but I wish she'd stop calling. If she calls Terry again when he's not here, I shall tell her."

"When did she last call him here?"

"Yesterday, while we were eating our dinner. On that," she said pointing to a mobile phone on the sideboard.

"Did Terry give you any idea of what she wanted?"

"Well, I did ask him because he finished saying to her, 'I'll see you tomorrow then', and I said, 'What did she want?' 'Oh, she wants me to help her with something,' he said. I said 'What?' He told me, 'Something about a property she wants to buy.'"

"Where?"

"In Ventnor, near the Tennis Club. That's all I know, Inspector."

"Okay, that's useful," said Andy.

"Have you any idea where he is now?" she asked Bruno. "He'd gone when I arrived to do his breakfast. I don't stay here at nights because of Mum."

Bruno did not answer her question, giving an impression that he didn't know where Matchett was.

"Well thank you, Miss Weller, we'll call again if we need to speak to you."

Outside of Matchett's home, Bruno said to Andy. "We couldn't take the phone, until we charge him. But it's helpful to know about it."

CHAPTER 37

BACK AT THE STATION, they decided to interview Matchett first, as he was likely to be the easier nut to crack. He was uncomfortably untidy for a dapper little man due to his early morning arrest.

Andy Bowen undertook the procedural formalities, informing him that this meeting was conducted under caution. It would be recorded and his answers could be used in evidence at a later time.

"Mr Matchett, our investigations into the cause of the Carnival Queen's float reveal that the braking system on the vehicle had been sabotaged while it was being prepared for the parade through Shanklin on the evening of 12th July this year. Can you tell us what your movements were on that day?"

"Unless I was away, and I don't think I was on that day, I was at work in Newport," Matchett replied.

"In the office?" asked Andy.

"Of course."

"Did you leave your office on that day for any reason?"

"No."

"Not for lunch or coffee?"

"I usually buy a sandwich from Graces the Bakers and bring it in. Sometimes I go for a walk. I might do some shopping, but I can't tell you about a specific day in July."

"Our evidence shows that on the day in question you were driven to Popham Road in Shanklin in a Renault Clio saloon car by Jane Martin at around 1 p.m., and while Mrs Martin parked alongside, you boarded the low-loader. Using your mechanical engineering knowledge, we believed you sabotaged the low-loader brake system. The loss of brake fluid in the hydraulic braking system caused the driver of the vehicle to lose control, once it turned onto the downhill slope of

Church Road that led to the Old Village, it increased speed rapidly, so the by the time it reached the chicane through the village with a failed braking system it was uncontrollable and crashed into the ancient stone wall that is the boundary to the Crab Inn."

Matchett was stunned by the directness of the police investigation. Fear crept into every sinew as he listened to his accusers.

"I don't know what you are talking about," he muttered.

"Do you want me to repeat what I have just said?" said Andy.

"What are you accusing me of?"

"Sabotage of the Carnival Queen's float that led to the death of two persons."

At this he stood up and said, "Is it because you can't find who really killed McClusky that you are accusing me?"

"We have a witness that watched you jump out of the car onto the Carnival float, disappear out of sight for five minutes, reappear, jump off the float, climb back into the vehicle and the lady driver, Jane Martin, drove you away."

"That person was not me, Inspector."

At that point Bruno produced the fingerprint evidence that Tommy Dodd's team had taken from the Clio, and highlighted Matchett's prints to him.

He did not show him Sam Levy's photographs of him at that moment.

"They are not my prints," he said. "I have never had them taken."

"We have your prints Mr Matchett, and if you don't accept that we have them, we will take them now and prove they match those from the car. So, what's it to be?" said Bruno.

"I think you have run out of ideas trying to find Mick's killer, and you're clutching at straws."

"How well do you know Jane Martin, the person who tried to buy 9 Harbour Lane?"

"I don't know her. Should I?"

"We intend to detain you for further questioning. You are entitled to speak to a lawyer of your own choosing or we shall appoint one on your behalf to be present when we continue this interview later today."

With that Bruno summoned two uniformed police officers to conduct Matchett to a police cell, where his fingerprints were taken. The desk officer then notified Streeter Horsfield, a firm of Newport solicitors, to provide a qualified representative to advise Terry Matchett.

Tom Horsfield arrived within twenty minutes and joined Matchett in the police cell, where he was able to listen to his defence against the police accusations.

◆

Jane Martin had already requested that a solicitor be present at her interview, and during the time she had waited, a court solicitor had arrived to be present and represent her.

After the preliminaries and the police reasons for bringing her in for questioning, Bruno asked her how well she knew Matchett, the Middleton's estate agent.

"I don't know him at all," she said.

"Strangers?" said Bruno.

"I always have to repeat myself to you, Inspector."

"You've met him though?"

"Not to my knowledge, Inspector."

"He was the person who took you to see 9 Harbour Lane when you agreed to buy it."

"I didn't know his name."

"But you know who we mean now?"

"Yes," she said.

"Did you drive him to Popham Road on 12th July, the day of the Carnival procession, so that he could sabotage the brakes on the vehicle that crashed in the Old Village, killing the driver and the Carnival Queen?"

"What on earth have you brought me here for, Inspector?"

"We have evidence that you drove Terry Matchett to Popham Road at 1 p.m. on 12 July, for the purpose of sabotaging the Carnival vehicle."

"Perhaps you could tell me what that evidence is, and where exactly is Popham Road?"

Bruno explained the location and produced a picture of the Clio.

"That is the car driven by you to Popham Road at lunchtime on Carnival Day, and to prove that it was you, we have matched your fingerprints to those found in the car. We also have photographs to support our accusations. This car belongs to a man called George Foley who is employed by Southbridge Motors. You took his car without permission on the 12 July, for the purpose of driving to Popham Road in Shanklin to inflict serious damage to a vehicle that you knew would be driven by Michael McClusky."

"This is bloody outrageous, Inspector! You may have matched my prints with prints you found in that car, but I can assure you I did not drive that man to sabotage the Carnival vehicle on July 12th. That car may have my prints on it because I could have driven it at Southbridge when rearranging cars in the car parking area reserved for staff cars. Now I'd like to speak privately with Mr Mercer, the solicitor you've appointed to protect me."

"Okay," said Bruno. "As long as you like," and they withdrew.

"That was a swift answer to our print accusation!" said Andy.

"Yes, it was unfortunate for her that by the time she got to Shanklin she needed fuel," said Bruno.

◈

It was thirty minutes before Mercer agreed to resume the interview, while Jane Martin sat relaxed, composed, answered his questions and listened. When the police continued their interview, Mercer spoke first.

"Mrs Martin denies the accusation that she drove the Clio to Popham Road on Carnival Day, for the purpose of sabotaging the Carnival with the help of Mr Matchett. She is familiar with the car as it was purchased by her employer, Southbridge Motors, in a new car sale trade-in. It is now owned by George Foley, an employee of the company, and because of employee parking restrictions from time to time she might take responsibility for moving parked cars in the outside staff parking areas, so her fingerprints could be found in any staff car.

"My client has admitted that she has met Mr Matchett once or twice in connection with a proposed purchase of a house in Bembridge, but had not known his name until now. Other than on those occasions, she has never had any contact with him.

"Regarding the man who died at the scene of the accident, Mick McClusky, she had never heard of him."

Bruno had not anticipated her response, expecting that revealing the fingerprint evidence to the two suspects would clinch it, and they could then charge her.

In respect of Matchett, he anticipated that in the next twenty-four hours he would admit his reason for his participation in the crime. The fact that she said she had previously driven the car did not alter anything. The Clio was the car that took Matchett to Popham Road. Bruno had proof that Jane Martin was the driver at 1 p.m. on 12 July, he had photographic proof of her refuelling the car.

"We should release her on condition she returns tomorrow morning for further questioning," said Andy, "when we've had time to check her contacts with Matchett on his mobile phone."

"Okay. You pick up the phone from his lady housekeeper."

Bruno left Andy to do that before they returned to Matchett to continue his interview. The local solicitor, Tom Horsfield, whom the police had summoned on Matchett's behalf, was present to ensure that the police investigation continued in accordance with correct legal procedures.

On resumption Matchett was not relaxed. Horsfield had clearly put him right regarding police procedure. The horror of being accused of the murder of Mick McClusky and Gillian Napier frightened him, to say the least, because he knew he was guilty.

"Let us set aside for the time being your participation in the sabotage of the Carnival vehicle, and understand your relationship with Jane Martin. When did you first meet her?" said Bruno.

"She came into the office one day in response to our window presentation in which we displayed a property for sale in Bembridge. She sat at my desk and went through the details, she asked advice about making an offer, and whether she could view the property. I called the vendor and asked if I could bring a potential purchaser to view it.

"There had not been massive interest in 9 Harbour Lane, so the vendor, Hilda Prescott, agreed to show it that afternoon. Unusually Mrs Martin made her offer during the visit and she accepted verbally, which I confirmed in writing when I returned to the office. We provided both solicitors with the usual information as we always do on a purchase.

"That was that as far as I was concerned, until two weeks later, when Jane Martin received a letter from her solicitor saying Hilda Prescott had withdrawn. Mrs Martin was not the sort to take the rejection lying down. She found out that it was her boss's wife at Southbridge Motors who had offered £25,000 higher than her offer."

"Who was she angry with?"

"Me, until she found out Mick had brokered the deal, he was already working for the Southbridges, buying up the harbourside properties to develop the harbour facilities."

"Why didn't Mick handle the sale of Harbour Lane from the beginning?"

"Because he was out when she came into the office."

"Nevertheless, was it unusual for you not to involve him?" said Andy.

"She can be a charmingly persuasive lady," he said, but did not elaborate.

"So you fell under her spell. And when she asked you to cut the brake cable on the Carnival float, you did it?"

Matchett squirmed but did not speak.

Bruno detected from his lack of response and the expression of fear in his face, he realised that the damage he had inflicted to the Carnival float had caused the death of Mick McClusky and Gillian Napier. After a word from his solicitor, he continued his silence, enabling Bruno and Andy to withdraw and let his legal adviser give him advice as to his position.

When they returned, he was frightened. If the police evidence was accurate, he knew he would be charged with murder, an outcome he would never have contemplated. It was never his intention to cause the death of anyone, and now he could not believe what he had done.

"Mr Matchett, we shall detain you in police cells overnight while we continue our investigation."

◈

"I think we will see a different man after a night in custody," said Andy.

Bruno was convinced that Jane Martin had charmed Terry Matchett into damaging the Carnival low-loader, causing the fatal crash. Matchett hadn't admitted being the passenger in the Clio and a good defence lawyer might successfully challenge Pimley's assertions that the brake cables were cut and create a sufficient doubt that they could have snapped, and they'd no doubt produce evidence from other road crashes, where the braking system had failed, so they needed more evidence.

CHAPTER 38

THE POLICE had fed Matchett at regulation times, and allowed him to wash up for his next interview. A night in police cells had chastened him.

His long-term girlfriend, Debbie Weller, had visited the previous evening from which he had derived some comfort. After explaining why he was being held in police custody she had made him see clearly what he had done, namely, that he was responsible for a double murder since he had been persuaded to sabotage the Carnival float by Jane Martin. After learning of the death of Mick McClusky, his friend and boss, he had lived in denial. When interviewed by Bruno he had denied anything to do with the acts of which he was accused. His misguided belief was that if he and Jane Martin stuck together, they would escape the consequences.

In reality, he knew he was done for. He now relied on Tom Horsfield to save him.

Bruno did not know what Matchett had told Tom Horsfield: very little, nothing or everything? He had told him that of the accusations made by the police, he claimed to be innocent. The police would rely on the prints in the car and he could not be identified from the photos they had.

Jane Martin, who had been released the day before, had agreed to return at 2 p.m. for what Bruno believed would be a critical interview. If the credit card used to buy the petrol was hers, then he believed they had the evidence they needed. And so it proved to be when Harry Wilson called Bruno at 1 o'clock with evidence that it was her credit card that had paid for the petrol.

As soon as he got the confirmation, he brought Matchett up from the police cell and sat him down. They had one hour before Jane Martin showed up, so there was no pressure.

Tommy Dodd confirmed that Matchett's prints matched

the prints found in the Carnival float vehicle that had been secured by Detective Glenn Pimley of the Met Police.

Bruno opened his interview with a summary of his understanding of his position. In front of him he had a nervous man, whose world had fallen apart during the night in police cells. Bruno sat watching him, while Andy Bowen read out the ritual caution notes, which were like a prayer. Each word had a meaning. Matchett knew that part he had played in the murder of Mick McClusky and Gillian Napier, and he was unsure what to do. It was never his intention to be involved in a murder. In the end he decided to deny any involvement and hope the police evidence did not stack up.

"We have evidence that at about 1 p.m. on 12 July, the day of the Shanklin Carnival, you were seen to climb onto the low-loader prepared to transport the Carnival Queen and her attendants throughout the Shanklin Carnival. In approximately five minutes you rendered the vehicle unsafe by cutting the hydraulic brake cable, and removing securing bolts from the stabilising lintel above the Carnival Queen's throne. Have you anything to say?" said Bruno.

Stubbornly, he said: "It wasn't me." And repeated the words, loud and emphatically, "It was not me."

"The evidence we have points to you."

A dishevelled Matchett stared defiantly at the two detectives. He was no longer the five foot five inch immaculately dressed dandy, as he had always presented himself, as Detective Inspector Bruno Peach charged him with the murder of Michael McClusky and Gillian Napier.

"You will be remanded in custody to appear before the magistrates in the morning."

Neither he or his solicitor spoke another word in their presence, as Matchett was returned to the station cell to await transfer to a local remand prison on the Island.

It had taken twenty minutes to charge Matchett, leaving forty minutes before the arrival of Jane Martin at 2 p.m.

◆

Having retrieved Matchett's mobile phone from Debra, Andy
Bowen had a report of the calls received. He had received
51 calls from Jane Martin in the previous eight-week period
which suggested there was more to their relationship than
Harbour Lane, and the elimination of McClusky.

"It looks like he took some persuading," said Andy.

It was difficult to identify a tangible gain for his behaviour. Matchett had succumbed to the charms of an attractive female and had participated in damage to a vehicle that
he thought would simply immobilise it in anticipation of an
exciting relationship with the kind of woman he had only
ever dreamed about. Now if convicted of murder he would
pay a heavy price for his involvement.

She was the root of the evil and had planned everything. A
good lawyer might get a murder charge against him reduced
to manslaughter as an accessory to murder.

"We will see," said Bruno.

◆

Jane Martin appeared at the desk ten minutes before 2 p.m.
with a partner from a Portsmouth firm of solicitors who was
a criminal specialist to represent her. She did not anticipate
being detained and charged with murder. She was charming,
pleasant and smiling, showing a side of her personality she
could turn on and off to suit the occasion.

After the usual pleasantries, she introduced James Dalmas
from Dalmas, Chandler and Brooks. Dalmas had travelled
on an early car ferry from Portsmouth to Fishbourne and
driven to Jane Martin's home in Shanklin, where she had
explained her situation. After Dalmas had distributed his
business card and Andy Bowen had made his introductory
cautionary statement, Bruno accused Jane Martin of the sabotage of the Carnival float.

"At about 1 p.m. on the day of the Carnival you drove
a vehicle parked in Popham Road next to the Shanklin

Carnival float whilst Terry Matchett, in five minutes aboard the vehicle, rendered it unroadworthy. You parked beside the vehicle and then drove him away from the site after approximately five minutes, once he had completed his sabotage and returned to the car."

James Dalmas responded to Bruno's accusation by stating that Jane Martin was working at Southbridge Motors on that day and could not have been driving around Shanklin looking for a Carnival float.

"We have evidence that you took a Renault Clio vehicle from the car park at Southbridge Motors without permission, met Terry Matchett, and drove to Popham Road, stopping en-route at Wilson's garage in Shanklin to put petrol into the car just before 1 p.m., before driving onto Popham Road where Matchett inflicted the damage to the vehicle, whilst you sat in the Clio, engine running. You then left the scene, returned to Southbridge Motors, dropping Matchett on the way, and placed the Clio back to where you had taken it.

"The damage inflicted on the Carnival float rendered it unsafe to drive. It did not affect the ignition so the driver was able to begin the journey from Popham Road. It was a slight uphill slope, but it gathered speed down the Church Road hill toward the Old Village, instead of maintaining the walking speed of the procession. By this time it was travelling fast and totally unstoppable. It swerved into the Old Village, through its double bend, before it crashed into the ancient stone wall at the Crab Inn.

"This accident was caused as a result of the damage to the vehicle by your accomplice Terry Matchett. The result was severe damage to the vehicle and the death of the driver, Michael McClusky and the Carnival Queen, Gillian Napier."

There followed a short pause, after which James Dalmas said, "My client maintains that everything you have put to her is fiction. She has stated that she was not the driver of the

Clio on that day and that you have mistaken her for another person. I would request that you terminate this interview now to permit you to find the real person responsible, and allow Mrs Martin to leave."

Bruno ignored James Dalmas, and from his brown folder took out three photo enlargements and laid them across the desk in front of Jane Martin, and allowed her and James Dalmas to study them.

"Mrs Martin, the picture on your right is a photograph of you at the petrol pump at Wilson's garage in Shanklin putting petrol into the Clio. You have removed your sunglasses, presumably to read the pump indicator so that you could put just four litres of petrol into the car, enough to cover the entire return journey of less than twenty-five miles. Sitting alongside you in the passenger seat, clearly visible, is Terry Matchett. The middle picture is a copy of the petrol receipt, timed 12.54 p.m. and dated 12 July, the day of the Shanklin Carnival, paid for with a credit card in your name.

"The third picture is the car driving slowly along Popham Road at 13.04 p.m. that same day, and stopping behind the Carnival Queen's float. A police witness saw Matchett alight from the Clio, driven by you, climb onto the float and remain out of sight for five minutes. When he reappeared he climbed off the float, got back into the Clio and you drove off together."

Bruno then produced enlarged copies of Sam Levy's photograph of Matchett jumping from the Carnival float.

Neither Martin or Dalmas uttered a word, during which time Bruno and Andy sat quietly waiting for a response.

Jane Martin was the first to speak, her voice cracking with anger.

"Those pictures are not of me, they are fake, anyone can produce those type of pictures, they are all fakes."

"What about this one?" said Bruno, pushing forward a copy of the credit card payment for petrol at Wilson's Garage.

"They are all fake," she said, seething with tooth-grinding anger, while Dalmas stared at Bruno, realising the he was defending the indefensible. "Anyone could have driven that car, but it was not me."

"We put it to you that for reasons unknown to us, that you, together with Mr Terry Matchett, undertook to render the Carnival Queen's float dangerously unroadworthy immediately prior to the Carnival whilst it was being made ready for the parade through Shanklin Town that evening. The damage inflicted by Matchett resulted in the crash into the Crab Inn in the Old Village, killing the driver Mick McClusky and the Carnival Queen, Gillian Napier.

"We are charging you with the murder of Michael McClusky and Gillian Napier on Tuesday 12 July, and you will appear at a special session of the Newport Magistrates' Court in the morning. You will be detained in police custody until the hearing."

Bruno believed the police had taken their investigation to that point where the courts and the wheels of justice would test the defendant's pleas of innocence under cross examination, and the police evidence would lead to a conviction.

However, they were too experienced to believe that they could win in court without collecting other evidence to prove their case and get the convictions, for example the evidence showing the Clio being driven past the Luccombe Grange at 12.59 p.m. and the gathering of the witnesses, some of whom might resist appearing in court on behalf of the prosecution. Bruno knew they still had work to do.

CHAPTER 39

DURING THE INTERVIEW Jane Martin had shown glimpses of her controlling personality and her ruthless nature that would be exposed by the prosecution case. Matchett, a small insignificant man, had succumbed to her feminine charms and done her bidding, lapdog style, one could only presume, without reward.

To assist the prosecution, it was Bruno's professional duty to provide detailed background to the case. He had seen the murder of McClusky as an act of revenge for slights, or perceived slights, by a person who harboured grudges, who saw actions as personal attacks on them in spite of evidence to the contrary. For Jane Martin this started when she discovered that McClusky had captured the attention of Alan Southbridge by persuading him that his future lay in leading the redevelopment of Bembridge Harbour. In fact, it was Alan Southbridge's ambition that had driven that activity. There had also been rumours that Alan Southbridge was planning to sell his motor company to raise cash for his property venture, thereby interfering with her plan to ultimately take over the business.

She knew that a sale of the motor business would mean a due diligence examination of the company accounts and expose the criminal activity of Jane Martin and Charlie Adams in extracting cash from Southbridge where he as the general manager and she as the company accountant were syphoning off cash into a newly formed company, Adams & Martin Limited, presumably for some joint endeavour unconnected with Southbridge Motors and without the knowledge of the its owners. The lawyers and the accountants on behalf of the purchaser who would descend on the business to undertake due diligence would expose their theft and bring their plans to an abrupt end and criminal charges would follow.

Undoubtedly Jane Martin would have planned the cash theft from Adams & Martin in a manner that she could claim no knowledge of the company Adams & Martin, shifting the full responsibility onto Charlie Adams. Regarding McClusky, her intention was in devising a way to stop Alan Southbridge pursuing his Bembridge Harbour venture which, without McClusky, she hoped would grind to a halt.

What convinced her that Mick McClusky was a sufficient thorn in her side to justify her taking some action was his intervention in her purchase of the Harbour Lane house in Bembridge. Terry Matchett had allowed him to knock her out of the transaction. It was a rare occasion when she did not get what she wanted. That it was bought by Alan Southbridge's wife Elizabeth using her maiden name tipped her over the edge.

The annual Shanklin Carnival event she would have known well, and that would include who was the driver of the leading vehicle, Mick McClusky. Working in the motor trade she'd have been able to find out all about how to wreck a float. The braking system would have been understood by anyone with an interest in commercial vehicles like Terry Matchett and he'd have bigged himself up with her by telling her about vintage buses. Just the man she'd have thought to cut the hydraulic cables on McClusky's vehicle and wreck his involvement in the Carnival and satisfy her demand for revenge.

While all this was going on she was conducting an affair with Charlie Adams, playing tennis for Ventnor Tennis Club, home and away, staying in hotels at away venues and secretly being tracked by George Martin's private detective gathering evidence for an early divorce petition.

"Do you think the evidence we have is enough to convict?" said Andy.

Bruno thought about Andy's question for a time before answering.

"With the revelations we came across yesterday I am certain we will secure the convictions we need."

Sally Bots had given cast-iron evidence to the detectives of Jane Martin's conversation to Terry Matchett in the restaurant at the Ventnor Lawn Tennis Club with a full recorded version of their conversation which was entirely self-incriminating. She was a respectable, credible witness, whose evidence could not be doubted by the defence lawyers. George Foley's discovery of the credit card receipt for payment of petrol just minutes before Matchett's attack on the Carnival vehicle and the evidence from Harry Wilson at the garage that the petrol was paid for by Jane Martin, with a photograph of her paying for the petrol, was irrefutable evidence for the prosecution that she had driven Foley's Clio.

"Surely they were 'bang to rights'?" he said.

"The evidence we have proves beyond a shadow of a doubt they are guilty. Guilty defendants do sometimes walk free, but not this time, I hope," said Bruno.

"The Clio came from where she was working that morning, both their prints are all over the car, very unthinking and careless. She put petrol in the car at Wilson's and paid for it with her card at the payment desk, she took off her sunglasses providing the CCTV camera a picture of her face. Minutes later the car was spotted travelling along Popham Road as far as the Carnival vehicle, where Matchett got out, climbed on board, and sabotaged the brakes, and extracted the bolts from the steel lintel, carefully jumped off the vehicle and got back into the Clio."

"Do we ever have enough evidence in our job?" he asked Andy.

"What about a guilty plea that they did not intend to murder the victims?"

"Don't know," said Bruno. "It could be their best shot at getting a lower sentence."

"Could it work for Matchett?" said Andy. " I am sure his defence will exploit that."

"Murders are often committed by people who only intend to cause serious injury, but they are guilty of killing and deserve the proper penalty. Their crimes are not accidents, they are committed by people who don't care about the consequences of their actions. Matchett's knowledge of commercial vehicles' braking systems, through his interest in old buses, enabled him to damage the vehicle in minutes. He'd be aware that such damage could have proven fatal to anyone involved in the inevitable crash. The Carnival was lucky that no pedestrians were injured by the runaway vehicle. Imagine the carnage had the driver not kept it on the road. My guess is that the driver was praying for an incline that might have stopped the vehicle, but it did not come."

◆

The Island's newspapers had got wind of the police action in the Shanklin Old Village murders, and were aware that two suspects had been charged with the killing of the driver and the Carnival Queen, and were due to appear before the Newport Magistrates at 10 o'clock the following morning. It never surprised Bruno that in an Island murder investigation, the mainland press were always fully represented by all the local Hampshire newspapers in Portsmouth and Southampton. The information must have come from the courts, because no one in the Newport Police Station would dare to inform the press of confidential information.

Bruno had kept Chief Superintendent Barlow informed of the progress of their investigation throughout, in advance of charging the suspects. With the conclusive evidence presented by the detectives he fully endorsed their action in charging the accused with murder.

The defendants appeared together at Newport Magistrates' Court the following morning, and through their legal representatives pleaded not guilty to the charge of murder of Mick

McClusky and Gillian Napier. Their pleas resulted in them being sent for trial at Winchester Crown Court. They were refused bail because of the severity of the charges and sent to the Island remand centre, part of the Parkhurst Prison complex. With the accused safely locked away to await trial, the detectives could switch off and take a holiday. It had been a bloodless investigation, with a positive outcome, but there were loose ends that needed explanation, which with a trial set for the New Year, gave them time.

With the evidence that Jane Martin and Terry Matchett had sabotaged the Carnival Queen's float there was no consensus between the police detectives on their motive for the killings. It could not be assumed that murder was not their joint intention when they conspired to damage the float. If it had crashed into Big Mead, the large expanse of open parkland on the way down the hill, and even injured the driver and wrecked the Carnival procession, all might have been achieved – certainly for Terry Matchett, who had given no sign during his interrogation that he thought he was becoming involved in a murder case. However, the courage displayed by Mick McClusky in steering the vehicle away from the crowds lining the route, keeping the vehicle on the road was deserving of a medal. It had saved many lives, but cost him his own life and the life of the Carnival Queen.

CHAPTER 40

For seven months on remand awaiting trial, in solitary confinement, they suffered the realisation that, if found guilty, life imprisonment for murder awaited them, which meant a minimum of fifteen years.

By then, if she survived, Jane Martin would be over sixty. For her scheming and disregard for every person around her, she would have received justice, and have ruined the remainder of her own life. Sadly Mick McClusky and Gillian Napier had been the unfortunate, innocent victims of her jealous and revengeful crusade.

It was the prosecution's task to prove that she was a woman whose only interest was herself. She used every person with whom she came in contact – family, friends and acquaintances – to further her own ends.

Terry Matchett became caught up in her web during a visit to the Harbour Lane property in Bembridge when he became infatuated with her, later agreeing to sabotage the Carnival float in return for favours he never received, that she never intended to give him. The prosecution evidence, expertly put together from Bruno's police report, prevented the opening arguments from the defence, who were unsuccessful in reducing the charges for both defendants to manslaughter.

Jane Martin's attempt to blame Matchett for the entire escapade backfired. She said he had asked her to take him to the float, to sabotage the brakes while she sat and waited for him in order that he might ultimately take Mick's job. She claimed that she had no idea what he was doing. The jury did not believe her.

"So, you admit that you were the driver of the vehicle that took your friend Mr Matchett to the Carnival float at 1 p.m. on 12 July 2022."

She answered that she was, and that left her completely confused.

The jury of twelve were like any jury, impossible to judge, but the mere fact they were on the jury guaranteed that the defendants would get a fair hearing and that the prosecution would have to prove beyond reasonable doubt that murder was intended. It was understandable that most police officers think a jury is on the side of the defendants, but it is their duty to achieve a fair verdict, and ensure that the prosecution do prove beyond all reasonable doubt the guilt of the defendants.

The lead barrister for the prosecution, Mr Solomon, took a considerable amount of time cross examining the defendant. During her time on remand Jane Martin had become more aggressive than she had ever been with Bruno and Andy during their investigation.

Solomon had a kindly manner and was intent on showing the court what kind of person she was. He was friendly and spoke to her as her equal to ensure she was relaxed, stripping away any airs and graces and pretence that she might have thought would persuade him to believe every word she said.

The first part of his cross examination concerned the period of her life when she was married to Jim Ridgeway, the father of her daughter, Elizabeth.

"Am I right in saying that your marriage to your daughter's biological father ended when his glass factory was destroyed in a fire?"

"That's correct," she said.

"Is it also correct that on the night his factory burnt down that you were sitting in your car at the factory exit one hour before the blaze started and saw it burn?"

"I did bring him home after the fire."

"That is when the police and fire brigade arrived?"

"Yes."

"I am correct Mrs Martin that you arrived at the Poole Glass factory well before the fire started?"

"Yes," she said.

"You didn't think to enter the building where you worked every day to speak to your husband and say you were waiting for him?"

"No, because I didn't want to disturb him whilst he was working at the furnace."

"So, you just sat and watched the fire take hold with your beloved husband still in the building?"

"I knew he would come out, and he did."

"Was the fact that you had already transferred the ownership of the factory to your sole name and recently had the building insurance increased so that the insurance claim would be paid to you alone, a factor in your behaviour?"

"What are you suggesting, Mr Solomon?"

"Soon after the fire, three months to be exact, you collected and banked the insurance cheque, sold the burnt-out site, divorced Mr Ridgway and married the insurance assessor responsible for certifying your claim. Is that correct Mrs Martin?"

"You are not suggesting there was anything dishonest, are you?"

"No, Mrs Martin, I am just trying to establish the timeline in your behaviour. Then did you move to the Isle of Wight with all of Ridgeway's money and his daughter to start a new life with Mr Martin, the man who was instrumental in obtaining a substantial cash payout from Zurich Insurance company?"

"I went home to where I was born and married George Martin."

It was clear from her uncomfortable countenance that if she could have killed Solomon, she would have.

"Mr George Martin is now in the process of divorcing you, you are aware of that?"

"I am."

"On the grounds of adultery with Mr Charlie Adams, your work colleague."

To that statement she gave no reply.

"Is that correct Mrs Martin?"

"Yes, he is divorcing me," she said.

"I understand that Mr Martin has allowed your daughter to move to Bournemouth and live with her father."

Her silence to Solomon's statements of fact concealed a level of anger that she dare not show, for fear of revealing the worst of her personality.

Ignoring the Shanklin Carnival completely he moved onto her attempted purchase of 9 Harbour Lane.

"All went well with the purchase, Mrs Martin, until Mick McClusky appeared on the scene, and persuaded the vendor to switch buyers with an improved offer of £25,000. We shall hear later from Hilda Prescott what happened after she accepted the higher offer.

"Mrs Martin, I would now like to move onto your relationship with Terry Matchett, who negotiated your failed attempt to buy Harbour Lane. What was your relationship with Mr Matchett?"

"We did not have a relationship," she answered.

"Can you tell us the subject matter of your 31 calls to him in a 14-day period prior to the Shanklin Carnival?"

"I don't recall speaking to Terry Matchett at all during that period," she replied.

"His mobile phone proves that you did. I put it to you, Mrs Martin, that the substance of your calls were to set up your plan to sabotage the Shanklin Carnival Queen's float."

Solomon continued to explain to the court how they conspired together, culminating in Terry Matchett's sabotage of the Carnival low-loader. Solomon was succeeding in exposing her evil, unpleasant and lying personality, and regardless of her behaviour towards everyone, which even though it caused the death of two innocent people she would not turn a hair. Somewhere inside her troubled mind she would justify her actions.

Was her behaviour that of a psychopath? Bruno didn't know. He liked to think that she was mentally normal and would receive the justice the victims' families deserved.

Solomon's treatment of Matchett was with kind ruthlessness. He portrayed him as a man who believed once he had set Jane Martin up to buy Harbour Lane that with his charm that she would reciprocate with more than just a goodnight kiss. After her attempt to buy failed, he remained under her spell willing to commit murder for her, in order for her to succeed in her quest for revenge against McClusky. The prosecution did not rely on her attempt at fraud and the stocking swindle using Adams and Martin Ltd., because it could involve a host of people unconnected to the murdered victims and it would have muddied the waters and involved the fraud squad.

Solomon did however, call Hilda Prescott to report Jane Martin's visit to Harbour Lane after she had decided to accept Mick McClusky's client's higher offer.

"Her manner was extremely aggressive," said Hilda Prescott. "I thought that violence could feature if I provoked her. She left my house shouting and screaming, 'If I set my eyes on that bastard McClusky, I'll kill him, you can tell him that,' she said. She truly frightened me."

The prosecution called Barney Puff to confirm that the cage encasing the Carnival Queen's throne was securely fixed and the Kennedy's service report was produced, certifying the serviceability of the vehicle.

The prosecution attack on Martin and Matchett was completed by the end of day two. On the third day of the trial the defence task to obtain a not guilty verdict for both defendants was immense. It consisted of a blanket denial of the prosecution claims. Sam Levy's photographic evidence was questioned, and the photos were passed amongst the jurors. They clearly showed Matchett climbing off the float at nine minutes past one on Carnival Day and being driven away by Martin in George Foley's Clio.

As for Alan Southbridge, in the six months the defendants had been locked up on remand, he had progressed his plans by securing the remaining waterfront building sites completing the deal to sell Southbridge Motors to Billy Sharp. He did not appear in court to speak on behalf of Jane Martin. In his mind she was guilty as charged and he was not prepared to defend the indefensible. He was also mindful of Adams & Martin Ltd.

The fact that the stocking issue was not raised as part of the prosecution case was a blessing to his deal to sell the motor business, and as a single man Charlie Adams was able to ignore all references to an affair with Jane Martin in spite of George Martin's divorce petition, which cited him as the correspondent on which Martin obtained his uncontested divorce.

Sally Bots had remained in court for the entire trial and although the telephone conversation she recorded was read out by the prosecution, her testimony was not challenged by the defence and accepted as bona-fide evidence. Bruno was pleased that she retained her anonymity as it did not enhance her public reputation to appear on the witness stand. After the trial she received from Chief Superintendent Barlow a letter commending her for her contribution to solving the Carnival float murders.

◈

The jury took three days to reach a verdict, during which time the detectives continued to work on their case load.

On the morning on day four of the jury's deliberations they were ready to deliver their verdict to the court. Bruno and Andy discussed the possible outcome of the trial many times, without agreeing on the verdict. They were aware that the prosecution had been invited back into the court on the previous day to discuss certain appropriate alternative counts to be added to the indictment, which provided the jury with clarification.

The court went completely silent before the judge, who had said very little to the lawyers during their presentations, as there had been few points of conflict in their respective arguments.

Addressing the foreman of the jury the judge asked, "Have you reached a verdict?"

The foreman replied, "Yes, Your Honour. In the case of Jane Martin, we find the defendant guilty of the murder of Michael McClusky and Gillian Napier on 12 July 2022."

After pausing, he continued, "In the case of Terry Matchett, we find the defdendant not guilty to the charge of murder- but, with the agreement of the prosecuting counsel, guilty of manslaughter."

Bruno knew that the rider referring to prosecuting counsel's agreement to the lesser conviction for manslaughter for Matchett, meant they would not appeal or request a retrial and accepted the lesser conviction.

At the sentencing hearing, Jane Martin was given the harshest possible sentence: a whole life order of not less than thirty years. Terry Matchett was given twelve years for manslaughter.

⸙

"What do you think, sir?" said Andy to Bruno on the Portsmouth to Fishbourne car ferry back to the Island.

"For us it's a job well done. I don't think either of them wanted to commit murder. Matchett certainly didn't. He is serving a sentence for stupidity, arrogance and his amorous desires for a woman who thought he was a fool. In fact, he was. On the other hand, she was no fool, but had all the traits of someone who is evil: greed, avarice, jealously. A woman with a single thought – herself. She was 'me, me, me' through and through, disregarding everyone who stood in her way. I think the jury saw that. Twelve different views united in their judgement of both of them."

"And ours," said Andy.